WHAT PEOPLE ARE SAYING ABOUT MARSHALL COOK AND "GLORIOUS":

"Marshall Cook has created a glorious cast of characters inhabiting a small Wisconsin town, from the joke-cracking radio DJ to the married owners of a diner. Beneath the surface of a town known for its Polar Plunge and Cow Chip Toss, readers will discover love and heartbreak, secrets from the past, the battle between the sexes, and even a dog named Frederick Douglass. With echoes of Sherwood Anderson and William Faulkner, Marshall Cook gives us America—and ourselves."
—Emily Auerbach, co-founder and director of The Odyssey Project, Professor of English at the University of Wisconsin-Madison, author of *Searching for Jane Austen*, and co-host of University of the Air on Wisconsin Public Radio.

"If you love baseball, rock 'n' roll and small-town diners, you can't do better than Marshall Cook's Glorious. Tempering wisdom with humor and humor with wisdom, Cook immerses us in a world where deeply-held values encounter a rapidly changing world. The result is a joy to read."
—Craig Werner, Professor of Afro-American studies, University of Wisconsin-Madison and author of *A Change is Gonna Come: Music and Race and the Soul of America, We Gotta Get Outta This Place: The Soundtrack of the Vietnam War* (with Doug Bradley), and others books.

Fun, small-town characters serve up big issues and entertainment for readers
"Marshall Cook aptly captures the essence of small-town Americana in this novel depicting the people of Glorious, Wisconsin. Cook has created an array of wonderful people with problems and dreams that are relatable in today's world. The author's laid back, often funny and always informative dialogue-driven style makes the reader smile, root for the characters, and feel good about small towns everywhere. Cook's novel will be especially appreciated by readers who loved books by Kent Haruf, Billie Letts, Clyde Edgerton, and Jan Karon. A highly recommended escape from our hurly-burly world."
—Christine DeSmet, faculty associate in writing and director of the Write-by-the-Lake Writer's Workshop & Retreat at the University of Wisconsin-Madison, award-winning screenwriter, and author of *Fudge Shop Mystery Series* and *Mischief in Moonstone Mystery Series*.

"Written with a nostalgic nod to baseball, radio, and apple pie, Marshall Cook's 'Glorious' paints a colorful landscape of small-town America, with its celebrated diner, folksy radio station, and likable characters. A midwestern version of 'Northern Exposure' peopled with characters who are as engaging as they are memorable. Marshall portrays the residents with such insight and realism, the government might be forced to include them in its next census. I don't think anyone writes about small town USA like Marshall does."
—Maddy Hunter, author of the *Passport to Peril Mystery Series*.

"They say write what you know, and Marshall Cook knows small towns, baseball, newspapers, diners, and most important, the vagabond ways of the human heart. He makes you care about his people and root for them as they stumble to find their way. I'd love this novel even if there wasn't a minor character named Joe Moe, which is what the nurses in the hospital called me when my parents couldn't settle on a name."
—Doug Moe, author of *The World of Mike Royko* and *Lords of the Ring: The Triumph and Tragedy of College Boxing's Greatest Team*.

GLORIOUS

(A novel)

GLORIOUS

(A novel)

Marshall J. Cook

Three Towers Press

Milwaukee, Wisconsin

Published by
Three Towers Press
An imprint of HenschelHAUS Publishing, Inc.
www.henschelHAUSbooks.com

ISBN: 978159598-613-9
E-ISBN: 978159598-614-6
Audio ISBN: 978159598-615-3
LCCN: 2018936030

To my Irish Rose-
always

"I made stuff up. I admit it.
"I had to. How could I know what people were thinking or
what they said to each other when nobody else was around?
But I've been pretending to be other people on the radio all my life, and
I think I've gotten pretty good at it.
"What I've never been so good at was figuring out who I was.
"But the story—it's all true. I swear to that. This is what really happened.
And it isn't really about me anyway."

—*Kenny Kellogg, KCOW Radio*

Chapter 1:
The Dinky

Let's start with the day Bee found out that her childhood crush, Ricky Nelson, had died in a plane crash the night before. That would be New Year's Day, 1986, the day events were set in motion that were to bump our little town out of its malaise, to use Jimmy Carter's word for the place we were in.

They say that sorrows come in threes, and that was sure true in Bee's case. She and her husband had finally got a baby cooking last spring, a not so minor medical miracle Bee had all but stopped praying for years before—and then Bee has miscarried. The doctor had told her that if by a second miracle she got pregnant again, it might kill her.

It was a long time before I finally found out from Jubal why he and Bee couldn't make any babies. The doctors had told them that Bee had a tipped uterus, and Jubal was shooting mostly blanks because of something called a varicocele that overheated his sperm, the poor little fellas.

Two weeks after the miscarriage, Bee's mother died.

Ordinarily, I don't think Ricky Nelson's death would have hit her near so hard, but this was a matter of kicking a woman when she was down.

Bee was born and raised right here in Glorious, Wisconsin, our town, a speed bump on the county highway between La Crosse and Eau Claire. How the town got its name is another story for another time. We're no more—nor less—"glorious" than the folks in Madison or Chicago or Sodom, I suppose.

Bee was a shining light among us.

Her full name was Brigid Mary Cooney, daughter of William Patrick "Red" Cooney and Degan Mary Cooney, nee Sullivan. We all just called her "Bee." Her husband, Jubal Early, called her "Rosie" because "Rose" was her confirmation name. Sometimes he called her "Irish," for the obvious reason. He said she reminded him of Maureen O'Hara in *The Quiet Man*. Jubal, of course, cast himself in the John Wayne role.

Little Brigid grew up in "Degan's Dinky Diner," which was and remains the heart of the town. Her parents owned it, and she started helping out before she could even see over the counter without a boost. The whole town knew her from the ground up. When she'd married Jubal instead of a local boy, folks thought it was a big mistake, and when she kept the name Cooney after they'd tied the knot, some started calling her a "feminist," which around here was tantamount to calling somebody a card-carrying member of the "Democrat Party."

I just figured she didn't want to be known as "Bee Early."

By any other name, most everybody in town loved her.

She and Jubal took over the diner when Degan died and Red could no longer manage and had to move into the old folks' home on the edge of town near the abandoned cheese factory. At that point, Bee and Jubal became sole proprietors of the Dinky, and later, when Red died, Bee owned it outright.

Jubal was born and raised in Pickwick Dam, Tennessee, so named after the Charles Dickens character. It was just a long throw from the borders of Alabama and Mississippi, so you could sit your behind on three states at once if you aimed just right, Jubal liked to say. If you asked him what else Pickwick Dam was near, he'd tell you the nearest town was Grump. I don't know who that was named after.

Jubal had been a professional baseball player, a pitcher, who'd bounced around in the minors before reaching the end of the line in Eau Claire, where a lot of screaming line drives and a chronically sore shoulder told him it was time to seek other employment. He met Bee at a barn dance there, and they fell in love. But if Jubal wanted Bee, and he surely did, he'd have to marry her, and to marry her, he'd have to convert to Catholicism. (He'd been baptized in an evangelical church in Tennessee.) Marry her he surely did, after taking the lessons and making the promises required to become a Catholic. The pledge he gave the priest to raise the kids Catholic turned out to be a moot point.

To marry Bee was to marry the diner, so he got himself a new vocation along with a bride.

Like any good son of the South, Jubal bore two first names, "Joseph" and "Robert" (no doubt "Joe Bob" back home). Bee called him "Lefty" because "That man bats, throws, and thinks left-handed," she said. Most of us called him "The Reb," or "Rebel," or "Jubal," because he claimed to be a direct descendent of Jubal Early, the Reb general from "The War of Northern Aggression." If he was related to a famous Civil War general, I'm Cleopatra's third cousin once removed, but everybody's entitled to be called what they'd like to be called, I guess.

Jubal usually manned the grill at the Dinky and otherwise sat at the counter shooting the breeze with the regulars. Sometimes he and Bee put on a nice little floor show for the paying customers, starting when, for example, she had to tell Jubal four times to get up off his lazy butt and go down to the basement to get more eggs or some such.

He became a hero in our town by turning the high school basketball and baseball teams, which had been a joke, into contenders. In his sixth year at the helm, the year I'll be telling you about, the baseball team even went to the state regional finals. This despite the sad fact that our athletic teams didn't have a name or a mascot, thanks to the governing board of the consolidated school district, which couldn't decide whether to have decaf or regular coffee at their meetings, much less whether we should be Lions or Tigers or Bears, oh my, or something else all together. This was all after they had caved in to outside pressure from the state to abandon the name "Chiefs."

That nameless baseball team would disrupt the whole town that year, thanks to The Reb and Bee and a student named Norah. I say "thanks" because if ever a town needed disrupting, it was Glorious, Wisconsin. I guess some of the credit goes to an old man named Burleigh, too, and I might have even pushed things in that direction a little bit myself.

But that's getting ahead of the story.

Glorious was mighty lucky to have that little diner. Every town's got to have pride and a heart, and for my dough, that nameless baseball team became the pride, and the Dinky was the heart.

But let's get on with the story. New Year's morning, 1986.

They'd kept the diner open till past midnight the night before for New Year's Eve and then opened up early and fed half the town breakfast. They'd then spent the morning and half the afternoon cleaning up the mess—with time out to watch the Tournament of Roses Parade and church for Bee and the Rose Bowl game on television for Jubal.

Billy had come in to help with the clean-up, as he always did, and to watch some of the game with Jubal. Billy did clean-up at the diner, delivered the newspapers, helped out at the post office, and several other odd jobs. He was what I guess now you'd call "intellectually challenged," but in 1986 Glorious, folks called him "Dummy" or "Billy Goat."

On top of all that work, Bee and Jubal had each run a basketball practice at the high school—Bee was volunteer coach of the lady's basketball club and also the softball club in the spring.

Now neither one of them had the will to get up off the stool, go back into the kitchen, and rustle up something to eat. So it was the perfect time for a game of "Whose Turn Is It?" Neither of them wanted to go first, because in this game, unlike tic-tac-toe, going first was a major strategical error.

It wasn't the cooking so much. Both of them could cook in their sleep (and Jubal often did for the early breakfast crowd). It was thinking about it, deciding what to have, getting up to get things started—just the idea of having to stand up once they had finally sat down was more than either could bear.

"I cooked last night, Lefty," she reminded him, giving in to hunger and firing the first salvo."

"And I cooked Monday and Tuesday," he shot back.

They had no energy for cooking but always held some in reserve for "Whose Turn Is It?" Most nights, one or the other would give up and go into the kitchen to throw something together without making too big a stink about it. But as I say, they were both especially tired and cranky and ready to try to out-reason the other. Both felt they had righteousness on their side.

"Scrambled eggs and toast isn't really cooking."

"I made pizza Tuesday."

"You heated up a frozen pizza."

"I chopped up peppers and onions and tomatoes for it."

"Those were left over from lunch."

"And I was the one chopped 'em up for lunch! Besides, you got to admit, I cook a pretty mean frozen pizza."

4

He had said it "AD-mit." When he was on a roll, his Tennessee drawl got a whole lot thicker.

They sat in silence on their adjoining stools at the counter, sipping the reheated coffee that had been sitting in the pot for hours while they each tried to wait the other one out.

"All right, Rosie," Jubal said, slapping the counter with his outsized left mitt. "A round of Tennessee Rotgut. Loser fetches dinner."

"No rotgut, and no going out back and playing horse in the snow, either. Not that I wouldn't whip your behind at either one. Go fix us something to eat."

Jubal sighed, shoved to his feet, and shuffled into the kitchen to rifle through the refrigerator. "I'll do it," he muttered, "but only because you're sad because your heartthrob died last night."

She let that pass. The only sound was Jubal rummaging around in the fridge.

"We still got some of Monday's hash," he called out. "With a fried egg on top? And some pear slices on the side? How about that?"

"Is there green fuzz on the hash?"

"Hardly so's you'd notice. I can scrape that off in a jiffy."

Jubal was color-blind, and the hash could have been ready to get up and walk out of the refrigerator by itself for all he'd care. But she said, "Sure. Sounds delicious."

Leftover hash with a fried egg on top was one of Jubal's specialities.

Jubal brought out the hash and eggs and two little bowls of canned peaches and presented them as he might have set the finest fare before Queen Maeve herself.

"I thought you said 'pears,'" Bee noted.

"Peaches, pears. They both start with 'p,' right?"

He took the stool next to Bee, put his hands together and bowed his head. "Bless us O Lord and these thy gifts, which we are about to receive," he intoned, just to get her goat. He considered such bleating to be "mumbo-jumbo," which he had rejected, he said, when he "became a grown-up."

"And when was that?" she'd said. "I must have missed it."

"Ha, ha."

"How'd practice go?" she asked when she had finished eating and was trying to fight off the urge to grab the last slice of Dutch apple pie, which was still sitting in the little cylinder on the counter by the cash register.

"Ragged," Jubal said, his usual assessment. "How about you? How'd the girls do today?"

"Good. Norah is like a second coach out there. And she's good enough to pitch on the varsity this spring."

Jubal choked on his coffee.

"Not a chance!" he said when he'd recovered.

"You haven't seen her throw."

"She'd get eaten alive on the men's team. Besides, this town would have my behind on a skewer if I tried to pull a stunt like that, and you know it."

"I'm not asking you to put her on the team. But you should at least see her."

"What, with the mush-melon the girls play with?"

"No. With a hardball. She can make it dance. She's got more break on her curveball and slider than you ever did."

"And I suppose she could match my heater?"

"Your heater wasn't that hot, kiddo."

"Hot enough to strike out 18 in one game."

"And how many did you walk, 19? In a park with lights so dim, the batters couldn't even see you, much less the ball. And that was how many centuries ago?"

Jubal grinned. He liked it when Rosie got her Irish up and gave him the business like that.

"You should let her try out for the team," Bee said.

Jubal's grinned disappeared, replaced by a scowl. "If I let her try out, which I'd never do, and she didn't make the team, which she wouldn't, you feminists would be madder'n hell."

She laughed at the notion of 'feminists' in Glorious. "Don't you want the best possible players on your team?" she goaded. "Don't you want them to get a chance to play in Eau Claire in the regionals—maybe even go to State?"

"'You mean the Division V *Men's* State Championship, where no girl has ever played or ever will?'"

"'Never has' doesn't mean 'never will'."

He turned on the stool and surveyed the little diner. The chairs were turned upside down on the tables. The floor was mopped. The salt and pepper shakers were full, the set-ups wrapped and stacked in their bin under the counter, ready for the morning rush. All was in order.

"I'm bushed," he said. "I'm going up to bed. How about you?"

"I'll be up as soon as I clean up in the kitchen."

"Leave it till the morning. I'll get it then," he said, knowing full well she didn't have "leave it till the morning" in her vocabulary. But it was fair enough. He'd cooked, after all.

He got to his feet and shuffled over to the stairway.

"Don't be long, Rosie. I'll warm up the bed for you."

She could see that his bum knee was hurting him bad. He wouldn't mention it, or go see a doctor about it, of course. If his leg fell off, he'd duct-tape it back on and try to pretend nothing was wrong. When anybody asked after his health, his invariably cheerful answer was always, "Still vertical and taking nourishment."

His theory, oft repeated, was "if it moves and ain't supposed to, use duct tape. If it don't move and it's supposed to, use WD-40. If it hurts, itches, or burns, Vaseline. That's all you need."

Bee would be up at 4:30 the next morning and ready to greet Billy delivering the day's bakery by 5:00, as usual. Jubal would join her in the kitchen about then to prep for breakfast while Billy got the chairs down and Bee got the set-ups and coffee cups on the tables. The regulars would start showing up about 5:30, even though the diner didn't officially open until 6:00. Then Bee and Jubal would both be on their feet until 2:00 p.m. closing, clean up and hurry over to the high school for their practices. It wasn't an easy life, but it suited them just fine.

The school didn't actually have girls' athletic teams. Bee had raised such a stink about that, the school board had finally gotten tired of hearing about it two years ago and agreed to allow girls' softball and basketball 'clubs,' but only if she'd coach them—without pay. "Coaching" in this case meant holding try-outs, ironing the numbers on the t-shirts she bought herself and washing them after each game, scheduling games with any other team that was within two hours' driving distance and would agree to play them, transporting the girls in the diner's van, and fighting Jubal for practice time in the gym.

The basketball club had lost all but one of its games the first year, and the softball club had only managed to win twice, but they did much better the second year, and this year the basketballers had won more games than they lost so far, thanks in large part to the aforementioned Norah Stoddard, a freshmen who played point guard, could shoot the lights out, delighted in setting up her teammates with pinpoint passes, and played ferocious defense, a coach's dream.

Bee sighed, got up, cleared the dishes, and carried them into the kitchen to give them a quick rinse before putting them in the rack under the bonnet of the antique dishwasher. She was getting the water hot to scrub out the skillet when she glanced up through the serving hatch—perhaps she had sensed his presence—and saw the spectral old man peering in at the window.

The first time he had shown up like that, years before, he'd frightened Bee half to death. But it was just old Burleigh, who ran the backshop at the town's weekly newspaper, the Glorious *INQUISITOR-NUGGET*. She'd let him in that first night and every time he'd come since, which was about once every other week. She'd give him coffee and maybe a piece of pie, and they'd sit at the counter, talking quietly, she mostly talking, he mostly listening and smoking one of his disgusting little "crooks" cigars—but only after having asked permission.

He'd gotten more talkative with her as time went on. As far as she knew, she was the only one in town he talked to, except she figured he and Carolyn Henniger must have talked some to get the newspaper out each week.

Drying her hands on her apron, she went back into the dining room and walked quickly to the door to let him in before he froze to death, and that's how her long day would finally end and this tale would truly commence.

Chapter 2:
Burleigh

We all called him "Burleigh." Burleigh Grimes.

Some believed he was a direct descendant of the Major League pitcher by that name, a Wisconsin boy who was known to be such a mean son-of-a-bitch, he'd dust his own grandmother if she crowded the plate on him. Our Burleigh once told me the other Burleigh beaned a batter who had tagged him for a home run his previous at bat, which of itself wasn't unusual, but this batter was still kneeling in the on-deck circle when Burleigh hit him.

Having seen pictures of the original Burleigh Grimes, I seriously doubt he's kin of our Burleigh, but kin or not, we all called him "Burleigh," and to my knowledge, nobody knew his real name or if he even had another name.

Every town has its character, like Billy and his telephone. (Billy often carried around a receiver and had "conversations" with folks, living and dead and products of his own mind.) "Character" was too weak a term for what folks thought of old man Grimes. Even "eccentric" didn't quite do him justice. He was something of a mystery to most folks and even threatening to many. That's the sort of judgmental small-mindedness you trip over three or four times a day in the small town—and I suppose the big ones, too.

You might notice his hands first—long, thin fingers, gnarled and crooked, fingers that were the only fast-moving thing about him. He was the fastest typist I've ever seen; that old man's fingers could fly. And that was on a Linotype machine, mind you, not a typewriter Linotypes! The most ridiculous, improbable contrivance ever concocted by the mind of man or woman.

He never seemed to make a mistake, either, even when he was drunk, which was most of the time when he first hit town. He was probably an even better typist drunk than sober, now that I think on it, because his hands didn't shake when he'd had a few.

I know what that's all about.

The rest of him was built like his hands, long and as lean as the pickings in Mother Hubbard's cupboard, with a horsey hang-dog face and a dour expression. He always wore an old black frock coat that went down to his bony knees and an old-fashioned wool baseball cap with a short brim. Old jeans, a flannel shirt, and a black vest completed his ensemble, even in the summer.

He'd always smelled of bourbon and cigars when he first appeared in Glorious, the smell as much a part of him as his crooked, veiny nose, the bushy, droopy mustache that obscured his upper lip, his rheumy eyes, and his grim slit of a mouth, the cracks spreading from his mouth like erosions in the hard-packed desert earth.

Burleigh had sobered up well before our story begins, with the help of Bill W. and his 12 steps. He once told me he'd tried every rational way he had heard of to get off the booze, and none of them worked. Then he went to AA, the most irrational mish-mash of pseudo-religion and self-help babble he'd ever endured—and damned if that didn't do what nothing else could. He'd been sober for over six years at the time I'm telling you about. He could tell you how many months, weeks, and days, too, and maybe even the minutes.

He told me I was one of him without benefit of the program, but he never preached at me or tried to get me to go to a meeting with him.

Burleigh and I talked quite a bit, usually late at night when the town was asleep. I'm about the only person in town he did talk to, except Carolyn and Bee.

Although most adults were afraid of him or held him in contempt or both, kids loved him and paid rapt attention when he talked to them. They begged him to teach them to whistle the way he did, too.

Oh, yes. That whistling. He could imitate any bird God ever made—and maybe made up a few of his own—and when he really cut loose, he could whistle so loudly, you could probably hear him across Lake Superior and into Canada. He would patiently demonstrate his bird songs for the children, let them see how he formed his mouth and such, but none of them could ever do it. And nobody, man or boy, woman or girl, could come close to his decibel level. It was just something he could do, not something he could teach.

Dogs seemed to love him, too, and he loved them. He had had an old black lab named Satchel when he first came to Glorious, gray at the muzzle and as slow moving as Burleigh, and Satchel went pretty much everywhere Burleigh did.

Burleigh never whistled loudly when Satchel was close by; he knew it hurt his ears.

Satchel died about two years before our story begins, and Burleigh buried him someplace in the woods, where, exactly, only he knew. I think he was still grieving for him.

I figured any man who was shunned by adults but loved by kids and dogs must be a good man, and you can believe me when I tell you that our Burleigh Grimes had as good a heart as any man who ever lived and a better brain than most.

He really knew his baseball, especially the art, craft, and guile of pitching. He and that other Burleigh were akin in that.

A devil, like some folks thought? Naw. Those burn marks on his hands and arms were from all those old Linotype monsters he'd wrestled with, not from the sulfurous fires of hell.

Our dear Bee took him in like a stray puppy when he showed up at her diner late at night, giving him coffee and maybe a piece of pie, and a dog biscuit for Satchel from a little jar she kept by the cash register.

Other than that, Burleigh spent long hours in that dingy back room of the newspaper. For the longest time I didn't even know where he lived or even if he had a place to live. He was a mystery, that Burleigh Grimes, even to me. All this was before all the ruckus with the high school baseball team, of course. After that, like it or not, Burleigh was a sure-enough hero around here to most folks.

But getting back to that New Year's Day night when our story begins—

Bee unlocked and opened the door for Burleigh, leaving the "Closed" sign undisturbed. He crushed out his cigar stub before shuffling in, clutching his old frock coat tight at his neck. The frock coat was much too light for the bitter cold of the first night of the new year, but she figured it was the only coat he owned. He proceeded slowly to the circular table in the middle of the dining room, the one the Ladies of the Quilt always commandeered in mid-morning because it seated six and gave them room to spread out the crossword puzzle so that everybody could participate.

Burleigh grabbed the legs of one of the inverted chairs, lifted and turned it, put it on the floor, and straddled it like a horse, folding his arms over the back of the chair and resting his chin on his arms. He seemed to be staring out or at least at the window, or he might have had his eyes closed. Poor tired old man. She wondered just how old Burleigh was. A hard life could have created such a man in just 60 years, she supposed, but he looked even older.

She approached him slowly, the way you would a deer you hoped not to scare away. She pulled down a second chair and sat on it in the conventional way, next but not too close to him.

"Would you like some coffee, Mr. Grimes?" she asked.

"Not if it's a bother." His voice was a dry croak.

"No bother. I've got one more piece of Dutch apple pie."

He nodded, and she went to fetch it and brew some coffee. Burleigh liked his pie cold, no cheese, no ice cream, just the pie.

Jubal had told her not to let him in if he wasn't home, but Jubal was upstairs in bed asleep. He usually fell asleep before his head even hit the pillow, an ability Bee envied.

She brought the pie and coffee, along with a set-up of knife, fork, and spoon wrapped in a paper napkin, and set them before him. Burleigh sat up and nodded his head thanks. The knife, fork, and spoon rode in a little pocket she had learned how to make from her mother. I've never seen them wrapped that way anywhere else, just like I've never seen the way Burleigh taught Billy how to wrap his newspapers anywhere else.

With his scarred, arthritic hands, Burleigh unwrapped the tools and lined up knife, fork, and spoon neatly. He tucked one tip of the napkin into the neck of his collarless shirt. Only then did he take his cap off and hang it on the back of the chair.

He paused, his head slightly bowed. She assumed he was praying. He clutched the fork like a club and peeled back the lattice crust and stabbed two of the soft, thick wedges of apple, which smelled of cinnamon. He chewed them slowly and then ate the rest of the filling, scraping the bottom of the crust clean. Last he ate the crust.

She wondered where he slept at night. For all she knew, he might stretch out on the composing table in the back room of the newspaper. She got an image of him there, arms folded over his chest, eyes staring at the ceiling. The image made her shiver.

"Good," he said. "Good pie."

"Kringla's best."

He dabbed at the crumbs on the plate with the tip of his index finger and lifted them to his lips before turning his attention to the coffee. He cupped the mug in both hands, brought the coffee slowly to his mouth, and sipped daintily, taking care not to let his mustache get wet.

"Good," Burleigh said, so softly she barely heard, and then, "Good" again.

Their eyes met, and she saw kindness there. "Something's troubling you," he said.

"What makes you say that?"

Burleigh shrugged. He always seemed to just know things like that.

"Oh, Jubal and I had a little spat, I guess you'd call it."

Burleigh looked at her over the rim of his coffee mug.

"I said one of the girls on the basketball team was good enough to play with the boys, and he got all humped up like he does. She wants to try out for the boys' baseball team in the spring, too. I said she was good enough and then some, but he didn't think…"

"Bee? You comin' to bed or what?"

Jubal was standing at the foot of the stairs.

Burleigh began the process of disengaging himself from the chair and standing. Both knees cracked, like shots from a cap pistol. He seemed to rise in sections. You forgot how tall he was until you were standing next to him.

"You don't need to rush off, there, Burleigh," Jubal said, his heart not in it.

Burleigh muttered something, rammed his cap low over his eyes, and, head down, shuffled to the door. Bee walked him to the door. He leaned down and whispered "Thank you for your hospitality" and then, so softly

13

she barely heard him, he added, "You should tell that gal to try out for the team, no matter what Jubal says."

With that he disappeared into the night.

"What was that all about?" Jubal said, still standing at the foot of the stairs.

"Oh, you know Burleigh," she said. "He just needed a warm place and a little apple pie."

"If you feed a stray, you never get rid of him," Jubal said.

"He's no stray. He's a very kind old man."

"What did you two talk about?"

"This and that. He doesn't talk much."

"You told him about that girl, didn't you?"

"I just told him what I told you."

"Bee!"

"What? There's no harm in that."

"I wish you'd engage your brain before shooting off your mouth."

Bee felt her face flush. "Don't you raise your voice to me, Joseph Robert Early."

"Bee, come on! A girl trying out for the men's team! We don't want that getting out all over town. They'd be a big stink, the town council would convene one of its 'special sessions,' and everybody'd..."

"Don't you 'come on' me. Old Burleigh wouldn't tell anybody, and even if he did, nobody'd listen to him."

"Burleigh works for the newspaper, darlin'. Remember? If Carolyn gets wind of this, she'll write about it, and then the horse is out of the barn and we'll have a big fuss over nothing."

"Burleigh never says two words to anybody, except Kenny and Billy."

"And Kenny does what? Oh, yeah. Talks on the radio for four hours every morning. Bee, you might as well put it on a billboard and..."

"There's nothing for anybody to talk about. Nothing's happened. Nothing will happen."

"Then why are you putting this Norah up to trying out for the men's team..."

"I'm not putting her up to anything!"

They were shouting now.

"Did you tell her she was good enough to make the men's team?"

"She knows how good she is."

"Did you encourage her?"

Bee started to reply, but the anger was draining out of her as fatigue overcame it.

Jubal seemed to sense the change. "Please don't sit down here and brood half the night, Irish. Come on up to bed and get your rest. You must be dog tired after the day you put in."

"I'll be up in a minute, Lefty," she said. "You go on ahead."

Jubal nodded, blew her a kiss across the room, turned and walked to the base of the stairs.

"I'm sorry about that singer fellow," he said. "I know you really liked him."

He trudged up the stairs, gripping the railing to pull himself up. She felt the pain he must be feeling in his bum leg and her heart softened. She walked over to the window and stared out into the night, trying to convince herself that Jubal was worrying over nothing.

But what if Norah really did try out for the men's team? Should she try to stop her? Would it do any good if she did?"

Jubal would be asleep by the time she got upstairs, she told herself. He'd get up tomorrow bright and cheerful as always, as if nothing had happened. They'd been over a lot of bumps in the road together, one a lot bigger than the others. They'd get over this one, too.

Maybe it *was* Ricky Nelson's death that had put her in such a melancholy mood. On her way back from practice, she'd stopped for a city newspaper at the honor box in front of the pharmacy, which, like most everything else in town, was closed for New Year's Day. She'd settled for the *Milwaukee Sentinel*, the *Journal* box being empty. The pharmacy was the only place in town that sold the big-city papers from Milwaukee, as well as Eau Claire, La Crosse, and Madison.

She had quickly scanned the front page, her eyes drawn to the little box in the lower right corner with the words "First 'Teen Idol,' Ricky Nelson, dies in plane crash. Story on page 17."

She had had such a crush on him, with his soulful, heavy-lidded eyes and long eyelashes, his sensuous lips and soft, smooth voice. He looked down as he sang, as if he were shy. When he sang of losing his heart to sweet Mary Lou, young Bee had felt as if he were singing to her, and when he had lamented about how lonely the life of a teen idol could be, even a "travelin' man" with a girl in every city, she had cried for him.

Her two older sisters had crushes on him, too. Almost everybody she knew did, except her dopey little sister, Rosemary, who thought Ricky's big brother David was dreamy. Rosemary had gotten polio when she was six and died when she was barely out of her teens.

Bee whipped the tears off her cheeks, angry at herself for crying. Jubal liked to tease her about what a gloomy race of people the Irish were, and here she was crying over a man she had never met and a little sister who had been dead for years.

And for her mother's death.

And for the child she and Jubal could never have.

She had often sought solace from her grandfather when childhood sadness threatened to engulf her. He had taken her onto his lap, hugged her, wiped away her tears, and told her in his thick Irish brogue that things would look better in the morning.

And they usually do, Grampa Cooney, she thought. They usually do.

She wished she could talk to Grampa Cooney right then.

Jubal would be asleep, his anger forgotten. How she wished she could be like that. Perhaps she'd be able to sleep now, and she had better give herself that chance. Tomorrow would come early, as it always did for her.

* * *

That's the way I figured it might have gone, anyway. As I said, I had to make some stuff up.

In our talks, Burleigh revealed himself to be an historian not only of baseball but of his trade, printing, and of newspapers in general—he being a living relic of that history. When we were both in our cups, he'd tell me stories about the old days, folks like Dan De Quille and Mark Twain on the old *Territorial Enterprise* in Virginia City, Nevada, the second bloodiest and drunkenst town in the old Comstock Lode days, of Pulitzer and Hearst and the creation of yellow journalism, of the great newspaper boys' strike in New York and New Jersey, about gun fights and assassination attempts on editors, a lot of whom were printers who just created newspapers to keep the press busy when there wasn't enough job printing to get paid for.

He left it to me to draw the moral of each story.

I never made sport of Burleigh, the way others did. That's saying something, because I guess I made fun out of most everybody else in town, from the mayor on up. I was the only one who'd listen to Burleigh back when he was drinking. I never betrayed his confidence, never made a joke out of him. I'm telling you about him now in tribute, not in jest. He was a good man.

Occasionally, I'd look in at the window of the newspaper at the time I'm telling you about, and I'd see old Burleigh and young Carolyn Henniger standing together, hunched over some copy Burleigh had set and run off on the proof press for her approval—old Burleigh towering over little Miss Carolyn, who went about four foot six on tiptoe. Carolyn was not liberally gifted in the facial features department, either, and she had a speech impediment, the result of a harelip that had never been properly taken care of. I guess they call it a "cleft palate" now. But that young lady had a body that would give any man who wasn't dead ideas you wouldn't print in her newspaper.

The two of them made quite the pair, and that's for sure, his Mutt to her Jeff—or was it the other way around?

She inherited Burleigh when she got the job of editing the paper fresh out of the university up in Eau Claire. He might have been the last man in America who could and would still run a Linotype machine.

Townsfolk used to say that if Burleigh Grimes crossed your path, it was seventy times seven years bad luck. That was before all this I'm going to tell you about, of course. After that there was talk of erecting a statute to Burleigh next to the one of General Hans Christian Heg that stood tall and proud in the courthouse square.

Burleigh would have made a mighty fine looking statue, too, but he would have hated that statue and any other fuss people made over him.

That was old Burleigh, and Burleigh was the one who put our little town on the map, he and the girl, Norah, of course, and Jeb and Bee, and to some extent, I guess, to me.

But I'm getting to all that.

Chapter 3:
Billy Goat

Burleigh always walked Billy over to the post office with the papers Thursdays around 11:00, and I would meet them there and walk Billy's route with him. We'd hump the bags of mailers into the post office, Billy keeping his unfolded papers to hand deliver in town, and Burleigh would drag the empty wagon back to the newspaper office.

Billy kept to a strict and rigorous routine. He'd spend his Thursday mornings, for example, fetching the pies, rolls, and bread from the Kringa Bakery at 4:30 a.m. sharp and help Bee and Jubal get ready for the morning rush. Then he'd go two doors down to the newspaper, help Burleigh gets the papers ready for mailing, take them to the post office, and then walk his town route, dropping off papers to sell at the grocery and the pharmacy. When he finished his route, he'd go back to the post office and put papers in the boxes of all those who got their papers that way, matching the numbers on the address labels with the numbers on the boxes. He did all that without being able to read or write, which was a miracle or at least a marvel, when you think about it.

Next he'd go to the Dinky to sell leftover papers to the lunch crowd and help Bee and Jubal clean up.

Then he'd head to Milkelson's to restock and tidy the shelves. I figured he put in as hard a day's work as anybody in town, and not being able to read and not owning a television, he went to sleep at sundown.

Billy was in his 20s, maybe early 30s, nobody knew for sure, and was what we all called "a little off," had been since he had fallen off the swing in the park and hit his head on one of the metal stanchions when he was a kid. He was "special needs" before needs were considered "special." The town accepted him as he was, and with a little help from folks like Burleigh and Bee, all his jobs added up to food, rent at the Curve, the by-the-week motel where I also lived, and a little walk around money. His needs were simple.

He wouldn't take your money unless he could work for it, and he'd only let you give him a coat or a pair of shoes if you convinced him that you really didn't want them any more and he'd be doing you a favor to take them.

His name was Billy Coates, so of course some of the what we now call "young adults" called him "Billy Goat" and teased and taunted him. Folks can be so cruel.

The only real quirk he had was that telephone receiver he carried around with him. Cell phones were beginning to catch on in the cities at the time, although they were still big and clunky, but Glorious, like most small towns, I suppose, was full of slow-to-never adaptors when it came to newfangled gadgets. What folks now call "rotary phones" or "dial phones," to distinguish them from the newer kinds, were plenty good enough for our town. The only two I know of who had cells then were the aforementioned Ms. Henniger and an awkward high school kid named Myron Mickelson, the son of the folks who owned the grocery. Myron was what today we'd call "on the spectrum," something of an electronic savant but as socially adept as a door knob. Billy had probably seen Carolyn and maybe Myron use theirs, although he never went near the high school, and that's where he got the idea to carry the detached receiver around with him.

Anyways, on this particular first Thursday of the New Year, Burleigh walked with Billy to the post office as always with the papers in that kid's red wagon Billy had picked up somewhere and always insisted on pulling himself. I met them there, having finished my radio show. Burleigh patted Billy lightly on the shoulder—Burleigh and I were the only people who could touch him without him cringing—and gave him a little pep talk— something along the lines of, "If anybody gives you any trouble, you tell them to go crap in their hats, you hear, now? You're just as good as any of them. Better!"

Postmaster Ole Olsen was sitting on his broad behind, elbows resting on the counter, head in his hands—he always looked like his back and neck weren't strong enough to hold his head up. We'd caught him many a time reading postcards, and I suspected that he steamed peoples' letters open sometimes and read those, too, though I never caught him at it.

"Here is the billy goat come a day late and a dollar short," Ole said, also part of the weekly ritual, "and with his pal the radio clown."

He made a sound like a goat and laughed, that little bark of his that was never happy. Billy had told me he thought Ole was hurt in his heart, and that's what made him mean. I suspect he was right. Billy could read hearts better than I could read words. Billy also said he prayed for Ole's hurt heart.

Ole shuffled around the counter, grabbed the bags, and dragged them back behind the counter, and we left, Billy still hefting his double bag of papers for his route. It was a big yellow contraption with *"GLORIOUS INQUISITOR-NUGGET"* printed in red on both bags. Billy would stick his head though the hole in the cloth between the bags and wear the thing like a serape, one bag in front, one bag in back.

Burleigh had walked the route with Billy his first day on the job, following the list the then-editor, a grump named Harold Starr, had given him, and together they dropped off the papers at the pharmacy and the grocery and at folks' houses and apartments and at the old folks' home. After that Billy walked the route alone, and then with me, without a list, which he wouldn't have been able to read anyway. In all the time he'd been delivering, he'd had maybe three complaints that he'd missed delivering a paper to somebody, and I suspect in those three cases, somebody probably stole the papers. As many times as I walked that route with him, keeping him company and trying to forestall any of the truants from taunting him or throwing things at him, I never came close to figuring out how he remembered who got a paper and who didn't.

As soon as we were clear of other people, Billy started chattering like a magpie. He never talked around most people, just stared at his feet if someone spoke to him, but with me, he was non-stop and barely took a breath.

People like Billy and Burleigh opened up to me because I was one of them, a bystander, an outlier, someone who didn't belong—not because we didn't want to and didn't try, at least in the beginning, but because we never could, no matter how hard we tried. Some outliers become writers and artists, but I think most of us just become cynical, even about cynicism, adopting a sour-grapes mentality. Most turned inward, but some, like me, developed a line of bull and a persona to keep folks at arm's length. None of us ever got society's answer key, so we were left with just the questions.

Folks didn't know what they were missing with the silent ones, like Billy and Burleigh, who were thoughtful, reflective, and observant. In a way they were both childlike, in that they'd never lost their wonder, their awe. The difference was, Billy was sometimes childish, too, and Burleigh never was.

"When I come in burley gives me the stink eye," Billy was saying as we climbed the steps to the second floor of the Curve, so named because it sits where the road curves as it leaves town to the north of Main Street. Across the street from the motel, a sign read, "Use your brakes! Do not downshift to slow down," but trucks invariably downshifted anyway as they approached the town from the north, making that growling noise that woke folks up.

"I am not late i tell him in my head i sweep up the cafe and come right over like always i am not late burley squints at the tube in his hand holding it like he is trying to remember what it is he chews on his cigar but doesnt light it he smells like cigar they say he is the devil but i dont think he is bout time he says his voice dry and froggy."

Billy choked on his saliva, having neglected to swallow during this deluge.

"Uh-huh," I said. I didn't need to say anything. Billy didn't need any spur. He needed to get it all said, as if things didn't really happen until he told me about them.

"He looks at me his one eye squeezed tight shut and his other eye cloudy like milk and snot and his other eye full of blood he nods toward the pile of tubes on the floor in front of him go to it he says we got it to get yet."

Billy's job at the paper on Thursday mornings was to take the label sheets, peel the labels off the backing, very carefully, so as not to tear them, stick a label on each tube in the space at the top next to the name, and then put it into the right pile depending on the zip code on the label. I'd watched him do it. He was amazingly fast and never made a mistake.

"I tear a label on accident slow down he says giving me the stink eye youll last longer if i tear a label i have to take the parts and stick them in their place so the two parts match like one of those puzzles they put out on the table in the dingy where everyone can play with them you are supposed to put all the pieces together to make a picture they put it out for everyone to play with but jubal and bee never play they are always too busy."

He dragged one of the newspapers out of the front pouch of the double bag. He carefully folded the paper in half the long way and then into threes the short way. He tucked one of the flaps into the other flap thus formed and creased it so it made a little square he could throw right up on the doorstep and not have to use a rubber band. That saved him money, because he would have had to buy the rubbers himself. He told me Burleigh taught him how to fold a paper like that. I've never seen anybody else do it.

At the motel, he balanced each square on a door knob of one of the by-the-week residents who subscribed. He didn't speak while he did all this.

"I am real good at putting the pieces together," he started up again. "I never look at the picture just the shapes of the pieces when i hold two of them in my hands i can see how they fit together in my mind and then i put them together i catch up and have to wait while burley makes them into tubes with a little bit of tape to hold each one shut i love burley he loves me too he never says he loves me i know he does even if he never says it his mouth is twisted like his face is made out of metal and someone takes a pliers and twists his mouth it looks like he smiles and frowns at the same time he says we have to hurry to get the bundles to the ghost office before the truck comes burley says the ghost master is by the book i do not know what book he means i cannot read they say i am too stupid."

He kept right on talking, lugging those two bags of papers, the front bag almost empty now, up the steps to the third floor, where it was all by-the-week residents. This floor required lots of folding and balancing, so he was mostly quiet until we'd finished with the motel. When we reached my door he smiled and handed me my paper in its neat little square. He always handed me my paper instead of balancing it on my door knob, and I'd shove the square into my back pocket for later. As soon as we started down the stairs, the monologue began again.

On the first day I walked the route with him, I'd offered to carry the sacks for him for at least part of the route, but he'd said it was his job and that he always did his job. I allowed as how the important part was that the job got done, not who did it, and that there was nothing wrong with getting a little help, but he stuck to his guns.

"Burley says I am strong like bull and can carry the load," he'd explained to me. That's why he'd always insisted on pulling the "wheel burro," as he called it, over to the "ghost office" with all the bags of papers in their mailing tubes, too. He was by god strong like bull and always carried his load.

We dropped off papers at the nursing home and emptied most of the second bag to the homes on the other side of the highway and the two blocks of homes behind Main Street. The rest of the papers would be Billy's to sell at the Dinky, his pay for the route. He usually wound up with few or none left after selling to the lunch crowd. Some of the locals who bought papers from Billy also subscribed. I guess they did it because they felt sorry for him and wanted to help him out. The helping out was a good thing, but they could have kept their pity. Billy was a happy soul, despite his situation and the abuse it brought him.

As we got back to what the locals called "the business district," Billy began to moan, "Uh-oh. Oh no."

I followed his gaze across the street, where three older teen boys were standing in front of the hardware store.

"Hey, Billy Goat!" one of them shouted over, and he and the others began making braying noises, apparently ignorant of the difference between a goat and a donkey. Billy dropped his head and fell silent. One of the toughs picked up a rock and chucked it in our direction. I pulled Billy back, the stone whistled by us, and the glass exploded behind us from the window of the quilt shop.

I must have gone crazy then, because I bolted across the street toward the thugs. A voice in my head assured me that they would kick my ass from here to Kalamazoo, but I was in a blind rage and didn't stop. I must have looked like the lunatic I was, because the three thugs took off, laughing and braying but still running away.

When I got back to Billy, winded even from such a short run, my heart pounding, he was standing, arms at his sides, palms of his hands turned out as if in supplication, tears streaming down his face.

"It's okay, Billy," I told him, touching his arm, a touch he accepted without flinching. "Those morons don't know their asses from their elbows."

I was hoping to get a laugh from him, but he kept crying and moaning.

I leaned in close. "Billy, you are strong like bull! Don't you forget it. And you're worth a hundred people like them. Probably a thousand."

The crying slowly subsided. He looked up at me, his eyes tragic with hurt. "Maybe two thousands?" he said.

"Maybe a million, Billy," I said. "Maybe a trillion. Maybe a gad-zillion."

He didn't say another word as I walked him to the Dinky, where he would help Jubal and Bee set up for the noon meal, which we all called dinner, and then sell his newspapers. Then he'd go back to the post office to stuff papers into the mail boxes that were supposed to get them, and I'd slink on over to Big Nose Rose's to have a couple of belts and some of the free nuts and hard boiled eggs before my afternoon nap.

Chapter 4:
Carolyn

T he town fathers of Glorious, Wisconsin had at some point proclaimed a decree, in language that strained the limits of pomposity, that henceforth and into perpetuity on the first Monday of each New Year, at 6:00 a.m., those citizens of that fair burg addle-minded enough to follow such a directive would meet at a designated spot on Lake Glorious, which was by then usually frozen to a depth of two or three feet, where a large rectangle shall have been carved out of said frozen waters, and that those citizens abundantly willing of spirit and able of body (though clearly not sound of mind) should jump into the "water" thus exposed, all in the cause of raising funds, previously extorted in the form of pledges from those citizens unwilling or unable to take the plunge themselves, for the town's "Special Events Fund."

This so-called "Polar Plunge" ("Lunatics' Leap" would be more like it) was, in my considered opinion, the second stupidest thing the Glorious Town Council had ever decreed. What could possibly top that? Why, the Cow Chip Challenge, of course, which took place in Fireman's Park every Saturday before Labor Day Weekend. The purpose? To see who could fling a dried cow pie the farthest and thus go to the State finals in Prairie du Sac the following weekend.

It was bad enough that we had a Polar Plunge. Even worse, I was charged with doing a live remote from the very lip of the ice hole.

"Yes, sir, folks, this is Kenny Koffee, your morning jolt of java, coming to you live and kicking on K-C-O-W!, six nine oh on your ray-dee-oh, broadcasting LIVE this morning from out here on beautiful Lake Glorious, where, in just a few minutes, this year's POLAR PLUNGE will take place! So get your buns outta bed and hustle on over here, folks! It's a brisk fourteen degrees above nothing, with that Canadian Express whistling through, and if I have to stand out here freezing my bonzos off, then why shouldn't you?"

However one defined "bonzos, "Carolyn Henniger was pretty sure she didn't have any, frozen or otherwise, but she would indeed have to hustle to get out to the wide bend in the river designated as "Lake Glorious" if she wanted any photos of the great splash.

If it's news in Glorious, she reminded herself over a still scalding mug of coffee, it was her job as editor, reporter, photographer, and writer to report it in the *GLORIOUS INQUISITOR-NUGGET*, formerly *The Glorious Inquisitor*, founded 1887 and *The Glorious Nugget*, founded 1906, and "the only newspaper in America that gives two hoots and a holler about Glorious."

The ink on her master's degree in journalism from the UW in Eau Claire still wet, she had applied for and gotten this her starter job, the one she hoped would one day—and oh let it please be soon—get her a job on a real newspaper, and from thence to a bigger, even realer newspaper, and, ultimately, a column in the *New York Times*.

This wasn't a dream, she reminded herself often. This was a goal, backed by a plan. Carolyn Henniger was not the dreamy type. She was an intelligent, ambitious, and gutsy young journalist, excellent, if still inexperienced at her chosen life's work, she told herself. She would hone her craft and pay her dues at the dumpy little weekly and then move on up.

So why would an intelligent, ambitious young woman such as herself listen to the local radio clown instead of to Wisconsin Public Radio, for example? To keep her finger on the pulse of "her town," she told herself. Actually, if she didn't want to face each new dawn with silence while she fortified herself for the invariably long workday with coffee and a slab of kringle with butter from Anne and Billy "Gunner" Tollefson's Kringa Bakery, one of the town's few bright spots, the options were few and the pickings slim. Her radio could pull in the aforementioned public radio outlets from Eau Claire or La Crosse, but they were currently conducting a cursed "pledge drive." (*"And, if you pledge right now, a generous donor has agreed to match that pledge. Thus, you pledge of $10 a month becomes $20..."*) That left country music (*"I got tears in my ears from lying on my back, cryin' my eyes out over you..."*), the farm report (*"Pork bellies are up* *three and one-eighth, while hog snouts are down a quarter...*"), or The Come to Jesus Hour ("*except ye be washed in the precious blood of the lamb and accept Je-he-sus Christ as your personal Lord and Savior, ye shall not have eternal life!*").

KK prevailed by default. Nothing he ever said was an improvement on silence, but she could usually screen out his nasal twang while she composed the day's to-do list, and sometimes he'd actually play a decent "golden oldie" as part of one of his "three-in-a-row to make you glow," commercial-free triple plays. Just now the operatic rock 'n' roll voice of Roy Orbison, backed by a pounding bass beat, was singing *Pretty Woman*, and Kenny had promised something by Creedence next.

She didn't know why she enjoyed the music of the 50s, 60s, and 70s. It certainly wasn't "her music," but she did enjoy a lot of it.

The rapping on the window by the kitchen door made Carolyn start and almost spill her coffee. She looked up to see Cecile Johnsrud's round face leering at her. *Great.* What already promised to be a horrid morning had just taken a decided turn for the worse.

Unlike pretty much everyone else in town, Carolyn kept her doors locked, even when—*especially* when—she was in the house. If she didn't, "Cece," as she insisted on being called, would have barged right in without knocking. At least this way Carolyn had the time it took her to get up and go to the door to steel herself and get her game face in place.

"I saw your light on!" Cece exclaimed as she bustled past Carolyn, a blast of arctic air close on her heels. That little kitchen suddenly seemed much smaller.

Cece owned the quilt shop, but her true vocation was to serve as the eyes and ears of Glorious. She was the town gossip, and she never "said" but only "exclaimed," reporting in italics and underlinings, peppered with exclamation points. Not that she ever actually ended a sentence. Her mouth, once set in motion, tended to remain in motion. She probably feared that if she stopped to take a breath, someone else might actually wedge a word or two in.

Carolyn endured Cece's almost daily assaults as she endured so many of her encounters with other Gloryoskians, because it was part of her job. Besides, occasionally one of Cece's trashy tidbits turned out to be a good story lead.

Such would in fact be the case this morning, and not just a good story, either, but a first step on her march to the Pulitzer Prize.

"We'd better *hustle* our *bustles*, young lady!" Cece exclaimed. "They'll be taking the Plunge any minute! I thought we could walk over together. I've got something I think you should know about! I wouldn't tell another soul, but you, as editor..."

Carolyn longingly eyed the remaining two bites of kringle on her plate and the still-steaming coffee in her mug as she pulled on her heavy boots and laced them up.

"...a real humdinger of an argument, is what I hear. I just hope their marriage can weather the storm. 'The course of true love ne'er runs smooth,' as Benjamin Franklin so wisely said."

Carolyn had snapped back to attention.

"Whose marriage?"

"Why, *Bee's* and *Jubal's*! Who do you think we've been talking about? The way they were arguing, you'd think they were about to come to *blows*!"

"Who told you this?"

Carolyn took her down parka from its peg by the door, struggled into it, snapped it up, pulled up the hood and snapped it securely shut over her throat, to try to keep the cold from burrowing into her bones.

"And over that trashy *Stoddard* girl at that! You *know* what they say about *her*." Cece's voice dropped to a confidential murmur. "I don't want to speak ill of her. Lord knows. With her family situation being what it is, it's no *wonder* she's turning out the way she is."

"It was Shakespeare," Carolyn informed her. "Not Ben Franklin."

"Who was... *What*?"

Carolyn flung the door open and willed herself into the bitter cold, walking rapidly, head down, her boots crunching the dry, brittle snow. She heard the door close behind her, heard Cece panting as she struggled to catch up as Carolyn marched down Main Street, right onto Water Street, and another 200 yards or so to the lake, all the while sorting through Cece's breathless stream of unconsciousness sputtered between gasps of air, her short, fat legs pumping furiously to try to keep up. Despite her short stature, Carolyn covered a lot of ground in a hurry.

The gist seemed to be that Norah Stoddard intended to try out for the men's varsity baseball team. According to Cece, who was known to mix conjecture with fact if it made for a tastier booyah, Bee was all for it, was probably behind the whole crazy stunt, just to draw attention to her precious girls' clubs. Jubal, who was, after all, the coach of the varsity and would have the last say, thank heavens, was dead set against it.

She'd have to check it all out, Carolyn knew. Cece was hardly a reliable source. But if it were true..."

"I never thought I'd accuse Jubal Early of having an ounce of common sense in him," Cece continued, "but I must say, he's right as rain about this. Why, the idea of a girl in the men's locker room..."

"Who told you all this?" Carolyn asked, putting a gloved hand on Cece's arm to try to stem the tide of words.

"I'd rather not say," Cece said.

The question seemed to curb her enthusiasm at least momentarily, and she fell silent except for the sound of her panting.

A crowd of around 200 Gloryoskians huddled around the "swimming hole" in the ice 25 feet from shore, their puffs of breath creating icy clouds above them. A bonfire sparked and popped a little ways from the hole. It was still an hour before sunrise, and when the sun did mount the horizon, it would bring little, if any, warmth.

Carolyn bit the fingers of the glove on her left hand and pulled it off. The cold air shocked her bare skin. She pulled off the other glove, let both drop on the ice at her feet, and popped the lens cap off the camera hanging from her neck. She already had it set for the scene as she had anticipated it, and she snapped off several shots. She quickly put her gloves back on and worked her fingers, trying to get the blood circulating again. Frostbite was an occupational hazard for a photographer in winter.

"Quiet down, everybody!" Glorious Town Council Chairman Norb Borstad blared through his bull horn, calling the gathering to order. First Lady Dagney Borstad had not accompanied him, Carolyn noted (a mental note, it being much too cold to use notepad and pencil). Other members of the council in attendance included Rick Clausen, Arvid Engebretsen, Ken Erickson, and Bjour Gundersen.

Norb presented himself as a good old aw-shucks midwestern boy, but he was faux folksy. In truth, Dr. Borstad had a PhD in botany and had taught science at the UW-Eau Claire until he retired four years previously.

He now launched into a story, about the time he "got so angry, I like to flang a plate of Bee's good biscuits acrost the room.!" He was not himself going to take the plunge, of course, but it was easy to spot those who were. They were shivering in sweat clothes (a sad misnomer in present circumstances) or other easily shed garb and were predominately male, many of them young high school bucks, who took up any challenge to their nascent virility.

Carolyn was startled when she spotted Myron Mickelson among them. He gave her a cheery wave when their eyes met. He wore a ratty white bathrobe and a tattered stocking cap pulled low over his ears. His owl eyes stared at her from behind his thick horn-rims, his mouth curled up at the corners, and his pimples seemed to glow bright red in the cold.

Norb had finished his folksy oration, praising one and all for "manning the oars, opening up your hearts and your checkbooks, and coming out on this rather nippy mornin'." He raised a hand in the air and checked his watch, about to give the signal for the madness to begin. Carolyn again pulled off her gloves and began circling the hole, snapping shots from as many angles as she could.

At Norb's enthusiastic "Let 'er fly!" Myron whipped off his glasses, shrugged off his robe, baring his broad shoulders, deep chest, and well-defined ab muscles, and leapt into the hole before anyone else could claim the honor of being the year's official First Fool.

She was pretty sure she'd gotten a shot of him in mid-air, mouth gaping, eyes squeezed shut, looking naked without his glasses, and another shot just as he had hit the water. She kept shooting as others joined Myron in the frigid water, a few taunting the crowd to strip and join them.

She stayed long enough to shoot everyone who jumped in and came back out again—the two events usually separated by no more than a few seconds and several shrieks—and collect a few clichéd comments from witnesses.

Cece was bending Norb's ear, no doubt semi-hysterically informing him of the looming threat to the peace and tranquility of Glorious and its precious men's athletic program. Relieved to be shed of the old gossip, Carolyn made her getaway, eager for the warmth and sanctuary at the newspaper office. Mr. Grimes would no doubt have the space heater roaring and the coffee brewing, bless his gnarly old heart. She would type up all she could remember, which would be a lot—she had studied the interviewing techniques of Truman Capote and Tom Wolfe and practiced watching the evening news and then typing up as much of it as she could, verbatim, without notes.

She would develop her pictures, choose which ones to run, one large on the front page, the others in a full-page spread inside, and write her captions while everything was still fresh in her mind.

She would of course write nothing about the rumor Cece had passed along, not that the whole town wouldn't soon hear of it anyway. "If your mother says she loves you, get a second source." That's what they'd told her in journalism school, and that was her credo.

The Dinky was lit up, the "OPEN" side of the sign in the window facing out. Bee and Jubal were ready for the post-plunge crowd.

A muffled ringing seeped out of Carolyn's parka pocket. She let it ring. It was probably Myron, the possessor of the only other mobile phone in Glorious. No one was worth peeling gloves off in the bitter cold, not even Myron, and Myron would call again.

Sure enough, the ringing started again as she reached the office. She wrestled the bulky phone out of her parka pocket.

"That was the coldest I've ever been in my life!"

"Hi, Myron."

"You should have joined me, Carol."

She didn't like being called Carol, but for Myron, she made an exception.

"No, Myron. I definitely should not have joined you. Listen, Myron, I've got..."

"I know, I know. You've got your story to write. Be sure to mention that I was the first one in. And spell my name right: M-I-C-K-E-L..."

"I've got it, Myron. I see the name on the grocery store every day."

"Right. I was just kidding. You always spell everybody's name right."

"When in doubt, check it out. That's the rule. But I really do have to..."

"I know. I just wanted you to be the very first to know that I finally finished it."

"Finished what?"

"My tower! My station is finally fully operational! I thought maybe you'd like to come over after school and see it, maybe stay awhile and see what we can pick up."

She supposed that was his version of "come over and see my etchings."

"You don't need to have an excuse to invite me over to the house, you know."

Myron had been working on a 60-foot tower in his parents' backyard for months. Now he would be able to exchange dots and dashes with somebody in Tokyo or Bora Bora on his ham radio "station." That boy was some kind of strange genius.

"Okay, Myron. I'll be over when I get everything done."

"Great! Great! I'll see you then!"

The warmth of her sanctuary drove the cold out of her, and a feeling of purpose settled over her. It would be easy enough to write the same story the paper had been running year after year—she had read enough back issues to know how it always went—but she wanted to make this story and everything else in the paper new, fresh, *hers*.

Mr. Grimes did have the space heater on and the coffee brewing, bless him. She could hear the infernal dragon clanking and banging in the back room. She half-suspected he slept with it—she had never managed to get to the office ahead of him in the morning—but she didn't want to know for sure, since then she'd have to do something about it. Maybe he just couldn't bear to leave the Linotype and his beloved job case and press alone at night.

She'd never found any actual evidence of full-time habitation, no toothbrush or the like in the little half-bath at the rear of the back shop. There seemed to be only one item that could be classified as "personal," a battered baseball mitt. He'd been a baseball player a long time ago.

"Any messages for me?" she called back, picking up her mug and going to stand by the coffee pot on the counter, willing it to finish its bubbling and snorting.

"What's that?" came the answer.

"Were there any *calls* for me?"

"*What?*" She turned to see him standing in the doorway, grinning at her.

"Very funny. You really do need a hearing aid, Mr. Grimes."

"Now what would I do with a hand grenade, Miss Carolyn?"

She snorted. Had anyone in town heard their exchange, they would have been astounded, for Mr. Grimes not only spoke, but joked with his young boss! Somehow the two of them, despite the difference in their gender and age and having nothing in common except the newspaper, had become comfortable with each other and often bantered like an old married couple.

"Agnes Cartwright called again," Mr. Grimes reported. "Says she might be a little late with the column this week. Says you should call as soon as you get in."

"'This week?' When isn't she late?"

"Later'n usual, I guess she meant. How were the festivities?"

"Cold! Did you write down her number?"

"4-25-6-3-7-8."

"How do you remember numbers like that?"

"I remember lineups. We've got Lou Gehrig leading off, followed by big Frank Howard from the Dodgers, and then Musial, Ruth, Mantle, and Berra, a real murderers' row."

"How does that help you remember the numbers?"

"It's their uniform numbers. Did you know that the Yankees were the first team to put numbers on uniforms? They gave the starters the same numbers as their places in the batting order. Ruth batted third, Gehrig fourth...."

"I did not know that, Mr. Grimes, but I'm not surprised that you do. But why are lineups any easier to remember than numbers?"

"They are for me. I can see ballplayers. I can't see numbers."

The coffee had finished. She took Mr. Grimes's mug down from its hook, filled it with the thick, steaming brew—Mr. Grimes made coffee plenty strong—and Mr. Grimes walked over to receive it from her. She poured a second mugful for herself, leaving room for her two teaspoons of sugar. Mr. Grimes immediately took a swig. The heat never seemed to bother him.

"Are you really related to that old ballplayer?" she asked when he didn't immediately duck back into his lair.

"Which one, Ruth or Mantle?"

"You know who I mean—that other Mr. Grimes you told me about."

"Did I mention him? Must be gettin' forgetful, as well as hard of hearing. Oh, I kinder doubt it, Miss Carolyn. I did used to be a pitcher, though, and I'm a mean old coot, and so was he, folks say."

"You're not mean. You just want people to think you are."

She took a tentative sip from her mug. It scalded her lips and burned her throat, but she knew she would feel the welcome jolt of caffeine soon.

"You've never told me your real name."

"Grimes is my real name."

"Your first name. It's not really 'Burleigh,' is it?"

"That name suits me fine."

"Why won't you tell me your name?"

"Because it's none of your beeswax. Everybody calls me Burleigh, and that's the way I like it. Besides, if I told you my name, you'd put it in the paper, maybe even on the front page."

"No, I wouldn't. And if I tried, you and that fire-belching monster would just drop it anyway."

Mr. Grimes took another swallow of his coffee, eyed the mug, finished the last of the coffee, and held his mug out for a refill.

"I'll bet you've got some secrets of your own, Missy," he said. "Something you're hiding."

"That's none of *your* beeswax."

She was rewarded with one of his little laughs.

"Stop evading. What's your real name?"

"Won't tell."

"You named for a bank robber or a horse thief?"

"Probably related to several of 'em, but none I could name."

"Oh, go play with that spitting monster of yours. As soon as I get the pictures developed, I want you to help me pick out the best and then make the matts. We've got the weekly miracle to start putting together."

"Aye, aye, captain!"

He did a smart military about-face, clicking the heels of his ancient boots, and disappeared into the back shop. Carolyn strode to her desk, plopped into her chair, and picked up her phone. The two had taken to calling the paper "the weekly miracle," because it seemed to them a miracle that they were able to get a new edition out each week.

"Mr. Grimes," she shouted over her shoulder. "What was that number again?"

"Gehrig, Howard, Musial, Ruth, Mantle, Berra," Mr. Grimes called back, punctuating the list with another laugh.

Chapter 5:
Norah

It was usually their favorite drill, the three-person fast break starting at mid-court, the one in the center handling the ball, leading the charge, with a teammate on each wing. Then the weave, the two wings crossing, and the decision, bounce pass to the open teammate cutting to the basket, kick out to the one free for an open shot, or pull up at the free-throw line for the jumper with two teammates crashing the boards in case you miss.

There was usually lots of yelling and clapping, exhortations to hustle, shouts of "You'll get 'em next time!" when the play went awry, a chorus of encouragement—"Atta baby" and "Good hit"—when the ball found its way into the net. But today they were just going through the motions. The spirit wasn't there.

It's because she's not here, Bee reflected from the sidelines, a rolled-up pad of paper in her hand, lanyard around her neck, whistle dangling between her breasts.

Where is Norah? The fear was always there, the dread that Norah's wretched home life and her incredible gifts would somehow conspire to ruin her, to corrupt what was so beautiful and pure in her.

They all felt her absence. That's why there was no joy, no energy. Without Norah, they stood no chance of playing as well as they knew they could—let alone winning. Without her, they were just ordinary, and sometimes less than ordinary. With her, they were a force to be reckoned with, and their play was a pure joy.

Winning wasn't the most important thing, contrary to what St. Vincent so famously preached to his Packers. She had told them this a hundred times, and she meant it every time.

What was the most important thing? Team first. Striving to be the best you can, learning, growing, taking joy in movement, the beauty of the game when played right, the feeling of being a part of something greater than yourself. Character. Integrity. Courage. Stamina. Being the same person whether you won or lost. All the things it was so hard to put into words.

Her heart filled with love for them, as it often did, and for a few blessed moments the love took away the cold stone of anxiety lodged in her chest.

She did love them, all of them, but perhaps especially Diana Stoshner, the quiet heart of the team, over six feet tall and acutely self-conscious about it, fiddle-bow thin, a long-legged colt who hadn't filled out yet, left a bit uncoordinated by a dizzying growth spurt, shy, but with a calm at her core that allowed her to focus when the pressure became intense. Diana didn't have a boyfriend, and Bee wasn't sure she even wanted one, unlike the others. This young lady knew who she was without a boy.

By contrast, how junior forward Mary Masel strutted her stuff when the boys were around! She already realized the power her developing body had over them and kept at least a half dozen dangling at all times. On the court, she was just okay at everything but not really above average at anything.

Bee loved her, too, and loved Janet Qualia, the other forward, also a junior, a stocky, powerful five foot six, muscular, relentless in her deter-mination to drive to the basket, an okay but not great mid-range shooter, fierce on the boards. She had been the team's star until Norah arrived. If she resented her demotion, she didn't show it. She never showed emotion. A grinder. Reliable. *She's one of the rare ones willing to play backup in Jesus's band*, Bee thought with a smile.

Little Kerrie Merry, just a sophomore, was the playmaker. Barely five feet tall and, as Jubal would say, "cute as a bug's ear," she was an excellent ball handler, a furious harasser on defense, more interested in setting up a teammate for a good shot than taking the shot herself, all about the team.

She was also the most sought-after babysitter in town, conscientious and reliable, and all the kids loved her.

As far as Bee knew, she was the only one on the team with a steady boyfriend, a junior named Mark Engels. Bee thought of him as "Angles," all knees and elbows, crew-cut, clean-cut, to all appearances a great kid.

But what parent would hang "Kerrie" in front of the surname "Merry"? If she'd been a different person, the name would have been a "kick me" sign on her back. But she was so enthusiastic, so genuine, so willing to laugh at herself, any kidding she got was always given and accepted in fun.

Who wouldn't love a person like that?

Norah completed the starting line-up at the other guard—their top scorer, top rebounder, tall, strong, smooth, coordinated, skilled, and savvy. The perfect player—and just a freshman.

But Norah was not here. *Where was Norah?*

Bee gave two quick blasts on her whistle, and they stopped, turned, and looked at her expectantly. She tossed the pad aside and trotted out to center court.

"Ball," she called out, and Kerrie gave it to her with a crisp bounce pass. "I'll run point. I want Annie on my left and Myra on my right. Q and Stosh defend the wings. Kerrie, you guard me. Mary, you sit this one out."

She had picked two of her three bench players to run the three-on-three drill with her. Hard-working Annie Clausen was limited in skill and athleticism but game and always trying. She took mistakes too hard, and Bee had often had to remind her that a player had to have a short memory. It was all about the next play, not the last one. Myra Jensen, clumsy and good-natured, got panicky on the rare occasions when she had to play important minutes in a game because someone had gotten into foul trouble and there was no one else.

That left Helen Reedy, the other substitute, standing with the starters who weren't involved in the drill. She was really more of a team mascot and manager than a player, an overweight, awkward senior who never saw important playing minutes. She made an eighth player for four-on-four drills in practice and didn't seem to mind not playing in the games.

That was probably part of her problem, Bee thought. She was okay with just watching.

She loved them, too, of course—Annie and Myra and Helen—and always tried to make sure they got to play for at least a minute or two.

After this drill, they'd have a four-on-four full-court scrimmage, and she'd send them home. Bee would fill in for Norah. She still loved playing, and it kept the weight off and her body in reasonable shape. She feared getting fat, feared it so much that it robbed her of the joy of eating.

It might have been better if she could watch so she could better instruct, but she thought it worthwhile to try to embody the way she was teaching them to play the game.

"Go!" she barked, slapping the ball.

Startled into motion, Annie and Myra took off, Janet sticking close to Annie, Diana playing off Myra, who wasn't a threat. Kerrie nipped and feigned at Bee, slapping at the ball, doing a good job of moving her feet. *You play defense with your feet*, she had told them many times.

Bee filled the center lane with a low, controlled dribble, the ball tattooing the ancient hardwood floor. Annie and Myra crossed ahead of her. Annie broke for the basket, with Janet all over her, while Myra drifted out to the elbow of the key for a possible jump shot. Diana reluctant to go too far away from the basket, played off her, leaving her open. Bee faked the bounce pass to Annie and whipped a no-look pass for Myra, who wasn't expecting it and let it carom off her hands. Diana, grabbed the ball and hugged it to her chest.

"Look alive, Myra," Bee heard a familiar voice shout from behind her. "You had an open deuce if you'd caught the pass."

Bee turned to see Norah leaning against the closed-up bleachers, dressed in cutoffs and tattered dark-blue tank top, which fit her like a tent. *Thank you Jesus*, Bee thought.

"Where you been, Stods?" Kerrie called out.

"Seeing a man about a dog," Norah called back before turning her attention to Bee. "Sorry I'm late, Coach," she said.

Anger, relief, and joy fought in Bee—anger for Norah being late, relief and joy that she was there and seemingly fine. She fired a chest pass to her star, who caught it nonchalantly and, grinning, fired it back.

"Stoshner, Masel, Merry, and Stoddard, you're defending that basket. Qualia, Clausen, Jensen, and I have the ball. Helen, you'll rotate in for whoever gets tired. Let's go!"

As soon as they were in position, Bee blew the whistle and began dribbling downcourt.

When they scrimmaged, they called fouls on the honor system, and Bee became just another player. For the next 15 minutes, they played hard,

Stoshner defending Bee and Qualia shadowing, bumping, and boxing out Stoddard. Even so, the talented freshmen got loose for several jump shots and one pretty drive to the rim and worked a perfect give and go with Kerrie and a neat pick and roll with Stosh.

"Time!" Bee called after Stoshner got a nice offensive rebound off a Masel miss and put the ball back through the hoop. "Ten minutes of free shooting and then shower up. I'll see you back here tomorrow. Stosh, help Helen round up the balls and bring them in when you're done. Norah, come see me after you've showered."

"Uh-oh," Kerrie called out. "Somebody was naughty and has to stay after school."

The 10-minute head start allowed Bee time to shower and dress before the others. She retired to her makeshift "office" to wait for Norah. Bee was allowed to use one of the classrooms across the hall from the gym as long as there were no club meetings or other activities going on.

She heard two boys walking down the hall, talking softly. They were early for the men's practice.

Her team was coming out of the locker room, chattering happily, their footsteps echoing in the hall, growing fainter, then ceasing as the door clanked shut at the end of the hall.

Frowning, Bee grabbed up her parka and clipboard and headed for the door. She'd been trying to devise a defense against their next opponent, a tough St. Barnabas team that had size and depth. How "Bee's Battlers," as Jubal called them, responded to the challenge would define them for the rest of the season.

Norah was waiting for her in the hallway. "You wanted to see me?" she asked, her voice flat, neutral.

Is that defiance or fear I see in her eyes? Bee wondered.

She quickly realized it was neither as Norah began to cry.

"What's the matter?"

"I don't know if I should tell you."

"Norah, did that man lay a hand on you?" She'd been dreading something like this.

"No!" Norah said quickly but then added weakly, "not exactly."

"Then *what*, exactly?"

"Can we go someplace to talk?"

"Of course. Do you want to go to the diner?"

"Will anyone be there?"

By anyone, she could only mean Jubal. The diner had been closed for two hours.

"No. We can be alone."

The air outside stung Bee's cheeks and nose, the only parts of her not covered up. The pale sun was already low in the sky. Only crows seemed to share the world with them as they walked rapidly to the diner, their boots crunching on the dry snow and ice shards.

"Would you like some hot chocolate?" Bee asked as soon as they were inside.

"Yes, please. Thank you."

Norah seemed to have rallied her defenses and raised the shield she usually presented to the world. She was silent as Bee peeled off mittens, muffler, and parka and piled them on a table. Norah had only a cloth coat to shed; it must have offered little protection from the cold.

"I'll be right back," Bee said.

While she waited for the kettle to boil in the kitchen, Bee ran through several possible scenarios involving Norah and the bum of the month her mother was currently allowing to infest their home. She didn't like any of them.

When she returned to the dining area with two steaming mugs of hot chocolate, Norah was still standing where Bee had left her.

"Sit down," Bee prompted.

When they were both settled, Bee blew on her drink, warming her hands on the mug. She ventured a cautious sip, waiting for Norah to begin. A sugary burn assaulted her throat.

"I'm sorry I was late. It won't happen again."

"You know my policy." Bee sounded more hard-nosed than she intended. "First time, you get a warning. Second time, you're suspended for the next game. Third time..."

"There won't be a third time. Or a second."

"Good. Can you tell me what happened?"

The story came in jerky bits and pieces, and strong, stolid Norah Stoddard broke down and cried again as she told it. By the time she finished, Bee had moved to the chair next to her and put her arm around the young woman's bony shoulders.

"Does your mother need to go to the hospital?" Bee asked when Norah had finished.

"Probably, but you'd have to drag her. She always says she's fine."

"Who is this creep?"

"Says his name is Joe Easter. I don't know anything about him except he's a drunken shit—sorry—the kind my mother always takes in."

"He hasn't done anything to you, has he?"

"No, but the way he looks at me, I know he wants to." Norah's eyes met Bee's but quickly looked down. "…wants to do things to me. You know."

"I know," Bee said softly. "But he didn't? Try to do things to you?"

"Not yet. Not with Mom standing right there."

"But you think he will."

Norah met Bee's gaze, her eyes refilling with tears. "Can I stay here?" she asked. "With you?"

* * *

When Jubal got home from his practice, Bee was still sitting at the table, her parka and Norah's cloth coat heaped up in the center.

"You getting ready to donate to St. Vinnie's?" he asked, sloughing out of his own parka and hanging it on its peg.

"Keep your voice down. I think Norah's sleeping upstairs."

"Norah Stoddard? What's she doing here? We taking in boarders now?"

"More like a refugee. She's afraid of her mother's new man."

"She's got a new one already?"

"Yep. There's always another low-life to take the place of the last one."

"How long's she want to stay? Norah, I mean."

"She'll stay as long as she needs to."

"Says you?"

"Says me." Bee stood and squared off in front of Jubal, as if daring him to object. "I figured you'd rather that than have it on your conscience when Norah winds up beaten and raped."

"Aren't you being a little melodramatic?"

"No. I'm being realistic."

"You coddle those girls. You know you do. Especially Norah. You're their b-ball coach, honey, not their mammy."

"They're vulnerable young women on the verge of adulthood, not just basketball players."

Jubal laughed. "'The verge of adulthood,'" he muttered. "Good title for a soap opera."

"Jubal, I can't just..."

"You can't deny you take a special interest in her. She's your star."

"She's something special, Jubal. When that women's pro league gets up and running, like they're talking about, she'll be good enough to play for it."

"And what good would that do her? The league wouldn't last any longer than that other one, what was it, the 'Ladies Professional Basketball Association'? Did they even finish one season?"

"It was a start, Jubal."

"It was a *finish*, sweetheart. Nobody wants to pay good money to see a bunch of women prance around on a basketball court, unless maybe they do a strip tease at half time. And the same goes for baseball. The only reason there was a women's so-called pro baseball league during World War II was because the men were all off fighting. And don't think I don't know you've been encouraging her to try out for the baseball team."

"It's her idea, Jubal. I'm only being supportive. I've seen her pitch."

"You're wasting your time, honey. Norah Stoddard could never play with the men. And besides, she'll probably turn out to be like her mother. The only sport she might go pro in is the oldest profession."

"That's a terrible thing to say, Joseph Robert Early," Bee hissed. "Terrible and rotten and wrong."

"Look at her, Bee! The boys swarm around her. I'll bet she'll be pregnant before her junior year."

"Oh, you've noticed her body, have you?"

"Come ON, Bee! I'm a man. I may be married, but I ain't dead."

"Keep your voice down."

Bee's heart was no longer in the argument.

"Look, honey," Jubal said, the fight seemingly gone out of him, too.

"I'm sorry I jumped on you like that. I was out of line. And you're right, that girl has some real moxie to go with her talent. She just might make something of herself."

"I'm sorry I told her she could stay before clearing it with you," Bee allowed. "But you should have seen her. She was crying. Norah! Crying!"

Jubal put a hand on his wife's shoulder, and she let it stay there.

"It's all right," he said softly. "We can put her up on the couch in the den. Or did you already promise her our bed?"

"No. There's that convertible couch in my home office."

"And if her ma's bum of the month comes looking for her, I'll grab Old Hickory and knock his melon clean over the right field fence."

"You always were a dead pull hitter, when you actually connected, that is."

"This is just for a little while, though, right? You aren't going to adopt her while I'm not lookin', are you?"

"No, Reb. I promise I'll let you watch."

They embraced and shared a brief kiss.

"I'll rustle up some dinner," Jubal said. "Will she be wanting dinner, do you think?"

"I can just make sandwiches with the beef left over from the lunch special."

The argument was over; they were both even volunteering to get dinner. But the main issue was far from settled. If Norah Stoddard still intended to try out for the varsity baseball team instead of playing women's softball, Bee was prepared to back her, even if Jubal tried to stop it.

Chapter 6:
Travelin' Man

"It's a nippy seven degrees here in beautiful Glorious, the Athens of the Trempealeau Corridor. And you are listening to the voice of Glorious, WCOW, the Mighty 690 on your AM dial. This is Kenny's Koffee Klatsch, the program where we spin the platters that matter, the tunes that make you swoon, the moldy oldies. Coming up, another three in a row to make your heart glow, all about l-o-v-e-. I'm going to hit you with Frankie Lemon and the Squeezers, who ask the burning question, 'Why do fools fall in love?' Then I got Chuck Berry's *Sweet Little Sixteen* for ya, and continuing our tribute to Ozzie and Harriet's little boy, Ricky, his *Travelin' Man*.

"We're looking for a high today of thirteen above. Winds are out of the northwest at 10-12 M-P-H. If they'd just give me a studio with a window, I'd tell you whether or not it's snowing. The seven-day forecast calls for continued weather, mostly dark skies, with sunshine about as likely as Aunt Minnie growing a mustache."

I dropped the needle on the first turntable, potted down the mic, whipped off the headphones, and leaned back, trying to keep my lower back from spasming. Most stations were using cassettes now, and some had even switched to the new CD format, but I played nothing but vinyl from my personal collection, some of which I had hauled from station to station for years.

The only trouble with the oldies was that the cuts were too damn short. Fella couldn't even run down the hall to the can and take a decent dump while a song plays.

I potted Frankie Lymon down, dropped the needle on Chuck Berry on the second turn table, and replaced Lymon with Ricky Nelson on the first, positioning the stylus directly over the cut I wanted. Then I put his headphones back on, leaned back again, and bounced along to Chuck Berry's opening guitar riff.

* * *

"Why do they play all that stupid old stuff?"

"I know. Chuck Berry. Give me a break." Norah reached over and stole a fry off Sarah's plate. "Why don't they play Sting or Prince?"

"Way too radical for the Dinky," Sarah said.

"Fancy has the same stupid station on."

"True. But Fancy has better burgers."

"Does not."

"Does so."

Norah reached for another fry, and Sarah slapped her hand, not hard.

"What's this I hear about your brother?" Norah asked.

"Matt? Why? What have you heard?"

"Not Matt. The other one. I hear he's been sniffing around Sylvie True."

"There's nothing to that. Those two can't stand each other."

"That's not what I heard."

Norah and Sarah were by now good enough friends to tease each other about almost anything. It had started the day they realized they both had a study hour second period, and Sarah, a savvy senior from Tierney, had convinced Norah to sneak over to the Dinky instead of holing up in the library or gabbing in the cafeteria. Norah didn't know anybody much except her teammates, and she was flattered that Sarah, a senior, would hang out with her, a lowly freshman. She liked Sarah, and Sarah seemed to like her, too. It was almost as if they were sisters, something that neither one of them had.

Norah talked a lot about her basketball coach, the lady who ran the diner, and Sarah talked about her Gram Lydia, about her brothers, Matt and Mickey, and about how her father had hit the road after their mother had died. Norah talked about the trashy guys her mother brought home, even told how most of them would rather get into her pants than her mama's. That's when Sarah had suggested that they both take a self-defense class for women being offered at the "Y" in Eau Claire on Saturdays.

Ricky Nelson came on the little radio perched on the ledge between the kitchen and the almost empty dining room. They'd heard he'd died in a plane crash, just like Buddy Holly.

"Coach is sad about that," Norah confided. "She had a big crush on him when she was a kid."

"Really? That drip?"

"I know!"

When the song ended, Norah leaned across the table and whispered, "Want to know a secret?"

"Sure."

"You promise not to tell?"

Sarah ran her thumb and index finger across her lips and leaned in eagerly.

"Pinky swear?"

"Pinky swear."

The two locked little fingers.

"I'm going to try out for the baseball team," Norah whispered.

"Big whoop. Why wouldn't you?"

"Not the softball team. The *baseball* team."

Sarah's eyes got big.

"I want to pitch on the men's team."

"They'll never let you do that!"

"Coach says I pitch well enough."

"I don't care if you can throw like…Jubal *Early* said that?"

"No! Lady coach. And keep your voice down."

"I never figured you for a woman's libber."

"I'm not!"

"That's a relief. I thought maybe you were going to stop wearing a bra. The boys look at you enough as it is."

"Sarah! Stop it!"

"They do. You know they do."

"I don't encourage it."

"They don't need any encouragement."

They both drained their Cokes.

"What are you trying to prove?" Sarah asked.

"I'm not trying to prove anything. I just want to compete against the best competition I can. That's the only way I can keep getting better."

"And then what?"

"What do you mean?"

"I mean, say you did make the team. And you keep getting better. It's not like you could go pro."

"I still want to play."

"You're really serious about this, aren't you?"

"When I'm leading a fast break or looking in for the catcher's sign, I feel like I'm exactly where I should be, doing exactly what I should be doing. I never feel that way anywhere else."

"I wish I loved something as much as you love sports. You won't make the team, though."

"Thanks for the vote of confidence."

"I mean they won't let you play, no matter how good you do. But I'm rooting for you anyway."

"Thanks."

The disc jockey had stopped babbling, and now Pat Boone was writing love letters in the sand.

"Oh, brother," Norah said, nodding toward the radio. "Gag me with a spoon."

"Definitely grody to the max," Sarah agreed.

They laughed, the serious mood broken. They collected their books and headed back to school to be on time for their third-period classes.

* * *

As Pat Boone finished his warbling and the El Dorados started lamenting the tears on their pillows, Scott Dupple sidled into the studio, several sheets of yellow copy paper in one hand, a mug of coffee in the other. Dupple called himself the "news director," but was in fact the entire news department and, not counting Loni Marlowe, the station's receptionist, the only other human being in the building besides me. Whoever got there first in the morning had to turn on the transmitter and get the station on the air. The station manager, Bob "Bottom Line" Briscoe, didn't usually show up until after I left the air.

After that, the rest of the day was all a syndicated music service out of Des Moines until Dupple popped back in for news updates at noon and again at 4:00. The station went off the air at sundown.

Dupple's job was a lot like a crossing guard's. He only got paid for being at his post three times a day but had to use up the whole day doing it.

"Hey, Droopy Drawers," I greeted him. "About that time, huh?"

"In four minutes and…" Dupple squinted at the studio clock… " 17 seconds."

There being only one mic and one seat in the studio, Dupple had to stand and wait for me to finish before sliding in for his news report. He was a round little man, wearing his winter uniform of rumpled cords, a baggy sweater no doubt knitted for him by his mother, and a pair of loafers he always slipped into when he got to the station.

"You leading with the Stoddard story I tipped you on? You've had an hour to get the details."

"We can't use that yet. No confirmation."

"Whattaya mean, no confirmation? I told you!

"And where'd you hear it, Cecile Johnsrud?"

"You know we journalists never reveal our 'souses'. So, if you're not going to use my hot tip, what are you leading with? Illegal poaching of ospreys? Has the cheese factory been caught curding up the river again?"

"Unfortunately, none of that happened."

"Don't let that stop you."

"The best I've got is the same DUI I used at 8:00 and 9:00. Mort Forbes drove his pickup into a tree on River Road at bar time last night."

"And you went out there at 4 a.m. and got an exclusive interview with the tree, right, Scoop?"

"Har, har. You're a riot."

"Follow that up with the school lunch menus and today's obits and I think you've got a Peabody pretty well wrapped up, Droop."

"I wish you'd stop calling me that."

"You've got the sense of humor of a plumbing fixture, Droop."

I jammed the birthday song cassette into the slot, potted down the El Dorados, and potted up the mic.

"It's 9:49 Central Farmer Time here at the mighty six-ninety, and we'll have all the local news coming right up at the top of the hour with our very own insipid reporter, Scoop Dupple. But first, today's birthday, brought to you by Casey's Carcass Removal. Got a cow that's gone belly up? Don't wait for the buzzards to start circling. Give Casey a call, and he'll make that dead meat—whoosh—disappear. You got a corpse, call Casey, of course. That's Casey's Carcass Removal."

I gave the phone number twice.

"Today's the birthday of Laura Ingalls Wilder, who, as most folks didn't know, was born in Wisconsin, and Sinclair Lewis was also born on this date, in Sauk Centre, MN. For those of you who slept through *Babbitt* in English class, Lewis wrote novels about all the small-town dopes he'd grown up with. For that they gave him the Nobel, a dynamite award, maybe even better than the Poultry Surprise."

I pushed the button on the cassette deck and potted up the *Happy Birthday* song. When that was done, I pushed the button and popped the cart, deftly replacing it with the one the Farm Babe had left off that morning, all while saying, "And now, without further flimsy flapdoodle, here's Scoop Dupple with the morning update and today's local birthdays."

I pushed the mic aside, swiveled out of the chair, and gave it a good spin, so that Dupple had to start his report standing up. When Dupple scowled at me, I whipped out my lighter and lit the sheaf of papers in Dupple's hand on fire, tore out the door, and went down the hall to take a dump, something I'd been needing to do for an hour.

When I got back, Dupple, still standing, was reporting on the sheepshead league scores from the previous week, a singed piece of yellow copy paper in his hand. The aroma of burning paper filled the little studio. He wadded up what was left of the copy, fired it at my head, missed, and stalked out of the studio. I pulled the microphone over and said, "Thank you, Scoop, for that fascinating report on the events that alter and eliminate our times. And now here's Eau Claire's own Fabulous Farm Babe, Pam Henke, with the morning farm report."

I stabbed the button for the cassette, and Henke started giving the prices of pig snouts and cow flop, as usual. Or at least I assumed that's what she was doing. Dupple had hidden the headphones.

The phone light lit up.

"Hi, Myron." I remembered to push the button that allowed me to take the call off air. "How's life?"

"Hi, Kenny. It's me, Myron. Your number-one fan."

"So how come you never call when I'm on the air? Are you shy, Myron?"

"I don't think anybody would be interested in what I have to say."

"That's where you're wrong, my boy. Things are so boring in this burg, folks will sit and listen to corn grow. I'm sure you're at least as interesting as the sound of corn growing, aren't you, Myron?"

"I just wanted to tell you. My station's up and running! I'm W6-IUL!"

"Well, welcome to the airwaves, Myron. I suppose now you're going to be my competition."

"My station isn't like that. I can't even talk yet. I have to get an advanced license for that."

"All code, huh? Well, give your dotty friend Morris my best. I gotta dash…"

"I just wondered why you didn't use the information I gave you about that girl."

"We journalists always have to confirm a story like that with a second source, Myron. Where did you get your information?"

On an impulse, I punched two buttons, one to stop the farm report tape, the other a red button on the phone console, which turned green when I depressed it.

"I'd rather not say."

"That makes me think you made it up, Myron."

"I did not!"

"Does Henniger know about this?"

"I don't know! It wasn't Carolyn who told me."

"Carolyn, eh? You and our Miss Henniger are on a first-name basis, are you?"

I could practically hear Myron blush through the phone line.

"She's the editor of the newspaper."

"I know that, Myron. Would you know if she intends to print that story in this week's edition?"

"I don't know. I told you, it wasn't her."

"Methinks thou dost protest too much, Myron. But never mind that. Just to refresh my memory, tell me again what Carolyn didn't tell you."

"She, I mean somebody, said Norah, Norah Stoddard, she's on the girls' basketball team, she's just a freshman and…"

"Get to the news, Myron. This is only a four-hour show."

I spotted my headphones, perched on top of the tape decks, stood up and grabbed them.

"She's going to try out for the men's baseball team!"

"Is that a fact? And what does Coach Early have to say about that?"

"I don't know. I don't think he knows about it."

"And where did Carolyn, I mean your source, get her information?"

"I don't know."

"Okay, Myron. Thanks so much. I gotta run."

I closed the phone line. *Now why did I do that?*

The light on the console started blinking again. I ignored it.

"That was Myron Mickelson, our high school campus reporter, with our hot tip of the morning. According to sources who are not Carolyn Henniger, Norah Stoddard, the star of our girls' high school basketball club, reportedly intends to try out for the men's varsity baseball team. Further bulletins as we receive them. And remember, you heard it first right here on Kenny's Morning Koffee Klatsch, the radio program that wakes you up each and every day and drags you through the morning. And now..."

I took the mic with me as I stretched to fish an album off the shelf.

"Why, it's Mr. Del Shannon, here to sing us off the air for the day with his big hit, run-run-run-run *Runaway*."

And with that, I disappeared into the ether, my day's mischief done.

Chapter 7:
Order in the Court

It was the first Monday in February, the beginning of the doldrums, that part of winter that strangles the soul, deadens the mind, and attacks the fortitude of even the bravest, stoutest, stubbornest among us. The Polar Plunge was a month in the past. The regional basketball tourney was a month in the future. The only thing anybody had to look forward to was the Valentine's Day Dance at the high school, and few, if any, of us had given much of a hoot or a holler about a high school dance since we been in high school, which was a long time ago for most of us.

It was the season of suffering, the days of darkness, "the winter of our discontent."

Ah, but we had been given an entertainment, a show to distract us from our ice-encased misery. The atmosphere in the Dinky, full of the smell of grease and cigarette smoke and humanity, felt something like the day the circus comes to town, the little diner already packed and people crowded in at the door, and still 15 minutes before it was officially open for business. When a fight's brewing, we tend to huddle together in some clean, well-lighted place, don't we?

It wasn't a circus, not a literal one. It was bigger than that. This must be what it felt like to be in Las Vegas on the morning of the big heavy-weight title fight. Not that anybody in Glorious would know what it felt like to be in Vegas on that or any other morning.

There was an air of expectancy, and Cecile Johnsrud's arrival on the scene made it unofficially official: the gunfight at the not-so-okay corral was at hand. Today was the day of the shootout, the showdown, when we would get the lowdown.

Cece stood for a moment in the doorway, surveying the mob scene she had helped create while allowing the bitter north wind to blow its soul-numbing cold into the room.

I'd figured out by now what must have been the chain of information that ended with me outing Norah Stoddard on the air. Cece had told Carolyn, who had told Burleigh, who had told me. And I, being the intrepid journalist that I am… Okay, I, being the loudmouth, pot-stirring clown that I am, told everybody—or rather, let poor Myron do it for me.

How Cece found out I hadn't yet sussed out, but Cece seemed to find everything out, including stuff that hadn't actually happened. You just know our dear Cece must have gloried in the excitement she had such a large part in generating. Norah Stoddard, a mere freshman of the female persuasion, intended to try to pitch her way onto the men's varsity baseball team! Did you ever hear of such a thing?!

The place to be that night, of course, would be the high school auditorium, for the meeting of the Glorious-Tierney-Whitehall-Blair Consolidated School District Board Meeting. (The order of the four towns varied depending on which town you were in. The district was simply called "consolidated.")

Such irony. Ordinarily you couldn't find two denizens of our little bump in the road to rub together at a school board meeting, for all the talk of the kids being our future. Tonight we'd be wall to wall, the contentious and the curious alike, generating enough heat, if very little light, to keep things toasty on a cold winter's night.

The challengers and decided underdogs, the "women's libbers," would be there to support Norah Stoddard, the best athlete the town had ever produced, in her apparent quest to play on the varsity baseball squad.

Such a quest flew in the face of *The Way It's Always Been and Always Will Be*—personified by the seven august worthies of the Consolidated School Board, a prohibitive favorite in the battle, having gone undefeated for decades.

Tryouts were still more than a month away, and neither Miss Stoddard nor anyone speaking for Miss Stoddard has said anything about trying out for the varsity, at least not in public. But never mind that. The news that she would do so was all over town and up and down the Trempealeau River Corridor.

See what a rumor hath wrought.

The three major figures in the anticipated battle royal were among the throng in the Dinky. One was of course Coach Jubal Early, who had brought respectability to a down-and-out athletic program that had been a joke and a punching bag since even before the state Department of Instruction had forced it to abandon the mascot folks had cherished for the seven decades the school teams had been known as the Glorious Chiefs. The town had then adopted the Glorious Generals, symbolized by crossed deer-hunting rifles, which was apparently okay with the DOI, as long as them Injuns didn't have the guns. And now, because of consolidation, they would have to change the name yet again. Students had already held a mock election, choosing Consolidated Cream Puffs over the equally tasty Cupcakes or Custards.

Whatever you called them, they had for years been the laughing stock of the Northcentral Wisconsin WIAA Division IV Conference. The turn-around accomplished in just five years by Coach Early had made him something of a hero.

Also present that morning, of course, was Jubal's wife, Brigid Mary Cooney, the queen of the deep-fat fryer, the town's unofficial hostess, who coached the women's basketball and baseball "clubs" and seemed to be the primary supporter of the assault on tradition and common decency in the person of Miss Stoddard, who was also on the premises, helping with the morning rush before school began for the day.

Just look at her. A girl in the men's locker room! Breasts on a baseball diamond!! The very idea. Shocking!

Bee had even taken the possessor of those interloping breasts under her metaphoric wing and her literal roof and had, for all the town knew, maybe even put her up to this nonsense in the first place.

Did Bee and Norah have a puncher's chance of winning this fight? There was just enough of a possibility to make it interesting. There were, after all, three women on the board and one man who had been known to cave in to the pressure when those three ganged up on him.

But more likely, the plucky challenger would be beaten to a pulp.

Either way, it was a fight not to be missed.

"Here we go," Rick Clausen muttered, having spotted Cece still surveying the room from the doorway. He was sharing the round table in the center with his fellow members of the Town Council, Arvid Engebretsen, Ken Ericksen, and Bjorn Gundersen, who were waiting for their leader, Council Chairman Norb Haas, to show up so their daily unofficial meeting could unofficially commence.

Joe Moe, who wasn't due to open the hardware store until 9:00, was there, as was Boomer Smith, the social science and health teacher and coach of the Glorious football team, along with Hjalmar Halvorson, the school's science teacher and husband of Hulda, president in perpetuity of the PTA. These three staunch Glorious athletic supporters now occupied stools at the counter usually covered by the ample posteriors of the coffee-sipping and snooze-dipping farmer trio of Stits, Schmitz, and Schultz, who, displaced from their rightful roosts, sulked on the three stools at the far end of the counter.

The third major character in the drama, the silent one, Norah Stoddard, now stood behind the counter, the coffee pot in her left hand hovering motionless over Coach Smith's mug as she watched Cece make her way from the door to the counter.

Bee burst through the swinging doors of the kitchen just as Cece arrived at the cash register at the end of the counter closest to the door, next to the plastic cylinder packed with fresh baked pies delivered by Billy Coates half an hour before. Bee was carrying six platters, one in each hand and two more defying gravity on each forearm. The two platters in her hands carried what looked to be a couple of layer cakes without frosting, but were in fact two orders of the "short stack," two of Jubal's enormous flapjacks, as he called them. The "short stack" was usually more than enough for most folks.

The yammering died down as a room full of people watched and listened while trying to appear as if they weren't watching and listening. The Dinky was all ears.

"It's not listed on the posted agenda," Cece hissed over the counter to Bee. "They're trying to keep everything hush-hush." Her hissing penetrated the thickest skulls and the deafest ears in the now otherwise silent room. Well, all but one of the thickest skulls.

"What'd she say?" Stits asked from his place in the cheap seats, loud enough for everybody to hear. Schmitz and Schultz shushed him.

Bee turned to Norah.

"Would you go in the back and help Jubal on the grill?" she asked.

Norah nodded, set the coffee pot on the counter, and made her retreat, not looking at anyone. Cece smiled smugly as she waited for Bee to deliver her platters to the middle table. When Bee returned to the counter to pick up the abandoned coffee pot, Cece waddled down the counter parallel to Bee, who topped off coffees for the counter clingers.

"Would you like some coffee, Cecile?" Bee offered with a smile, acknowledging her presence for the first time.

"No, thank you, dear. I haven't time."

"How about a nice kringle, then?" Bee offered. "They're still warm from the oven."

"Not for me," she said, sniffing. "You know what they say, 'a second on the lips, a lifetime on the hips.' I suppose you'll be attending the meeting tonight?"

"I guess I might," Bee said. "If there's nothing good on television."

"And your hubby? He'll be attending as well?"

"You'd have to ask Hubby. You sure you wouldn't like a piece of banana cream pie?"

"No, dear. I really must be going. So much to do."

"I can imagine."

"It promises to be quite contentious, wouldn't you say?"

Bee frowned as if confused. "Why would that be, dear?" she cooed.

Somebody snorted, then tried to cover it with a cough.

Cece had to refrain from pounding her hip with her fist, her way of exhibiting exasperation. "You know very well why," she said, her voice rising.

"Oh, *that*? I don't see why a simple thing like that should be such a big problem."

Cece gave Bee her best so-you-want-to-be-that-way-about-it look, made a huffing noise as she pivoted, and flounced back out into the frozen wasteland.

At that point, I had to skedaddle to the station to conduct the Koffee Kvetch. Billy later told me that Cece next surfaced at Bufford's Barbering, along with Stits, Schmitz, and Schultz, who usually made Bufford's their second stop of the morning.

For 47 years, Jan Stenerud had been the town's barber. Before him, the original proprietor, Bufford K. Langerhorn, has presided for nobody knew how long until he was found in the spare barber chair—the place had two chairs but never a second barber—a heart attack having dispatched him to that great tonsorial paradise in the sky. Jan had opened up way early this morning, figuring lots of folks might want to spruce up for the big doings that night.

The two hand-printed signs in the windows, bleached by the sun, had never changed.

One said,

"COME ON IN AND GET CLIPPED"

The other said,

"IF YOUR HAIR ISN'T BECOMING TO YOU, YOU SHOULD BE COMING TO ME!"

Inside, nothing else had changed much in all those years, including, some would swear, the magazines and comic books on the squat table next to the floor-stand ash tray—*WHIZ KIDS, ARCHIE, BATMAN, SUPERMAN, RAWHIDE KID, THE CISCO KID*, and *BOY'S LIFE* for the boys, *FIELD AND STREAM, OUTDOOR LIFE*, and *THE POLICE GAZETTE* for the bigger boys.

Jan was at the moment servicing the town's banker, Hiram Knutson, whose meager gray-yellow fringe of fur clung from one large, floppy ear to the other along the back ridge of his otherwise bald dome with the tenacity of spring dandelions. Barber Stenerud was in the midst of snipping at the air for 15 minutes so Hiram could pretend he was actually getting a haircut.

Banker Knutson claimed to be a direct descendent of the town's founder, Ansten Knutson. He was not, and in fact, Ansten Knutson had never taken a wife and thus left no known descendants, at least none that bore his name.

Mike Mickelson, who with wife Maddie ran the general store, was waiting his turn in one of the chairs not occupied by Stits, Schmitz, and Schultz. He was studying a battered edition of *THE POLICE GAZETTE* and puffing on a stogie, which he never touched with his hands, leaving it to wobble on its own. From his vantage point just inside the side door, broom in hand, waiting for some actual hair to sweep up, Billy stared at that cigar, studying the ash, now an inch, now two, now three inches long, waiting for it to break off and fall into Mickelson's lap.

Glorious

Mickelson's General Store stocked milk, cheese, butter, eggs, and bread, along with a fine assortment of junk food and soda pop. Folks also had Tollefsen's Bakery and Rink's Deli for consumables, but most did their big shop at the Piggly Wiggly in Eau Claire or the A&P or the Red Owl in La Crosse.

Now entered Father Patrick Healey, one of the few Irishers in town besides Bee and shepherd of the Catholic flocks in Blair, Whitehall, and Tierney, as well as Glorious. Father had lived in the little corridor between the Mississippi River in La Crosse and the Chippewa River in Eau Claire all his life, except for his years away at the seminary. He always brought with him a bountiful stock of good cheer, jokes, and stories, all of which any good Catholic in the area would have heard in a Sunday sermon many more times than once.

Right behind Father Healey came the honorable Circuit Court Judge Harlan Bristow, President of the Consolidated School Board.

Grocer Mickelson snuffed out his stogie in the ash tray and decided he'd come back for a haircut another time. Stits, Schultz, and Schultz got up as one man and followed him out, carrying their coats. His Honor the Judge would receive his trim with only Father Healey for company.

A dog howled outside, and a combination of sleet and hail began to fall.

All afternoon, Glorious was a ghost town, Main Street deserted. Even Cece seemed, for once, to be home tending to her knitting. The hail pinged a few cars, and the sleet laid down an ice sheet on walks and roads before the storm turned to snow, the little, hard-pellet kind that doesn't make good snowballs or snowmen but that gets caught up in the tree branches and glitters when the sun comes out again.

It was the easy shoveling kind, but it kept falling, four then five inches of it, turning to fat, slushy mush as the wind shifted to the southwest and the temperature rose, almost all the way up to freezing, so that by the time the kids got out of school, the buses were running late, and the young 'uns who walked home had to slog through knee-high drifts.

By nightfall, which came even before suppertime this time of year, eight inches had fallen, and folks stayed by their radios to see if the school board meeting might be cancelled. But there was no real chance of that happening. If a meeting was scheduled, and Judge Harlan Bristow was involved, that meeting would be held, come hell or high snow.

As folks bowed their heads in prayer over the evening meal, the lights flickered, lightning flashed, fat, heavy snowflakes continued to fall, and thunder rolled over the Mississippi River and up the Trempealeau River Corridor.

Surely nobody would venture out to something as mundane and potentially soporific as a meeting of the Consolidated District School Board. Ordinarily, good weather and the promise of free beer and brats wouldn't have attracted much of a crowd to *that*.

But these were no ordinary times. This promised to be a showdown, the kind of thing about which folks would forever say, "I was *there!*"— even if they weren't.

Besides, these were hardy Wisconsin folk, perverse enough to fight through ice, sleet, snow, and the possibility of being struck by lightning just to show how tough they were.

Thus the auditorium was crammed well before the announced 7:00 p.m. starting time. Coach Jubal Early was there, of course, as was volunteer "club coach" Bee Cooney, along with most of the members of their respective teams.

The press was well represented, with the county weekly, dailies from Eau Claire and La Crosse, and, of course, Sylvie True of the *Lighthouse* and Carolyn Henniger of the *INQUISITOR-NUGGET*, plus station WCOW's Droopy Drawers Dupple, who, aside from being the "news director," also hosted a Saturday morning kiddie show.

Under old business, item VII on the agenda, the board had listed "Discussion of a name for the consolidated School District athletic teams." But that had been listed for eight consecutive months with no promise of a consensus being reached or action taken.

It was item VIII, the ambiguous "New business," that folks had come for.

Judge Bristow and the six other worthies of the school board mounted the stage at precisely the appointed hour, drawing a few hoots and jeers, and took their places on seven metal folding chairs behind two portable tables, Chairman Bristow seated in the center with three on his right hand

and three on his left. His honorable buttocks perched on a cushion, his the only chair so adorned.

The judge banged the gavel, glanced at the three members to his left and the three members to his right, and surveyed the crowd like a quarterback studying the defense and preparing to call an audible.

Court was in session.

Somehow the judge, a tall, fat, jowly man with thick glasses that made his eyes look like enormous, unseeing agates stuck in the snow, made his lowly folding chair look like a seat on the U.S. Supreme Court ,if not a king's throne, thanks to his regal bearing and that royal purple cushion that kept his kingly keister from making contact with harsh, unyielding metal.

Thereafter followed an hour and three quarters of old business—budget bagatelle, reports from the Curriculum Committee, the Standards and Testing Committee, the Parent-Teacher Association Steering Committee, and the ad hoc committee appointed to study the question of determining a new school mascot, which, for the ninth consecutive month, reported having failed to reach a consensus on a list of names for the board's consideration.

Names that had been previously discussed and rejected, as dutifully reported in the *Lighthouse* and the *INQUISITOR-NUGGET*, included the Trempealeau Tigers, Titans, and T-Rexes, the Trempealeau Corridor Chorus Line (the high school music teacher, Greg Benedict, had suggested that one), and the Kickapoo Joy Juicers (an anonymous submission).

Motion made, seconded, and carried to table the matter until the following month.

The chairwoman of the Committee on Student Dress Code, Henrietta or Hazel something from Whitehall, took a full 15 minutes to report that the committee had nothing to report. The crowd grew ever more restive as the packed hall filled with smoke and the smells that humans in a hot room emit, especially humans whose diet included beans, bran flakes, and sauerkraut.

Finally, the board, apparently having used up every trick it knew to try to bore the throng into submission, at last got to "New Business."

"Is there any new business to come before the board?" intoned Judge Bristow, whose training as a trial lawyer had taught him never to ask a question for which he had not already planted the answer.

The crowd hushed. Many leaned forward in their chairs.

Blair's lone representative on the committee, a skinny, knobby, little man whose name perhaps two or three people in the room knew, came shakily to his feet.

"Mister Chairman," he squeaked, "I move that the board go into closed session to discuss a personal matter."

"Second," an older woman from Whitehall immediately chirped.

"Do you mean a 'personnel' matter?" Judge Bristow scowled as he asked.

"Yes, sir. A 'personnel' matter."

"Does the second agree to this change in the original motion?"

"Yes, I do, Your Honor."

"All in favor, signify by saying 'Aye.' Opposed? The aye's have it," Judge Bristow banged his gavel. "The motion is carried. The auditorium will be cleared of all except the following people, Mr. Jubal Early and Mr. Frank Walkup," the latter being the high school principal.

It took a moment for the judge's pronouncement to sink in. Then the room broke out in raucous shouts of protest.

Judge Bristow pounded his gavel mightily once, twice, thrice. On the upswing after the third blow, the business end of the gavel flew over his shoulder and landed with a soft thud 20 feet behind him.

It took over 10 minutes for the room to empty. Many simply kept walking, angrily fighting their way into coats, hats, gloves, and boots while expressing their outrage and disgust in mutters and snorts. But most stuck around, despite being jammed into a narrow foyer like 10 pounds of bratwurst stuffed into a three-pound skin.

Three minutes later, the door opened, and Marvin Englehoffer, Judge Bristow's factotum, cautiously announced that the board had gone back into open session and adjourned the meeting.

The foyer exploded. The door slammed shut. If it hadn't been so noisy, Marvin Englehoffer's footfalls could have been heard pattering down the long aisle and out the side door, through which the board and its two guests had already escaped into the cold, snowy night.

Bee and Norah were among the lucky ones who had only a short walk home.

"What just happened in there?" Norah finally managed when they were a hundred yards from the warmth of what was now her home.

Bee knew exactly what hidden ball trick the board had just pulled. "I'll tell you what happened," she said, trying to keep her anger under control. "The board affirmed its unwritten, unlawful, and ungodly 'men only' policy for the baseball, basketball, hockey, and football teams."

Warmth enveloped them as they reached the sanctuary of the diner.

"Jubal! Get down here!" Bee shouted.

"What's the policy for our teams?" Norah asked. "I mean, could a boy play on our team if he wanted to?"

"Oh, honey," Bee said. "Girls' softball and basketball aren't even 'teams.' They're 'clubs.' I'm sure the school board couldn't care less who plays on them. Jubal! Get DOWN here! Norah, you go upstairs please and get ready for bed. Jubal and I need to talk."

"I'd rather stay."

They had both shed their snow gear and piled it on one of the tables. Bee gave Norah a quick one-armed hug, knowing it would embarrass her but needing to do it anyway, for her own sake as much as for Norah's. "Don't worry," she said. "Jubal isn't going to hit me. He's not that kind. And I'm going to try real hard not to mop the floor with him."

She had hoped for a laugh or at least a smile, but Norah looked deadly serious.

"You sure?"

"I'm sure. But thank you."

Jubal was slinking down the stairs, each step clearly the product of iron will fighting against self-preservation instincts.

"Hey, Norah," he said as they passed on the staircase.

Bee went into the kitchen. Jubal walked to the window and stared out at the bleak snowscape. It had stopped snowing, but the strong wind had shifted again and was bringing the so-called Polar Express from the north, blowing the snow off roofs and out of trees, giving the effect of horizontal snowfall.

Bee came out of the kitchen carrying a glass of tomato juice.

"Have you at least got the balls to turn around and face me?" she said from across the room.

Jubal turned slowly. "You know I don't like it when you use language like that," he said.

"Tough shit! Is swearing for boys only, too?"

"This is not that big a deal. I told you what would happen. They aren't about to change the rules just so..."

"They didn't even listen to us! They didn't even have the nerve, let alone the common decency, to do their dirty work out in the open, where we could see them."

"They have every right..."

"No, they don't! The open meeting law says you have to declare your intention to go into closed session 24 hours in advance, and then only to discuss personnel matters."

"Where'd you get that?"

"From the Wisconsin Blue Book."

Jubal snorted air through his nose. "Big deal," was the best he could come up with.

"Did you at least say something on Norah's behalf? Did you at least do that for her?"

"You mean for you, don't you?"

"You think I'm doing this for myself?"

"Aren't you?"

"Jubal Early, you know damn good and well Norah Stoddard is good enough to make the team! Isn't that why they have the stupid rule in the first place? So a girl won't show up the boys?"

"She's good for a girl! That doesn't mean she could compete with men who are bigger, stronger, better trained..."

"They're better trained because you won't let girls compete on your teams with them! And just why are your players 'men' and mine are 'girls'? Girls mature faster than boys."

"Keep your voice down, Brigid Mary. That 'woman' of yours upstairs doesn't need..."

"You know I'm right, don't you? You're afraid to let Norah try out for the team because you know she's good enough to make it."

"If you'd let me get a word in sidewise..."

"You should have done your talking to the board."

"Look, this isn't my decision to make. The school board makes the rules. If I don't obey them, they can me and get somebody who will."

"If it were up to you, would you put her on the team?"

"I'd let her try out. If she was good enough, yeah, I'd put her on the team. I want to win games!"

"Then you should have fought for her, you gutless coward!"

Jubal's eyes narrowed, and his words ran together as they tumbled out. "I'm gutless, huh? And what are you? An ex-athlete trying to recapture former glories by using this girl..."

"Using her! You think I'm USING her?!"

"Yes, using her!"

Bee crossed the room and stood nose to nose with Jubal.

"You never left much of a mark," Jubal went on. "So you think you can get a share of her glory now."

"That's not fair!" Bee screeched.

"No? Well, then, maybe that's not the real reason why you're up on this soapbox of yours over something silly like this."

"Silly? You think equal rights for women is silly?"

"Oh, for corn's sake, Irish! We've got real problems in this town. We can't be wasting our time fussing over this."

"I know we have real problems. People are losing their farms. If the farms go, the farmers go, and if they go, the town dies. And we're denying women equal rights in our schools. That's a real problem, too."

"If you mean the Haskins, Kirsti and Annette will pay them a bundle so they can have another cranberry bog. And the Haskins boys aren't interested in keeping the farm going anyway."

"What about the Haskins girl? Or doesn't she count."

"She doesn't want to run a farm! And as for Kirsti and Annette, now there's a great example of women's rights! It's one thing to be lesbos, but to openly flaunt it like they do..."

"Go ahead, Jubal. Say what you really think."

"I'll tell you what I really think. I think you're trying to make Norah into your daughter because we couldn't have kids of our own. You'd better face the fact that Norah already has a mother."

"You son of a bitch!"

She turned and walked away. Jubal flinched at each step as she mounted the staircase. He jumped when he heard the bedroom door slam. Moments later, it flew open, cracking into the wall. A pillow and blanket tumbled down the steps, stopping in a heap a third of the way down.

"Aw, come on!" Jubal called up.

But Bee had already gone back into the bedroom. This time, she closed the door gently.

Jubal stomped up the stairs, gathered the blanket and pillow, stomped back down. As he reached the foot of the stairs, he glanced up and saw Burleigh's baleful face staring in at him through the window, a coil of smoke curling up from the cigar in his mouth.

"Get out of here, you old soak!" Jubal shouted. "Show's over!"

The face disappeared. Jubal wasn't even sure he'd seen it. He's like a stray cat, Jubal thought. Bee gives him a saucer of milk and a couple of pats and he keeps coming back for more.

Jubal arranged the pillow and blanket on the bench by the door where folks waited to be seated when the diner was full. He had to assume the fetal position to fit all of him on it, and the hard wood dug painfully into his hip and shoulder. He welcomed the pain, figuring he probably had it coming for saying what he did to Bee. He always felt awful after losing his temper and saying hurtful things that he wasn't even sure he meant.

For an hour or more he lay there, running the argument again and again in his mind, thinking of things he should have said to make Bee come around to his point of view.

He heard a door creak upstairs, followed by slow, careful footfalls on the stairs. He stayed still, pretending to be asleep. The girl crept to a table in the center of the room, making rustling noises as she struggled into her jacket, secured the hood, and pulled on her boots. She walked right past him. He could have reached out and touched her. The door opened, the slap of cold shocking him.

When the door clicked shut, the silence she left behind was denser and darker than it had been before he'd heard her door open upstairs.

It's probably for the best, he thought. She didn't really belong here with them. But he didn't feel like it was for the best. He didn't feel good about things at all.

Chapter 8:
Teen Idol

"This portion of Kenny's Koffee Klatsch, your morning cup of Joe with your favorite schmo, is brought to you by Michelson's Grocery. If you can't find it at Michelson's, you don't need it and couldn't afford it if you did. Also brought to you by Moe's Ace Hardware. Ace is the place.

I punched up my sound-effects tape. "How'd you like a bucket of hog's livers?" a woman's gravely voice rasped.

"Not much, but thanks for the offer. Now here's a live report from our bureau chief, Martin Van Bureau, live in the news room."

"This breaking news, KK, just handed to me." Me in my Yosemite Sam voice.

"Well, glue it back together and read it!"

"Moe reports that he finally got in a new shipment of snow throws! Also shovels, for those of you who'd rather call a spade a goldarn shovel. If you missed out on the big sale back in September, you can finally get your mitts on the goods now. Except it's too cold for blowing, throwing, or shoveling this morning."

* * *

He's got that right, Bee thought as she drove down the familiar Main Street, slowing for the bend in the road at the old folks' home where her parents had lived, and gently eased down on the accelerator as Glorious fell away behind her. Jubal's beloved '57 Chevy, which he and his brother had restored and Jubal had kept running all these years, took forever to warm up the interior. Bee willed it to hurry while the cold penetrated her layers of clothing, and her puffs of breath fogged the inside of the windshield.

Jubal didn't like her driving the car in the winter, but she had convinced him that the road would be well-plowed—there were dairy farmers on this route, after all—and promised she'd be extra careful.

"Now here's Willa Raines with the weather."

"Thank you, Kenneth." KK in his Maude Frickert voice. "It's cold out there, Honeybuns, and dry, very dry, with winds at approximately 10 to 15 mph from the north." Kenny whistled into the microphone to make the wind.

"Whoa. Did you just break wind there, Willa?"

"I did not, Kenneth. But the wind should keep us in the icebox for the formidable future."

"While we contemplate our frosty future, here's the sports, with our resident sport, Baxter Backcourt. Baxter, what's the word?"

"In sports news, Kenny, we have this late score to report: St. Louis Browns 5, Kansas City Athletics 3." KK doing his best Foghorn Leghorn, Bee's favorite of his voices.

"Boy, that is a late score. Anything else?

"This partial score, just in—the Boston Celtics 97."

How many times had Kenny greeted her in the morning and kept her company with his corny jokes, constant patter, menagerie of voices, and the "solid gold to make you feel old"? He felt like a friend, a familiar voice to carry her through the first part of the day.

One of her favorite songs filled the frigid car, Ricky Nelson's *Teenage Idol*. He was her first crush, this boy-man, with his long eyelashes, soulful eyes, and languid smile. Her parents didn't have a television then, but her across-the-street friend Claudia Woolery did. Bee's father said Mr. Woolery sold pharmaceuticals, and that's why they could afford a TV. So she went over to Claudia's house to watch, and that's where she had fallen in love with Ricky on the show with his parents and big brother David.

She was still mourning the singer's death—and, with him, the death of her youth.

She thought of the words of another of Ricky's songs, the later, more mature reflection that *"You can't please everyone, so you got to please yourself."*

Unfortunately, she wasn't pleasing herself or anyone else just now. She was upset with herself for fighting with Jubal and frantic with worry that their fighting had driven Norah from their home three nights ago.

Norah's mother apparently hadn't even noticed that her daughter was missing. *Probably too drunk*, Bee figured. Reluctant to get the girl in trouble, Bee had held off for a full day before calling the sheriff, who was now supposedly looking for her.

As the song wound down, Ricky's sweet, sad voice lingering on the words "*How lonesome I can be*," a prayer formed in Bee, for Ricky's soul, for healing in her relationship with Jubal, and for Norah's safe return.

* * *

I potted down the Nelson and punched up Gene Chandler's *Duke of Earl*. I charged down the hall to the toilet , but the door was locked. Loni again. When not camped out in the head, Loni answered the office phone—I had my own line in the studio—"received" anyone who happened to wander into the station, and otherwise filed her nails, gabbed with her friends on the office phone, and read romance novels. When the phone rang when I happened to be out in the lobby, all I usually heard her say was either "He's not here right now" or "I don't know."

How the mighty have fallen. I had to run my own board at a little two-bit, five-watt station in Bumluck, WI. I even had to bring his own coffee, in a thermos I filled each morning at the Dinky, before it officially opened, on my way to the station. I'd been big-time once, or at least semi-big-time. Top-rated morning drive-time DJ for WLOL in Minneapolis-St. Paul, a top 40 format in the rockin' '50s. But top 40 and, for that matter, WLOL, were long gone. It had been a long slide from there—smaller markets, rigid formats, corporate ownership, the heart and soul sucked right out of radio.

I might as well be a farmer. Like them, I'd soon be extinct.

I'd been fired twice for showing up for my shift polluted. I'd also been fired because of format change, fired for telling that stupid joke about the two guys taking a leak off the train trestle, and fired for no reason at all that I could figure.

Each time, the next station, the pay, and the audience were smaller, the bosses less competent, and the listeners dumber.

At least I got to create my own format and use all my voices in glorious little Glorious, only because nobody at the station much cared what I did as long as people listened and I didn't screw up my live ad reads and station IDs.

I'd started doing the voices on my first real radio job, in Covington, Kentucky. There was never anybody else at the station when I was there, either, it being the middle of the night, and nobody would come on the show to be interviewed, so I'd just started interviewing myself using different voices. Turned out I had a knack for it.

Chandler was duking his final earl as I potted down the song and opened my mic.

"That was, of course, *Duke of Earl*, in case you somehow missed the title. Before that we heard Ozzie and Harriet's little boy, Ricky, complaining because he's sooooo lonesome being a rich, famous teenage idol. Poor kid.

"If anybody knows what Ozzie Nelson did for a living on that show, please phone in, willya? He never seemed to have to go to work. Maybe he was a sweater model?

"Now, here once again is our beat reporter, Wally Barnsmell. Trust me, folks. Wally really looks beat this morning. Tough night, Wally?"

"There's still no sign of our little runaway, Kenneth, missing high school freshman and basketball stand-out Norah Stoddard," I intoned in my Elmer Fudd voice, not my best impression, but serviceable."Folks, if you have any information about her whereabouts, please notify the sheriff's office immediately.

"Said sheriff has probably already heard plenty of theories about alien abduction and Russian plots to overthrow the government, so please keep those to yourself," I interrupted himself in my own voice.

* * *

Bee's attention had snapped back to the radio at the mention of Norah's name. Her throat tightened, and her eyes welled with tears, which she fought back.

"Now here's our local correspondent, Glorious' own Gloria von Goldfarkle, to dish the dirt. Gloria?"

"Kenny," KK cooed in his Marilyn Monroe breathless whisper, "a little birdie tells me that Coach Jubal Early is holding down the fort at the

Dinky all by his lonesome this morning while our Queen Bee is taking the morning off and motoring to our neighbor just to the north. Could she have gotten a lead on the Stoddard girl's whereabouts? Leave us hope so."

Bee turned into the driveway at the Haskins' farm, put on the emergency brake, and sat for a moment collecting herself. You couldn't take a step without everybody hearing about it!

"And now here's another great platter that matters, this one coming at you from Nor'leans and the fabulous fat man, Antoine Domino himself, taking us on a little hike up Blueberry Hill."

I punched in the sound effect for a needle scratching a record, glass shattering, a gunshot, and Bugs Bunny chomping a carrot and asking, "Eeee, what's up, Doc?"

"I've told you a million times, you stupid rabbit. 'Updock' is what you do in the late fall before the lake freezes. Now here's Fats, and oh look, he brought his pie-anno with him."

I potted up the song.

The light for the phone line began pulsing. I took the call off air.

"What's up, Myron? You got a hot tip for me on the Stoddard kid?"

"You shouldn't make jokes about her."

"That's what I do, kid. I make jokes about everything. Say, have you got the hots for this Norah chick, Myron? Maybe you've got her locked in your basement and are grooming her to be your sex slave."

"This is serious. She could be in big trouble or hurt or something."

"I'd call being locked up in your basement big trouble."

"It's disrespectful."

"Okay. I hear you, Myron. Maybe I was a little over the top. But I don't get paid to be respectful. I don't get paid much anyway, truth to tell."

Myron started to respond, but I plowed on. "I know this is serious, kid, and I'm trying to remind folks to keep an eye out. I urge you to do the same."

"Nobody listens to me."

"When this song's over, want me to put you on the air so you can make a pitch yourself?"

"No! No! And you shouldn't have put me on the radio like that before. You didn't even tell me!"

"Don't worry, kid. Nobody listens to this show anyway. Talk to you tomorrow."

I punched the button, and the green light flickered and turned red.

The song was over.

I took a deep breath and potted my mic back up.

Bee snapped the radio off. She lifted her head, dabbed at her eyes with her handkerchief, and took a deep breath. *Gran Lydia will know what to do,* she thought. *She always does.*

She took another deep breath and realized she was shivering. More of the words of an old Rick Nelson song came to her. *"If all I sang were memories, I'd rather drive a truck."*

She turned the engine off. *Lord knows Lydia has enough troubles of her own,* she told herself. She doesn't need me crying on her shoulder this morning.

She opened the car door and stepped out into the frigid winter air.

* * *

I potted up the computer feed and tossed my headphones on the table next to the board. Another barrage of babble had bled out into the ether and was gone and, no doubt, already forgotten.

I recognized the old enemy, the darkness, the weight on my heart. *Been here before, and I'll be here again,* I told myself. This, too, shall pass. A belt or two at Big Nose Rose's and some blessed sleep would fix me. I decided to skip walking the route with Billy today. Too damn cold.

This, too, shall pass.

And so will you. So will you.

I struggled into my parka and tied the hood tight. Still, the cold ripped the breath out of me the moment I stepped outside. I lowered my head to the wind off the lake and stepped off the boardwalk into the street, unmindful of the man walking toward me until he plowed into me.

"Whoa. No harm, no foul," I said, holding out a gloved hand to steady the other man. "Mr. Marisnik. What are you doing out on a morning like this?"

"I was comin' to see you, actually," the old man said. "I got a favor to ask ya."

Mr. Marisnik was short and lean, with a gray little beard and squinty eyes, the only other colored person in town besides old Burleigh. Colored *persons*. Mr. Marisnik had a wife. They lived on the east side of the tracks with the rest of the poor folk. Mr. Marisnik did odd jobs, repaired things, fished all summer for food, and opened up his store when he felt like it.

"I'm on my way to the drinkery to see a man about a dog," I told him.

"Mind if I walk along with you?"

"Free country."

"So they say."

I had to slow down to match Mr. Marisnik's short, choppy strides as we reached the boardwalk on the other side of the street and tromped together to Rose's, where warmth and whiskey awaited.

I headed straight for my stool at the bar, but Mr. Marisnik put a hand on my arm and nodded toward a booth.

"Do you mind? I want to keep this just between me and you."

"Sure. No problem."

I surveyed the otherwise empty room. Fast Freddy had the radio on behind the bar. Lawrence Welk and the Orchestra. *Calcutta*. Mush with bubbles. The robot in Des Moines had lousy taste in music.

I fought my way out of my parka, hung it on the hook by the booth, and settled in across the table from Mr. Marisnik, who kept his coat on. Wasn't much of a coat to keep a skinny man warm.

"I hope whatever you've got for me today is good news or money," I said.

Freddy approached.

"You should be careful the company you keep, Mr. Marisnik," he said. "This guy will ruin your reputation."

He set a glass down in front of me. "Your usual, I presume. What'll it be for you, Mr. Marisnik?"

"Just a cup of coffee, please," he said.

"Anything in it?"

"Just coffee."

"Put it on my tab," I said.

"Naw, naw," Mr. Marisnik said. "This one's on me." He dug deep into his pants pocket, pulled out a couple of rumpled bills, and set them on the table.

"Black man's money's good as white, ain't it?" Mr. Marisnik said, grinning up at Freddy.

"Hell, yes," Freddy said.

After Freddy brought the coffee and disappeared into the back room behind the bar, Mr. Marisnik leaned over the table, keeping his voice low. "It's about that Stoddard situation," he said.

"What about the Stoddard situation? Do you know where she and her situation are situated?"

"Yes, sir."

"You wanna tell me?"

"No, sir. This ain't about that. It's about her wanting to pitch for the boy's team."

"Is she alright?"

"She's just fine." Mr. Marisnik sounded like he knew for sure. "That's what I wanted to tell you, so you can tell the people on the radio."

"And you know this because…?"

Instead of answering, Mr. Marisnik took a sip of his coffee, which must have been scalding hot but didn't seem to bother him. I drank off half my whiskey, the cold liquid making my throat spasm slightly.

"She's just off getting some expert coaching, is all," Mr. Marisnik said. "So she'll be ready for the tryouts."

"They're not going to let her try out."

"If Coach would just give her a chance, see what she's got, why, he'd see she'll take that team all the way to the state tournament. Then nobody'll care if she's a girl, a boy, or a jackass mule. They'd be willing to make a 'ception to the rule."

"You've seen her pitch?"

"Yeah, I seen her pitch. She makes that ball dance, just like old Satchel used to, back in the day. I seen Satchel pitch, you know. His fastball didn't have much getty-up on it by that time, his bee ball didn't buzz no more, but he could still make that ball do tricks. The old Bat Dodger, the Midnight Creeper., the Wobbly Ball, the Whipsy-Dipsy-Do. Oh, and that Hesitation Pitch. Ball liked to hang in the air for two minutes. Batter swing once, swing twice, swing three times before the ball even got to the plate— strike out on one pitch!"

The old man was having such a good time, I just sat and listened. Why call him a liar? Wasn't the old fella paying for my drink?

"And the Stoddard girl's got the old Whispy-Dipsy-Do, does she?" I finally asked when Mr. Marisnik ran out of pitches.

"Damn right!"

"Shouldn't you be telling Jubal all this instead of me?"

His grin faded, and his brow furrowed. "You know Mr. Jubal. He might not take kindly to a black man making a suggestion as to what he ought to do."

"Naw. He's not that way. Besides, you're too old, you and Burleigh both, too old to rape their women. And you keep your place. You aren't a threat to anybody. Some of the yahoos in this town might object to your presence on general principles, but they won't do anything about it."

"Jubal's from the South, ain't he?"

"Yeah. And he was born in a barn. But that doesn't make him a cow."

"I just don't want to cause no trouble."

I finished my drink and looked around for Freddy.

"You need some more coffee?" I asked.

"Naw. I'm coffee-ed out. I'd better get to gettin'. Jasmine, she'll be commencing to worry about me about now."

"Thanks for the drink."

"It was my honor, sir."

I watched Mr. Marisnik shuffle across the room and out into the cold. Two old farmers had come in and were sitting at the bar, nursing a couple of beers and shootin' the breeze with Freddy while I pondered what Mr. Marisnik had said. Maybe he could have been telling the truth about seeing Norah Stoddard pitch. He probably hadn't really seen Satchel Paige, though.

I finally caught Freddy's eye, pointed to my glass and made a circle over it. Freddy grabbed the bottle from where he's left it on the bar and started across the room with it.

Chapter 9:
Everlovin'

When she reached her car, Bee turned to look back and saw Lydia standing at her upstairs window. Lydia lifted a hand and nodded her head slowly. Bee waved back.

Such a friend, Bee thought. A brave, wise, dear friend. And now a very ill one.

Bee had fully intended to hurry back to the diner to help Jubal, who would soon be dealing with the lunch rush. But the peace that Lydia's wise and loving words had brought her was already dissipating, leaving the emptiness that had been growing inside her for several weeks. She just couldn't go back and face Jubal and their troubles yet.

She had been waking at least once a night, her heart fluttering, her mind instantly alert as if to some danger, and been unable to get back to sleep for what seemed hours and sometimes not at all, at least not that she was aware of. The last few nights, her first waking thoughts had been of Norah. She tried not to think the worst, that Norah was badly hurt or even dead, but she worried about repercussions Norah might suffer for running away and missing school—assuming, of course, that she was all right and would have a future.

But she'd been visited nightly by some formless fear for several weeks even before Norah had gone missing. Her life, her marriage to Jubal, everything seemed to be slipping away, and something dreadful was about to happen.

Her sense of responsibility, of doing what needed to be done, had always kept her moving forward, but for once she felt helpless, and all activity seemed useless. She had nothing but prayer, and her prayer was nothing but "Help."

Shivering, she buttoned the hood of her down jacket and drew the strings taut so that only her eyes and the top of her nose were exposed to the air. She began walking rapidly up the road, facing any traffic that might come. The landscape matched her inner world—bleak and barren, cold and empty, no breath of life to stir the air, skeletons of trees etched against the horizon.

She heard a strange noise and looked up to see two crows perched on the power line paralleling the road. The larger of the two crows was emitting the sound, which had more of badger or raccoon than crow, a guttural growl unlike any noise she'd ever heard a bird make.

"What's the matter, crow?" she murmured, and the crow, seeming to understand, looked at her, tilted its head, gave one last low growl, and took flight, the smaller crow quickly following.

Bee shuddered again. *An omen? Some sort of warning?*

Silly, she told herself, trying to shake off the feeling. It's a loud-mouthed crow, nothing more.

As she watched the crows fly off, her gaze fell on the path leading off the road and winding past the shed that had been destroyed by a still-unidentified arsonist, perhaps in protest to the Haskins selling their farm. In the distance, a pile of rocks held up a worn wooden cross, and behind the cross, a small white building blended in with the white waves of snow that seemed to engulf it.

It looked like a miniature house, but Bee knew it was Lydia's Shrine to St. Joseph, patron saint of fathers and workers. Lydia had first taken her to it years ago. That had been in spring, when flowers bloomed in front and warm sunshine filled the building's one room. Now nothing about it looked at all inviting; snow covered the ground, and the blank window promised nothing but emptiness. Still, Bee turned onto the path, her boots squeaking on the ice, her body warming with movement now infused with purpose.

A small plaque still hung to the left of the door. Bee wiped the snow off clumsily, her fingers helpless in her fat, well-insulated gloves, to reveal the words carved in the wood, so weather-worn as to be barely legible: "In Memory of Jacob Haskins."

Bee braced herself to tug hard on the door, figuring that blown snow had probably turned to ice in the narrow gap at the top of the frame, but the door yielded easily, with a shriek, causing her to stumble back and almost fall.

She left the door open to admit as much light as possible as she stepped into the little sanctuary. The worn floorboards creaked in protest under her boots. Two tiny pews faced a large wooden crucifix on the wall opposite the door.

Bee jumped when the door banged shut behind her. A gust of wind. Just as well leave the door shut to keep the wind out, not that it was any warmer inside. She was panting little puffs of frosted air and willed her breath to slow, her heart to calm. She took a step, another, and sat, her jacket emitting a sigh as it pressed against the hard back of the pew. The weak rays of sunlight filtering through the frost-covered window offered no more than a candle's worth of illumination to dispel the darkness of the cold, little room.

The wall to her left held the pictures children had drawn for "Gran's chapel." Bee remembered more than saw them in the dim light, childish renderings of Jesus as a baby with Mary and Joseph, a picture of a tall man with a staff and a long beard, stick-figure people, people with large heads and potato-shaped bodies, people with the names "Gran" and "Grampy" and the children's names printed in shaky letters above them, pictures with a little white house with a cross in front and a huge, spiky sun above.

Bee felt that she should pray, for Norah to be found safe, for Gran's recovery—she couldn't bear the thought of her dying—for her marriage and for Jubal. Prayer had been difficult lately. All that came out were complaints and begging, no praise and thanksgiving. She felt neither lifted by these prayers nor assured that her words were going anywhere but around in circles in her head.

With difficulty, she got on her knees, her hands resting on the back of the pew in front of her. She was aware that the wind had picked up outside, pushing the frigid air through the cracks in the walls and making the little chapel creak with its gusts.

Always pray, whether you feel like it or not, a voice told her. She recognized that voice, dear Sister Olive, her favorite teacher in grade school, the sound of Ireland never having left her voice despite all her years in America.

But what if I'm having a hard time believing that God cares about me?

Pray anyway.

She recited the Creed, the Our Father, and was halfway through the Hail Mary when she stopped. The words seemed to fall in a puddle at her feet.

I'm mad at you, God.

Then let that be your prayer. Tell God you're angry.

God wouldn't like that!

God is not Monsignor Bradstone. Stop trying to impress God. You might have fooled Monsignor Bradstone with false piety, but you certainly can't fool God with it.

Monsignor had always frightened her when she was a girl. He was tall and fat and loud, and he talked about the wages of sin a lot.

Bee reached up to flick at something on her cheek, her fat glove scraping at her face, and realized that what she had felt must have been a tear. She supposed that a good cry might make her feel better, but she hadn't let herself really cry since she'd been that frightened child.

She got up slowly, approached the crucifix, and stood, hands palms out by her side, and stared at the crudely carved face of Jesus on the cross. "Here I am, Lord," she murmured, "ungrateful mess that I am."

Something about the way Jesus's arms were extended and the look on his face seemed to suggest quizzical concern, as if Jesus might be saying, "That's life. What are you gonna do?"

* * *

At the moment, Jubal sat on the bank of the river a few hundred yards in back of the diner. The water was frozen over at the banks but still open in the middle. This was his spot, where he often came to fish and think or just think. If he found someone sitting there, he felt trespassed against, but there was no one else foolish or desperate enough to be out on such a cold day, so he had the spot all to himself.

He hadn't planned to come, but when the morning crowd had moved on and only Jonesy and Wilmar, two of the regular knights of the counter stools, remained at their posts, Jubal had asked them to keep an eye on things, dug out a hole in the jar of wrapped mints by the cash register for folks to put money for anything they took, and left, promising to be back in 15 minutes.

Grabbing only his light baseball warm-up jacket and a pair of knit mittens off their pegs by the door and wearing only jeans, tattered sneakers with no socks, a cloth shirt, and his baseball cap, he'd lit out for the river.

He and Bee seemed to do nothing but argue lately. It had gotten worse with Norah living with them, but things had been tense before that. He'd try to hear her out, like you're supposed to, but he always wound up snapping at her. She'd goad him into an argument, they'd wind up nose to nose, and he'd blurt out nasty stuff he didn't even mean. He wished he could take it all back, but it was too late.

That wasn't really him talking. If he only had time to think first.

He had plowed this field of thought many times before, but it had never before yielded a crop.

Even when he hollered at his players when they screwed up, he wasn't mad at them. Not the way Bee made him mad. When he coached the little kids in his baseball camp every summer, he was patient and gentle with them, loving every blessed one of the little snot-nosed buggers. It was easy to be patient and gentle with little kids. They didn't push his buttons the way Bee did.

He supposed he ought to pray but felt wholly inadequate to the task.

"Help me," he murmured. "I'm in over my head."

He sat on the bank watching the strip of open water in the middle of the river push sluggishly westward, bent on meeting up with the Mississippi at La Crosse. He burrowed his left hand into the snow beside him until he encountered a small stone, which he pegged as hard as he could. The stone cleared the open water but scudded on the ice near the far bank. He dug out another stone, this one slightly larger than the first, and sent it on a low arc completely over the river, to bury itself silently in the snowbank on the far side.

Now the mitten was wet and his hand colder than if he weren't wearing mittens at all.

One of the quilters who came to the diner every mid-morning, nursing her coffee and her "maybe just this once" bakery sweet roll, had knitted the mittens for him. Annie something. Annie Shawl, he thought her name was—something like that.

The sweet young girls used to give him the eye and smile when they'd catch him sizing them up. Now old ladies knitted him mittens and mukluks.

He was supposed to be thinking about what to do to make it up to Bee, but his nimble mind slipped the collar and escaped to the current Dinky crisis, the raccoon spending its nights in the heating duct in the basement. He'd been putting off confronting it for several days, but it was only a matter of time before the varmint pulled the pipe away from the wall and escaped into the basement searching for food. He had moved everything that wasn't canned or in a barrel up to the kitchen closet, but the raccoon still returned to the duct every night for refuge from the bitter cold outside.

Almost slipping as he stood, Jubal swept the snow and ice off his butt, jammed his hands into his windbreaker's pockets, and limped back up the hill to the diner.

* * *

When Bee left the chapel, she noticed a fresh set of footprints leading up to the door from around the side of the building and then leading away again. Someone had come while she was inside! She walked in the footprints around the building and saw someone fleeing toward the line of red cedars that Lydia and Jacob had planted along the river decades ago to serve as a wind-and-snow break. She plunged into the snowy field, shouting "Stop!" and "Wait!" The footprints were far apart, and she had trouble matching the long stride.

Realizing that she was falling farther behind, Bee turned and ran as fast as the snow and ice would permit back to the country road. One of the crows started up again as she neared the road, but she ignored it. Her heart was pounding when she reached her car. She drove as fast as she dared up the road to where the paving ended. On the rutted dirt beyond where the county plowed, the snow had been worn to glare ice, and once Jubal's old Chevy went into a skid and almost left the road. Creeping forward, Bee edged the car beyond the windbreak, now a hundred yards distant, and she could see behind the curtain of trees. But there was nothing to see. Whoever it was had disappeared.

She saw no signs that a car had been parked anywhere nearby, but a car wouldn't have left tire tracks on the parts of the road where the snow had turned to ice anyway.

Bee got the car turned around, crept back to the county highway, and headed back toward Glorious. Out of habit, she clicked on the radio. The station happened to be playing another Ricky Nelson song, *Everlovin'*, which sent a shiver through her, and she again felt like crying. When the song ended, she clicked the radio off, grimly hung onto the steering wheel, and concentrated on her driving.

When she pulled up in front of the Dinky, the "CLOSED" side of the sign in the window was facing out. Frowning, she got out of the car, almost slipping on a patch of ice in the road. She found the diner door unlocked and walked into the dining room, where Jonesy was clearing dirty dishes from one of the tables. Back in the kitchen, she found Wilmar scrubbing a dirty pot in the sink, a stack of dirty dishes awaiting his attention.

"Where...What's happened to Jubal?"

Wilmar jumped and dropped the pan into the sink, splashing soapy water on himself.

"Oh, hello, Bee," he said, wiping his hands on his baggy corduroy pants. "I didn't hear you come in."

"He's fine, Missy," Jonesy said from behind her in the doorway. "He said he had to duck out for a few minutes and kind of left us in charge. We don't know how to cook, and when he didn't come back right away, we just closed her up and started to clean up for him."

"Where did he go? What's wrong?"

Jonesy, who was shorter than Bee, bald, hard of hearing and nearly blind, even with his thick glasses, shrugged his shoulders and grinned. "Didn't nothing seem the matter," he said. "Just said he'd be right back."

"Didn't say where he was going," Wilmar threw in.

"How long ago was this?"

Jonesy shrugged again.

"Oh, maybe half an hour, more or less," Wilmar said.

Dizziness swirled through her. She stumbled back into the dining room and sagged onto the closest chair, still so bundled in down, wool, and cotton she could barely bend in the middle. She might have sat for a few seconds or several minutes, her mind too dazed to keep track or care.

"You all right, Missy?" Wilmar asked from the doorway. "There's coffee, if you'd like some."

"No. Thank you. I'm all right."

Dishes clattered as Jonesy loaded them into one of the washer racks.

The front door rattled, and Jubal burst into the room.

"There you are!"

"Jubal! Where were you?."

"Sweet Bee, I'm so sorry. It was all my..."

"I think I saw her!"

She jumped to her feet. He came and put a hand on her arm to steady her.

"Saw who?"

She glanced toward the kitchen.

"She ran away before I could talk to her. We've got to find her, Jubal. I'm sure it was her. I called to her, but she kept running."

"Are you talking about Norah?"

She shushed him. "Yes!" she hissed.

"What would she be doing...?"

"Never mind. We've got to find her."

"You're sure it was her?"

"Yes! Well, pretty sure. I think I saw a flash of red sticking out from under her hood. And who else could it have been?"

"What would she be doing over at Gran Lydia's?"

"I think she was visiting the shrine."

"Shrine? There's a shrine at the Haskins' place?"

For the first time, she took a close look at him. Ice still hung from his eyelashes, his cheeks were red from wind burn, and his nose and ears were a creamy white with the onset of frostbite.

"What were you doing outside dressed like that? Are you out of your mind? Come on! Get your coat. Let's go!"

"Go where?"

"Back to the shrine."

"Well, we'll be on our way then," Wilmar said, leading Jonesy out from the kitchen.

"Thanks, fellas. I appreciate you holding down the fort," Jubal said.

"No problem. We'll pay for what we ate."

"It's on the house today, boys."

"Get your coat," Bee said, as soon as they were gone.

"Honey, you said she ran away from you."

"Yes! We need to hurry."

"Hurry where? She'd be long gone by now."

"But I saw her."

"Which means she's alive and still nearby. That's good news."

"Yes, but we have to ..."

"Honeybee, if she'd wanted to talk to you, she wouldn't have run away, would she?"

"Maybe she didn't realize it was me." But the rightness of what Jubal had said seeped into her, and all her energy drained out. She sagged, and Jubal helped her out of her heavy jacket and back into the chair.

"Why don't you lie down upstairs for a bit? I'll finish here."

She shook her head weakly. "No, I'll help."

"You sure?"

She nodded.

"Yeah, okay. As soon as we close up, I'll go out looking for her."

"I'll go with you."

"Let's see how you're feeling."

"We have to find her."

"We will."

The moment was past, and with it a chance for Jubal to tell his wife how sorry he was for the way he'd acted. He was so much better at actions than words anyway. He'd just have to let his all-out effort to get the diner back in shape and resume the hunt for Norah speak for him.

As for the raccoon, she'd have to wait.

Chapter 10:
Friends

Heart pounding, she waited in the darkness.

A dog erupted in startled barking, which quickly turned into deep, throaty baying. Sound traveled so well in the cold, brittle air, she couldn't tell how far away the dog was but guessed the Underdahl's hound had treed a raccoon or maybe a possum. She waited to see if a light went on in the Underdahl's house. One did, and moments later, the door flew open and a gruff voice hollered, "Shut up, Matilda." The noise ceased. After a pause, the door slammed. The night was still again.

In the glare of the floodlight, which played on the front of the high school all night, Norah saw the blue and gold "Glorious High" cloth bag hanging on the door knob. Thank you, Sarah. Still she hesitated. When she reached the door, it would be like stepping into a spotlight on stage. If anybody saw her, they might try to catch her or call the sheriff. She had to be sure no one was coming.

When she had been walking, it hadn't seemed so cold, but now she began to shiver, and the air stung her lungs. She pulled the balaclava down so that it covered her face.

A truck thundered down the highway, downshifted as it neared the town limits, and rumbled up Main Street one block over. She waited until it had again regained speed, the town behind it. She had to be so careful. Bee had almost caught her out by the Haskins' chapel.

Without consciously deciding to do so, she took off sprinting for the door, almost tumbling on the top step, unhooked the bag from the door knob, replaced it with an identical bag she'd been carrying, and sprinted back behind the hedge that marked the boundary of the school grounds.

All was as before. Safe. She waited for her heart to slow, then began the walk back to the little cabin on the river that was her temporary home.

Sarah was a good friend, the only real friend she'd made at school. She loved her teammates, of course. They went through battle together every Friday night and spent long hours practicing. But she'd never confided in any of them the way she had with Sarah, never had a serious conversation with them other than about basketball. She hadn't even told them what she intended to do; they were just as surprised as everyone else when the news spread through the school.

She had only told Sarah, had only enlisted Sarah to help her, and now she saw that she had put Sarah in jeopardy by doing so. She prayed no harm would come to her.

Sarah had confided in her, too, telling her about her grandmother's cancer. Norah had been praying for 'Gran Lydia' ever since.

She remembered the first day she and Sarah had really talked. Sarah had suggested they study together in the cafeteria, and Norah, surprised and happy that anyone, and an upperclassmen at that, had asked, eagerly said "yes."

She usually packed a lunch and ate alone in a vacant classroom, but this day she left her lunch in her locker, stood in line with Sarah, and got a steaming tamale wrapped in corn husks, a bowl of peas, right out of the can and into the steamer, a square of Jello with little chunks of pineapples suspended in it, and a carton of milk.

They found an otherwise unoccupied table and ate side by side. But they didn't get any studying done, and their friendship got off to a somewhat rocky start when Sarah said something about Norah being "lucky."

"'Lucky'? You think I'm 'lucky'?" Norah had said.

"Yes! Everybody does. They call you 'the natural,' like in the movie."

"What movie?"

"You didn't see *The Natural*? With Robert Redford! It's about this baseball player who nobody's ever heard of, and he's the best player anybody ever saw, like God's gift to baseball."

"And they think I'm like that?"

"Yes. Well, that and they also say you seem pretty stuck up."

"Who is this 'they'?"

Sarah shrugged. "Just kids. You know how kids talk."

"Well, you can tell them for me, I'm no natural."

"Norah, I've seen you play. You must know how great you are. You're famous! Everybody says you'll put our school on the map."

"They shouldn't put all that on me."

"Don't raise your voice. People are looking at us."

Norah lowered her voice, but it lost none of its intensity. "It makes me feel like I'm some kind of freak."

"You are a freak—freaky good."

"I just work harder, practice more." Norah stopped, embarrassed by her own anger. When Sarah didn't respond, she went on. "I'm not a freak," she said, "and I'm not a hero. I just love playing."

"Norah, you'll probably be famous, play in college, maybe even become a pro."

"Fat chance. My mother has never even seen a college, much less gone to one, and even if she had the money to send me, which she doesn't, she wouldn't 'waste it' like that."

"Couldn't you get a scholarship? You're smart enough."

"What would be the point? I could never make a living playing sports. Women only play tennis or golf professionally, and those are rich peoples' sports, not for folks like me. Not from a town like Glorious. No, I'll just play for dear old Glorious for four years and then get a nothing job, living from paycheck to paycheck like my mother, stuck in the town where I was born."

The first bell rang, warning them that they had five minutes to finish lunch and get to their next classes.

"I guess we're not going to get any studying done," Norah said, embarrassed at having talked so much about herself.

"Maybe after school?"

"I have practice."

"How about before school tomorrow? I could meet you here."

"Yeah. Okay. I guess so."

"Good. I'll see you tomorrow morning then," Sarah said.

"What time, 7:00?"

"I'll be here."

"Great. And thanks."

"For what?"

Norah shrugged. "For listening, I guess."

Lame, she had scolded herself as she hurried to her Wisconsin History class.

* * *

She was nearing the shack now, could see the light in the window and smell the smoke from the fire. He might be waiting up for her, reading from his old, battered Bible. It had a soft black cover with gold lettering, and he licked his thumb every time he turned a page. Occasionally, he read something to her. Micah 6:8 seemed to be his favorite. *Love what is good. Do what is just. Walk humbly with your God.* Something like that.

He had insisted she take the bed, and he slept on a thin pallet on the floor. He got up really early, while it was still dark, and would wake her up to have breakfast and go to school But first they'd grab their gloves and go out and have a catch in the predawn light. He had put a strip of reflecting tape on his glove so she could see it better and cleared out a strip 20 of his paces long, built up a mound, and carved out a home plate. After they'd warmed up, he'd start calling the pitches he wanted her to throw and telling her what she was doing right and what she needed to correct.

Then he'd leave for his job, and Norah would clean up in the shack, do her homework, and read the journal he'd kept on the art and craft of pitching. He had said she could read it after she found it on a shelf with some other journals and books. She couldn't read the other journals, he'd said, but it was okay to read this one. He trusted her, so she didn't read the others, but she poured over the one on pitching. He seemed to know everything there was to know about it.

She quietly lifted the latch and opened the door of the shack. In the flickering light of the candle he had left for her, she saw him curled up on the pallet underneath a rough woolen blanket, and in that moment, Norah was filled with the thought that she had not one, but two, good friends now, three counting Coach.

CHAPTER 11:
The Old Man in the Stands

The world moved on, as is its wont. Even if some in Glorious took no note of it, Carolyn Henniger insisted on trying to keep those who cared informed. When Ryan White, the boy with AIDS, returned to classes at Western Middle School in Indiana, she ran a four-paragraph Associated Press story on page two. Same when Imelda and Ferdinand Marcos fled the Philippines, reportedly with $5 billion bled from the country and Imelda's 5,400 pairs of shoes. Carolyn put George O'Keefe's death at age 98 in Santa Fe, New Mexico on the front page, with a thick black border, because the artist had been born in Sun Prairie, Wisconsin. ("Always look for the local angle," a community journalism prof had taught her.) And she wrote in her "From the Editor's High Shaky Stool" column about the nine Navy divers who found the crew compartment of the ruined spacecraft *Challenger*, along with the remains of the astronauts who died in it.

She also published the news everyone wanted—a front -page story and a page of pictures on page three, for example, from the high school regional basketball tournament, where our boys were rudely whupped by the Bloomer Blackhawks in the first round. She also ran a large picture on page one of the fight between the two squads that broke out after the game, clearing the bleachers for a brawl that most observers agreed was also won by the Blackhawks.

To add insult—and a bit of sheer terror—to the considerable injury to the egos of the townsfolk, a blizzard struck just as they were attempting to make their way back home to Glorious. Carolyn ran a story with a picture of the blizzard on page one, jumping to more pictures of the snowfall in Glorious on the center pages.

Fortunately, all were home and accounted for the next morning.

The emergency closed-door joint meeting of the school board and the town council the following Monday made the front page, even though the news was already stale by the time the *INQUISITOR-NUGGET* hit the streets Thursday. Everybody pretty much already knew by then that the confederacy of dunces had affirmed the district policy: only students of the male persuasion were allowed to participate on the men's varsity teams, just as God had ordained.

Norah's disappearance warranted the first extra edition of the *INQUISITOR-NUGGET* anyone could remember. Her whereabouts remained a mystery for two weeks, while the story remained on page one with the news that two Sundays in a row, someone had hung a bag on the handle of the front door of the school, presumably Norah herself, to be found by the janitor who opened up the school and fired up the furnace Monday morning. Each bag contained Norah's completed homework assignments for the previous week, written in her small, precise hand.

Which brings us to the tryouts for the high school men's baseball team, held, as tradition dictated, on the Ides of March. The town's run of bad luck continued when a heavy snow fell the day before the tryouts. Coach Early had to move the competition to the stock pavilion on the fairgrounds in Chippewa Falls, north of Eau Claire. That meant that Jubal and his volunteer assistant coaches, Billy "Gunner" Tollefsen, Julien Rink, and Jan Stenerud, had to drive up on Friday, Gunner hauling the batting cage, bases, limer, balls and bats, and the rest of the equipment on his flatbed trailer. They worked four hours Friday night setting up pitching mounds and a diamond in the pavilion, then got up early the next morning to lead a car caravan to get all the prospective players up to Chippewa Falls.

With Jubal, Gunner, Julien, and Jan thus occupied, the diner, the bakery, and the deli were running with only their wives to handle the trade back home. That wasn't a big problem, though, since the wives usually did most of the heavy lifting anyway. The barbershop was closed outright, but that wasn't a problem either, since most of the menfolk joined the parade, so they could make their own decisions about who should and shouldn't make the team.

Jubal already had most of the roster assembled in his head: returning players from last year's squad and five or six kids ready to make the jump from the junior varsity. Even so, each had to earn his place on the team. *You never value anything that was just handed to you*, was Jubal's thinking. And there was always that chance that a walk-on would dazzle them.

Jubal had been worried about the Stoddard girl's showing up, but with her disappearance, that worry had moved to a spot at the far end of the bench in the dugout of his mind. Not that he was happy she'd gone AWOL, of course, and not that he didn't pray every night for her well-being and safe return. He even went out twice more asking at local farmhouses up and down the corridor if anyone had seen her. But he was relieved, too, since he hadn't relished the idea of having to ban her from tryouts. As long as she showed up safe and sound later, it would all be fine with Jubal.

The Saturday morning in question dawned clear and cloud free, even if still not quite within hailing distance of freezing, and the parade of cars made it the 64 miles to Chippewa Falls without problems any worse than Coach Smith's young son, Sammy, getting car sick and throwing up all over the back seat of the family station wagon.

Eulalia McKenzie Bledsoe was among the faithful in attendance, of course, waving her old "Chiefs" pennant and cheering for all 'her kids' to do well. Eulalia, 85 years old and 32 years a widow, had attended every tryout and every game, home and away, for as long as anybody could remember, even though her younger brother, Hazel, 84, had to drive her now.

Eagle-eyed Eulalia was, in fact, the only one to spot the strange duo, a coltish, long-legged kid and a tall, thin, stooped old man, walk into the pavilion as tryouts were already underway. She recognized the man, old Burleigh Grimes the printer, but the kid, who was almost as tall as Burleigh, was wearing a hooded sweatshirt, hood up. Some wanna-be player Burleigh had taken a special interest in, Eulalia figured.

Jubal was catching the pitching candidates and had his back to the entrance, so he didn't see the strange pair stop at the edge of the arena, the old man talking, the youngster listening, didn't see the old man climb up into the stands and sit apart from the others, only caught a glimpse out of the corner of his eye of the late-comer walking out to take a place in line with the other pitchers.

But Eulalia saw, and from that point, on she watched nothing but the old man in the stands and the walk-on at the end of the line.

"Just a game of catch," Jubal hollered out to the kid currently toeing the improv pitchers' rubber, a sophomore named Eddie LeFaye, a starter on the junior varsity last year who had good velocity and movement on the ball, although his wildness kept him from winning more games than he lost. "Hit the mitt. No batter up there," Jubal chattered.

There was, in fact, a batter, if not a hitter, Father Healey, who each season picked up a bat and stood in the batter's box, first as a left-handed hitter, than as a righty, while the pitchers threw to Jubal. Father had played varsity and American Legion ball many decades ago, before he went away to the seminary in Madison. Those who remembered said he was a pretty fair hitter, even had a little pop in his bat, especially for a short, scrawny Irisher. But now he simply stood, grinning out at the pitcher.

Eddie LeFaye nodded as Jubal gave him the sign for fast ball, went into his rather elongated wind-up, and promptly plunked Father Healey on the right shin. The good father hopped around on his left foot, manfully keeping his thoughts to himself. Gerry "Moonlight" Graham, who had earned his First Aid merit badge decades ago and was thus qualified to serve as the volunteer team doctor, came out of the stands to minister to the Padre, and Hiram Knutson, the town banker, took his place in the batter's box.

One by one, Jubal put the chuckers through their paces, ending each one's turn by rolling the ball out a few feet in front of the plate for the kid to charge, pick up barehanded, and throw to first baseman Don "Boomer" Smith, the high school football coach. By the time the last candidate, the kid in the hood, finally took the mound, Jubal's knees were aching and his throwing arm, still not right since the raccoon he had finally managed to extricate from the basement had gashed it, felt like an overcooked noodle. He was anxious to dispatch the kid, a walk-on who didn't look like much of a prospect, and hang up the pancake glove for the day.

The kid threw a few warm-up tosses, and Banker Knutson stepped back into the left-handed batters' box, his belly hanging out dangerously near the plate.

"Let's see your fast ball," Jubal instructed.

The kid, a lefty, pitching out of a stretch instead of using a full wind-up, kicked and fired. The ball hit Jubal's glove right where he held it, but it didn't have much mustard on it. Jubal fired the ball back to the mound.

The kid caught it nonchalantly, then worked the baseball with both hands and looked in for a sign.

"Another heater," Jubal said.

Again the ball was accurate, but Jubal figured even Knutson could have caught up to it. Jubal stood, pushing the catcher's mask up off his face, and was ready to dismiss the kid when a high, impossibly loud whistle pierced the stale air of the pavilion. "Time out, coach!" Burleigh Grimes called out from Jubal's right, and Jubal turned to see the bent old man trotting slowly out toward the mound.

"What gives, Burleigh?" Jubal called out.

"I just need a second, Coach," Burleigh called back. "I been working with this kid."

"All right. Snap it up."

When Burleigh reached the mound, he spoke briefly, the pitcher listening intently, head down. Then Burleigh stepped back behind the mound, where the other pitching candidates sprawled in the dirt.

"Come on, kid." Jubal instructed. "Let's go. A couple more tosses."

"How about a breaking ball?" Burleigh said.

"You got a breaking ball?"

"Slider, curve, circle change, and screwball," Burleigh said.

Jubal snorted, but just in case the kid could actually throw any of those pitches, he said, "Okay, kid. Let's see the 'yacker'," that being slang for curveball, also known as "Uncle Charlie."

The kid kicked and threw a rainbow curve, what they call a 12 to 6, that started out head high but, with a huge late drop, cut into the strike zone knee high on the corner.

"Wow," Banker Knutson murmured.

"I'll be hogged tied and slathered with butter," Jubal muttered.

"How about a slider?" he said, firing the ball back to the kid.

At first, the pitch looked like it would be way inside, prompting Knutson to drop the bat, stumble backwards, and fall on his rumpus. But the ball broke back across the inside corner of the plate for a strike. When Jubal looked up, the kid was grinning at him.

In that moment, he recognized her.

"How about...?" He had to stop and clear his throat. "How about the change?"

Norah Stoddard took her abbreviated wind-up and, with the same motion and arm speed as for the other pitches, tossed a ball that came in much slower and had good late movement.

Last came the screwball, which went in right down the middle but then broke not out but in, nicking the inside corner of the plate as Knutson again bailed out of the batter's box.

"Well, I'll be switched," Jubal muttered.

He rolled the ball out in front of the plate. As Norah charged and pounced on the ball, her hood flopped off, allowing a long red braid to tumble down her back. She picked up the ball, whirled, and fired a strike to Smith at first, but Smith was just staring at her and didn't even put a glove up to protect himself. The ball bounced off his stomach, where his glove should have been.

"It's her!" Eulalia McKenzie Bledsoe screeched at the top of her lungs. "I knew it! I just knew it!"

Reaction rippled through the crowd. Jubal's right knee popped as he jumped up and strode out to the mound. Norah had retreated to the back of the mound, where Burleigh stood beside her, his hand resting lightly on her shoulder.

Eulalia began chanting "Norah! Norah! Norah!" Soon most of the women in the stands and quite a many of the men joined the chorus. None of them had ever seen anybody, man or woman, boy or girl, make a baseball do tricks like they'd just seen.

Perhaps the news was carried to Glorious on the cold north wind. More likely, Myron Mickelson, Carolyn Henniger, or both had used their portable phones to call the diner and tell Bee what had happened. By the time Jubal got back to town after helping repack the equipment, the welcoming throng already packed the Dinky.

People started shouting questions at Jubal the moment he emerged through the kitchen doorway into the dining area.

"One at a time!" Jubal shouted, rather enjoying the fuss. "Yeah, Arvid. Go ahead."

The noise subsided, Eulalia's by now delirious "I knew it!" being the last shout heard.

"What are you going to do?" the councilman asked.

94

"Do? Why, I believe I'll crack open a beer, if you-all don't mind."

"About the Stoddard kid!" Cece Johnsrud hollered, unable to contain herself.

"Oh, her," Jubal said. "Well, what do you think I'm going to do? I done found me my starting pitcher for opening day."

Chapter 12:
Clever as Snakes, Innocent as Doves

All was in darkness when he crept in at the side door. He groped his way to the stairs and climbed to the balcony, slouched down in the last pew, and let the darkness engulf him.

What do you expect to find here? There's nothing here for you.

It didn't matter if his eyes were open or closed. The darkness was absolute.

That other darkness was on him again, in his head and in his chest, a weight pressing against his heart. The voice in the darkness counseled him to go get stinking drunk and then kill himself.

Go ahead and do it. Who would care?

Thoughts of Grace came to him. Mrs. Walker's little girl, just three and then four years old. He'd been six, maybe seven. She called him "big brother." She would cock her head and ask "Why?" in her sweet little voice, and he'd try to explain things to her, and she'd ask "Why?" again and again. Another lifetime ago.

Then this good memory too got sucked into the darkness.

Mrs. Walker had been different frfom the others. She had talked to him. Sung to him. Kept her man from beating him, taking the beatings herself. She had taken him to her church, a black Baptist church on the south side of Chicago. Baptized him in the dark, in the empty church. She squeezed her eyes tight shut and moaned when she prayed.

Said, "Sweet baby Jesus."

"My Lord and my God."

Said, "Lord, have mercy."

Her man had come home very drunk and beaten Mrs. Walker nearly to death, and Burleigh had had to go to another foster home, and another, and another. The others wanted the money the state paid them, or a little slave to boss around, or someone weak and vulnerable to hurt. One of his "fathers" locked him in a closet. Locked him outside in the snow. Put cigars out on his arms. Came at him in the night. Climbed into his bed.

Another threw him across the room, giving him a concussion when his head slammed into the wall.

Another hammered on his left hand, breaking his little finger. It never healed right and wouldn't bend to this day.

These memories made him grab his head with both hands, his fingernails digging into his scalp—as if he could rip open his skull and let the darkness out.

Burleigh couldn't remember anyone teaching him how to talk, or walk, or read, or pitch a baseball. He must have just watched and listened and taught himself.

His first drink of alcohol, sipped from an abandoned glass of one of his "fathers" after the latter had passed out, had made the darkness go away. He had been 12 years old.

In time, he found that drinking made him feel warm and safe and happy—at first, and only for a little while. But as more time passed, drinking only made the darkness worse, became part of the darkness, and he drank to lose consciousness.

When he turned 18 and aged out of the foster system, he had lived on the streets of Chicago for a time and went to a tech school to learn the printing trade. He had to learn to touch type with nine fingers. It was the second thing he'd ever excelled at, the other being throwing a baseball, and he loved how his fingers, nine of them, anyway, could dance on the keyboard of the old Linotype machine, just as he loved how his fingers, four of them, could make a baseball dance.

His instructor, a short, bald, round little man named Salvadore Dominico, "Mr. D," helped him get his first job with a small weekly newspaper in Hoffman, in southern Illinois.

He drank away that job, and a second, and became an itinerant, working his way west. He was always skilled enough to get another job but always too drunk to keep it. Often he slept in the woods and survived on garbage, petty theft, and begging until he could find another job.

He had been one of the lucky ones. He had hit bottom before he died.

He woke up in a county lockup in Spanish Fork, Utah, to learn he was serving a 90-day sentence for vagrancy and public indecency. He had apparently urinated on the sidewalk, right outside a flower shop, and the girl behind the counter had seen him and called the police. He shared a cell with an enormous young black man named Eugene Robinson, who read his Bible aloud every night.

His withdrawal from alcohol was worse than the worst bodily sickness he could have imagined, but after a few days, the agony started to lift, and he and his cellmate started exchanging their stories. Eugene had literally been born in a prison cell. He had been in a street gang, sold drugs, stolen, had already been jailed twice and sent to a home for juvenile offenders before he was 16. When he was 27, he had found Jesus.

The night before Eugene was to be released, he told Burleigh (who had given that name to the policeman who hauled him in and decided to keep it) that he was "a friend of Bill's," which meant he went to Alcoholics Anonymous meetings. Three times he had "gone out," as they called it when you went back to drinking, and three times he had come back. He had been sober for 17 months this time and thought he could make it now, one day at a time, but he knew, he said, that his addiction, instead of withering, just got stronger while he abstained. He had to keep working the steps, he said, and said that he always would have to. He said he wanted to be a prison chaplain, to help others like himself.

Eugene sat on his bunk, Burleigh on his, their knees almost touching in the narrow cell. Eugene had his Bible open on his lap. It had a soft black cover with gold letters and showed signs of heavy use. He recited several Bible passages for Burleigh, scriptures about drinking, without once looking at the book. He had "got 'em up by heart," he said.

"Wine is a mocker, strong drink a brawler, and whoever is led astray by it is not wise," he said. Proverbs something something.

Burleigh nodded and said, "That sounds about right."

Eugene had a deep, resonant voice that had the South in it. He spoke softly and slowly, especially when proclaiming scripture.

"Do not look at wine when it is red, when it sparkles in the cup and goes down smoothly," he said. "In the end it bites like a serpent and stings like an adder. Your eyes will see strange things and your heart utter perverse things."

Another proverb.

Burleigh again nodded in agreement. That one sounded about right, too, he said.

"'Be sober minded,'" Eugene proclaimed. "'Your adversary the devil prowls around like a roaring lion, seeking someone to devour.'"

Something stirred in Burleigh's memory. A lion had often prowled in his dreams when he was a boy, blood dripping from its long, sharp teeth. Burleigh knew it was the devil and that it was after him, in the way you just know things in a dream.

Mrs. Walker had read that same Bible passage to him! He hadn't listened, not then. But he had heard.

She told him to be as clever as a snake and as innocent as a dove. He hadn't understood it then, but when it came to him now, he understood, and something moved inside him. He needed a child's heart and a man's head.

Eugene told him about an AA meeting he went to, in the basement of a Baptist church a couple of blocks away. Then he reached out, the Bible in his hand, bridging the narrow cell.

"Take this," he said.

"I can't take your Bible!" Burleigh protested.

"That's all right," Eugene said. "First thing when I get out, I'll get me another one."

After Eugene was gone, Burleigh read in that Bible while sitting out his 90 days; there was nothing else to do. Mostly he read Matthew chapters six and seven, because Eugene had told him that's where Jesus taught us the right way to live. Mrs. Walker had read this to him, too.

When he got out of jail, instead of heading for a bar, he had gone to a meeting. He didn't know what to expect. Even so, he was surprised, relieved. People, many of them more messed up than he was, just told their stories. Nobody had a last name. After the meeting, Eugene sought him out and asked him if he planned to come again.

"I'll be moving on now," Burleigh said. "Gotta find work."

"There are meetings everywhere. You can find one any day of the week."

Burleigh found that this was true. There were AA "clubhouses" everywhere he went, even in little towns. In Plymouth, Indiana—he was working his way back east now—Burleigh did his 90-90, a meeting a day for

90 days, staying sober the whole three months. He thought he'd won the battle and celebrated by going to a bar, to have no more than two drinks, he told himself.

It took him two more tries, but something always brought him back to AA, wherever he was. He finally earned his first-year coin, and then his second and third.

He got in the habit of reading from Eugene's Bible just before sleeping each night and again first thing upon waking.

The darkness still came at times, and the voice still told him he should kill himself. He learned not to try to argue with it. Like his drinking, he couldn't defeat it, not by himself. He turned it over to God and endured until it went away.

He stayed sober, but the newspaper where he was working converted to cold type and, with no need for his skills, let him go. Again, he moved on, and the voice followed him wherever he went.

It was with him now, in the loft of the Catholic church in Tierney, Wisconsin, telling him he was doomed. He had only made things worse for the girl, Norah, the voice said softly, and now she'd be arrested, too, and put into the foster system like he had been.

When she had come to him, he had tried to do the right thing and turn her in to the sheriff, like he knew he should, but he couldn't do it, even if it meant that the lion would devour him and he would go to hell.

He lay down on the pew in the darkness. He wept. Then he must have slept.

When he opened his eyes, sunlight was seeping through the stained-glass windows. He covered his eyes with his hands, but he still saw the light. When he uncovered his eyes, the light looked like milk that he could scoop up in his hands and drink.

He wanted a drink more than he could ever remember wanting one.

He saw Jesus hanging on the cross on the wall behind the altar below. Jesus had big hands and long, bony fingers.

"My God, my God. Why hast thou forsaken me?"

A door opened, closed. A white-haired woman with powdery white face and hands had appeared at the side door of the church. She carried several books clutched to her chest. She dumped all but one on top of the organ, the noise outraging the silence. She opened the last book and plopped it on the music rack. She took off her shoes. She was wearing stockings.

She settled in on the bench like a bird fluffing its feathers before sitting on its eggs. She began to play.

The music got mixed up in his thoughts, and he was in a grassy meadow surrounded by pines and aspens. Columbine Lake, Colorado. He was the typesetter for a little outfit in Granby. He was still young then, still strong. He took long hikes at dawn; walking through the forest made him feel clean and free.

Every afternoon in the summer, storm clouds blew in from the west, the warm rain fell for maybe 20 minutes, and the skies would turn blue again, with puffy white clouds.

He started awake. Kids were pouring into the church and up both side aisles. Nuns in full habits led them, each sister carrying a box of tissues. Like mother ducks with their ducklings.

He was trapped. They would see him if he tried to leave. Someone would call the sheriff, and he would be caught.

An older boy in a white surplice much too small for him lit the candles on the altar and a tall candle by the baptismal font.

The front of the church filled first, the littlest ones up close. Then the older ones, the oldest ones last—gangly boys with pimples, their white uniform shirts untucked, and girls with long, coltish legs and the beginnings of breasts. Some seemed so fragile, they would shatter if they fell. The oldest ones kept coming, up the stairs and into the loft, where Burleigh hid in the last pew. The pews creaked under their weight. Two boys with nasal voices talked softly, bringing down fierce shushing on themselves.

He dared a peek over the back of the pew in front of him. There were four empty pews between the last row of students and him. His heart was beating as if some insane drummer were pounding on it with the flat of his demented hands in a harsh, irregular beat.

Altar boys in their cassocks processed in, the tallest one coming first and holding a large golden cross. The priest came at the end of the procession and the children stood with a great rustling like the wind in the forest. Burleigh stayed slouched in his pew.

He knew the song they were singing. *They'll know we are Christians by our love.* Mrs. Walker had sung it. He had sung it, too.

"*We will walk with each other, we will walk hand in hand. And together we'll spread the news that God is in our land.*"

He saw things in the worn, dingy carpet at his feet, children singing, swaying with the music. They turned into men playing basketball, repeating the same moves over and over.

He couldn't remember when he first realized that other people didn't see such things, and he thought he was crazy because he did. He had stopped telling anyone about them. Sometimes he'd try to draw the things he saw, but the drawings were never the same as the images.

Another great rustling as the children sat. The priest said something about it being the solemnity of St. Joseph, spouse of the blessed Virgin Mary. His amplified voice banged around in the rafters above Burleigh's head. He was hearing a different song, now. Mrs. Walker singing "*Hang Yo hand on the plow, Lord!*" as she did the ironing. She had cleaned other peoples' houses, taking him along with her until he had been old enough to go to school.

The darkness was gone. Tears welled up in his chest. Something thrummed his heart the way the wind had thrummed the leaves of the quaking aspen in that long-ago Colorado forest.

The darkness would come back. It always did. But it was gone now, and he would hold onto that plow!

"*I know my robe's gonna fit me well, cuz I tried it on at the gates of hell.*"

Sudden awareness made him open his eyes. One of the boys four pews ahead of him was staring at him.

"What are you looking at?" Burleigh said, his voice cracking from disuse.

All the boys in the back row turned to stare at him. Their eyes licked fire on him, and he willed himself to disappear. When he opened his eyes again, they had tired of him. Only a puny boy at the end of the pew glanced at him and quickly looked away.

"*Before I'd be a slave I'll be buried in my grave*
And go home to my Lord and be free."

Where had the music gone as he had gotten older? No, not gone. Still in him. After all the years, all the dark nights, all the bloodless dawns, still in him.

When he had awakened, screaming that the lion was going to eat him, Mrs. Walker had come to him and stroked his forehead and held his hands in hers. He could remember the feel of her callouses. She told him that before he was born, "In your mother's womb, God sent you an angel, bearing your soul, and put it in your body. But before God had given the angel the soul to bring to you, God kissed that soul! And that angel sang to your soul all the way from heaven down to earth. And now she is your guardian angel, keeping you safe from sin and death."

A great gabble of voices swelled. The children were shaking hands, laughing, bubbling. The church expanded, grew deeper, more colorful. The little ones were so happy. The older ones in front of him stood, arms crossed, too big and smart for joy. The puny one was watching him again. Their eyes met. The boy detached himself from the others and moved up the aisle toward him.

Burleigh shrank back as the boy came nearer. The boy held his hand out. Burleigh saw his own hand reach out, saw his gnarly fingers and his burn scars on his wrist and the part of his forearm sticking out of his coat. The boy's hand was soft and cold.

"Peace-a Christ be with you," the boy murmured.

Their eyes met briefly.

"Yeah. You, too."

The boy went back to his pew, probably knowing how much the others would mock him later for his gesture of kindness.

The children stood row by row, a wave rolling toward the back of the church, with a great thumping and banging as they shoved the kneelers up. The organist played, and they sang a song Burleigh didn't recognize. They moved in two lines down the center aisle, shoes sussing on the naked tile. He was hearing a different song than the one the organist was playing and the children were singing.

"Tired of livin' but feared of dyin'."

The big ones in front of him stood, slid out of their pews, began descending the stairs. The short one on the end looked back at him, and he felt himself stand and shuffle forward with the rest, the last one in line.

Ahead of him, the priest intoned, "The body of Christ. The body of Christ. The body of Christ." Then Burleigh was standing before the priest, a tiny man with a hawk's beak for a nose. A short altar boy stood at the priest's side, holding the flat, golden paten on a stick under Burleigh's mouth.

Burleigh reached out to take the host.

"Put your hand down," the priest snapped. "Do you believe that Jesus is the Son of God?"

"Yes, sir," Burleigh said. "I do."

Stick your tongue out," the priest commanded. He reached up on tiptoe with the wafer.

"Should have brought a step ladder," he muttered. "The body of Christ."

He placed the wafer on Burleigh's tongue.

"Thank you."

"Say 'Amen'."

"Amen."

The wafer lay on his tongue. Burleigh opened his eyes.

"That's it," the priest said. "One to a customer. Come see me after. Now move along."

Burleigh followed the children up the side aisle. The little ones were singing, *This little light of mine, I'm gonna let it shine,* pretending their fingers were candles and holding them out for all to see. Tears streamed down Burleigh's face. He turned and pushed his way out the side door and into a cold north wind. It was starting to snow. Crocuses and daffodils were already pushing their heads into the light, and the magnolias had budded and would soon bloom, and yet it was snowing. He started to laugh, laughed harder and harder, the tears pouring out of him and running over the deep creases of his face, a flash flood washing the cracks and fissures of a trackless desert.

He laughed until he became breathless and dizzy. He sat down on the thin dusting of snow on the grass beside the pathway. It looked like when Mrs. Walker buttered bread and sprinkled sugar on it. He reached down and got some on the tip of his finger. It tasted like cinnamon, just like Mrs. Walker had said it would.

Glorious

The children came streaming out of the church, the bells ringing, the mass over. He got up slowly, spanked the snow off the seat of his pants, and began to walk toward the Tierney mission. He would go to a meeting, and then he would go back to Glorious and see through what had already begun. He didn't know how it would end, but he didn't need to know. Now was all he had, and it was all he would ever have, and it was everything.

Chapter 13:
Calypso

"It's a balmy 17 degrees here in beautiful downtown Glorious, the Athens of the Trempealeau Corridor. You, of course, are listening to the voice of Glorious, WCOW, the Mighty 690 on your AM dial.

"Now here's your traffic and weather, all jammed together. Traffic—none to speak of, just the semis rolling through town. Weather—we're looking for a high today of, ummmm, let's see, maybe 18, 19 if we're lucky. Winds are out of the northwest at 10 to 12 mph, so we'll be taking another trip below zero tonight. How many of you are sick of this weather? Raise your hands. Little higher. Yeah, I thought so, but you know what complaining about it will get you. Just button up and bear it.

"If this studio had a window, I'd tell you whether or not it's snowing, but it don't, so I won't. The seven-day forecast calls for continued weather, mostly cloudy skies, with sunshine about as likely as the lunch plate special at the Dinky being steak tartare, which is Latin for, 'we forgot to cook the burger again'."

I punched up the sound effects tape, and Bugs Bunny asked, "What's up, Doc?"

"I've told you a million times, Bugs, 'updock' is when you take the pier out of the water for the winter. And 'paradox' is, of course, two docks."

I punched the tape player again, and gunshots rang out.

"That's our resident cowboy, Rick O'Shay, reminding me that it's time for me to shut up and play some music. Don't worry, he only winged me, folks. Now here's the Fat Man himself, Antoine Dominique Domino, Jr. his own self, back to ask the rhetorical question, *"Ain't that a shame?"*

I dropped the needle on the spinning vinyl on turntable one, potted down my mic and brought up the music, which began with Fats wailing,

You broke my heart—bomp bomp—*when you said we'd part*—and then jumping on those triplets of his. Great stuff.

The phone light turned from red to blinking green.

"Not now, Marvin," I muttered as Scott Dupple entered the studio, several sheets of paper clutched in one hairy paw, his coffee mug in the other, and stood next to me, there being no other place to stand.

I sang along with Fats while Dupple studied his notes. I potted down the music slowly as the song ended and potted up my mic. "Yes, folks, love is a losing game, and ain't that a shame, and who's to blame, and that song's pretty lame.

"On a serious note, here's our news director, the ever-earnest Horace Hangnail, with this final news update for today's edition of the Koffee with Kenny Radio Program, brought to you by Bee and The Reb and all the good folks down at the Dinky, where today the plate special is meatloaf, with mashed potatoes and gravy, green beans, a roll, and a slab of pie all for just $3.95. Whattaya got for us, Horatio?"

I shoved the microphone over.

"Of course, the big news today, Kenneth, remains the ongoing hunt for Norah Stoddard after her dramatic appearance at the baseball tryouts Saturday in Eau Claire," Dupple began in his basso, for-radio voice. "The sheriff is also looking for Burleigh Grimes, who was with the Stoddard girl at the tryouts. As we reported earlier this morning exclusively on WCOW, your community radio station, they were seen leaving together, and Grimes did not show up for work this morning, putting into jeopardy publication of this week's *INQUISITOR-NUGGET*. Again, if you have any information about the whereabouts of either Norah Stoddard or Burleigh Grimes, please contact the sheriff's office immediately."

"What about the almanac, Huffenpuff?"

"Coming right up, Kenneth. Did you know that on this date in 1776, General George Washington drove the British troops out of Boston?"

"I did not know that, your Duppleness. Atta boy, George!"

"And in 1969, Golda Meir was elected the first female prime minister of Israel."

"Any truth to the rumor that Golda Meir was actually Lyndon Johnson in drag?"

Dupple choked on his saliva and had a coughing spasm.

"I ask you, folks, have you ever seen Lyndon and Goldie together? Anyhoo, right after this next song, I'm going to turn you back over to harsh reality. In weather, it's still cold, and in traffic, Baudelaire was seen snowmobiling down Main Street a few minutes ago wearing nothing but his long johns."

Dupple managed to stumble out of the studio while I was bloviating.

"And now here are the Weavers with our goodbye song, *So Long, It's Been Good to Know You.* but what say we meet under cover of darkness, right back here tomorrow morning at the ungodly hour of 6:00 a.m. for another thrill-packed edition of The Koffee with Kenny Radio Program, on the mighty 690, radio most glorious?"

Five minutes later, I climbed onto my stool at Big Nose Rose's Saloon, where the morning man, Fast Freddy Osterberg, had my post-show beer and a bump ready. The Statler Brothers' *The Class of '57 had its Dreams* played on the radio behind the bar. When Freddie spotted me, he went to turn the radio off.

"Leave it up," I said. "They're actually playing something good."

"Who decides what they're playing when you're not there?"

"A robot plays music all day, same music they're getting in Illinois and Indiana and Iowa. I'm the last human being at the station."

"What about the news guy?"

"Like I say, the last human being."

"So, how is it today for the 'Voice of Glorious'?"

"I'm suicidal. Thanks for asking."

"What else is new?"

"I hate mornings. Especially this one."

"What's special about this one?"

"Nothing. It just happens to be the one I'm stuck in at the moment."

"Why don't you quit the station and do something else?"

"I wouldn't give them the satisfaction. They'll have to fire me."

"They'll never fire you. You're an institution in this town."

"You mean I oughta be in an institution, don't you?"

"Everybody listens to you and you know it."

"Yeah, and if they canned me, nobody'd even notice."

"You underestimate what you mean to this town."

"Tell you what, Freddie, my good man. Come spring, we'll go down to the lake and both stick our hands in the water."

"And we'll do this because...?"

"When we take our hands out, you'll see how much of a hole we leave behind when we're gone."

Fast Freddie had gotten his nickname because he was so slow, that being this town's notion of a good joke. He was a slow talker, a slow walker, a slow tap-puller, a fat, slovenly man with sagging eyelids and perpetual beard stubble. He smoked Wolf Brothers' Rum-Soaked Crooks and had been known to take a second drink, just to keep the solitaries company.

The song ended. The robot went right on to Johnny Mathis and *Chances Are*.

"Now you can turn it off," I said.

Freddie did so, brought me another bump to keep the rest of my beer company, and went back to drying glasses.

The door opened, and in walked a woman, 25, maybe younger, a compact model with hazel eyes and a nose, mouth, and ears, all in just the right places. She wore her long blonde hair in a ponytail that swayed as she crossed the room. Even with her coat on, I knew by the way she carried herself that she had a good figure and was proud of it.

Freddy met her at the cash register.

"Good morning," she said in a voice that sounded like birdies in spring. She glanced over at me, and I nodded, touching the brim of my cap.

"What can I do for you, young lady?"

"I'm looking for a fellow."

"From the looks of you, you shouldn't have to look very hard."

"Not that kind of looking."

"Did this fellow happen to get you in the family way?" Freddie countered with his usual tact and diplomacy. "I just ask because that's usually the only other reason a young lady comes looking for a man in a bar."

"No, this fellow didn't get me 'in the family way,' not that it's any of your business."

"Atta girl," I called down the bar. "Don't take any guff from that big ape."

She looked over at me. No smile, just a glancing blow.

"Where you from, Missy?" Freddie pressed on, ignoring the interruption.

"I just hitched from the next town up the river. Something that sounds like 'tyranny.'"

Freddie guffawed. "It's 'Tierney.' But no, I mean, where are you from originally?"

"Someplace you never heard of."

"Try me."

"Boomer, West Virginia."

I sat up straight, having lost interest in my drink.

"You're half right. I have heard of West Virginia. Where's Boomer?"

"'Bout 25 miles from next to no place."

"Sounds like. So, what's this guy's name?"

"Joe Bob."

"What's he look like?"

"Damned if I know."

"Come on down here, miss," I called over. "I think I know who you're looking for."

She really checked me out now and then looked back at Freddie.

"It's alright, little lady. He's harmless, mostly, and he probably does know the guy you're looking for. He knows everybody."

She walked down the bar to where I was now riding my barstool side-saddle, facing her. I slapped the stool next to me, and she climbed up and perched on it, her feet not touching the rung.

"I'm Kenny. I tipped my cap and put in on the bar. "And you would be...?"

"Calypso."

"Say again?"

"Calypso."

"That's what I thought you said. Very unusual name. I suppose you've got a brother named Odysseus."

"I'm an only, and my mother never read *The Odyssey*," she fired back.

"I'm impressed," I said, meaning it. "Until you arrived, I figured I was the only one in Glorious who knows that Homer was something other than a four-bagger in baseball."

"My real name's Corrina, Corrina Durnion."

I stuck out my paw, then wiped it on my shirt to get the moisture from the beer mug off it. "Kenneth Kellogg," I said.

Her hand was tiny but her grip firm.

"My mama took to calling me Calypso when I was a kid because I liked to sing a song she played a lot. She had the record."

"Ah. *Jamaica Farewell*. Harry Belafonte."

She frowned. "I don't think so. I think it was called *Kingston Town*."

"Nope. He had to leave a little girl in Kingston Town, and that's why he was so sad, but the song's called *Jamaica Farewell*."

"Now I'm impressed. Are you a musician or something?"

Freddie had wandered over within listening range and was rubbing a hole in the bar with his rag. "This guy's been playing platters on the radio since your grampa was in diapers," he told her. "He knows all the songs."

"I'm sole proprietor of the Koffee with Kenny Radio Program on the mighty 690, 6 to 10 in the a.m., Monday through Saturday. At your service."

"So that was you I heard doin' all that silly stuff on the radio on my way down here."

"That's him, lady," Freddie confirmed. "The Voice of Glorious."

"You don't look like you sound."

"I know. I'm much better looking on the radio."

Calypso shrugged out of her jacket, confirming my speculation about her body, and laid it on the empty stool next to her.

"Can I get you anything to drink?" Freddie asked.

"Another round, barkeep."

"I was asking the lady."

"Do you serve coffee?" Calypso asked.

Freddie snorted. "Of course. Whattya think we are, savages? Anything with?"

"Black."

"Coming right up."

He went to get the drinks. Up close, Miss Calypso was even younger than I'd first thought—and even better looking.

"So tell me about this guy you're looking for, Calypso," I said when Freddie was back out of range.

"Mama said he was a ballplayer. He'd just been promoted from A to AA and was passing through Boomer. They took a likin' to one another."

Freddie returned with the drinks, the fastest he'd moved in memory, and walked a few steps away before resuming giving the bar a deep massage. I picked up my shot glass, tossed it back, and took a swig of beer.

"And this fella got your mama in the family way?"

"If you mean did he knock her up? Yep. And here I am."

Freddie whistled through his teeth. He'd figured out who her mystery man was, too.

"You sure you can hear okay there, Fred?" I said without taking my eyes off Calypso. "Maybe you should come on over a little closer."

"It's alright," Calypso said. "I got nothin' to be ashamed about."

"You know something? You've got your daddy's hazel eyes, but they look a lot better on you."

"You do know him then?"

"Oh, sure. Most everybody in town knows him. He and his wife run the diner. He coaches high school basketball and baseball. Only he calls himself Jubal now."

"Do they have any children, he and his wife?"

"Nope. I gotta say, Jubal never struck me as the kind of man who'd get a woman pregnant and then leave town."

"He didn't know Mama was pregnant. He doesn't know I exist. Mama said I could go looking for him when I came of age. All she really knew about him was that he was a ballplayer and he was from the south. She said his name was Joe Bob Early. I guess she kind of followed his career after he left, because she gave me a list of the teams he'd played for. Eau Claire was the last name on the list. Somebody there said there was an ex-ballplayer in Glorious."

"You've got some gumption, Calypso Corrina Durnion," I said, "tracking him all the way here from Boomer, West Virginia."

I reached to pick up my beer bottle and knocked it over.

"Damn it!"

"I'll clean it up," Freddie said, putting his rag over the spill to try to keep it from dripping off the bar. Fortunately, I'd finished most of the beer.

"You got a pretty good load on for so early in the morning," Calypso noted.

"I'm fine. Getting to be time for my morning nap is all."

"So, is this diner he and the wife run the one right up the street?" she asked.

"Yep. Only one in town. I'll walk you over there and introduce you to your daddy."

"I can't now. I need to go back up to Tyranny for a meeting."

"You have an appointment in Tyranny?"

"AA meeting. I asked somebody last night, and he said there'd be one at the mission at 11:00. Do you have a car I could borrow to get up there? I'm a good driver. If I have to hitchhike, I might not get there in time."

"I'll do better than that. I'll drive you up there myself."

She frowned. "I don't think you should be driving, Mr. Kellogg," she said.

"I'm fine. And call me Kenny."

Calypso again looked at Freddie, who had returned with some towels for the beer that was dripping from the bar onto the floor behind.

"He's not anywhere near's to being baked, Missy," Freddie said. "This guy can really drink."

"Practice, practice, practice," I said.

And that, friends, is how I ended up driving to Tyranny with Jubal Early's illegitimate, gutsy, pretty daughter, Calypso Corrina Durnion, who Jubal'd yet to meet or even know about. And that's how I found Burleigh and knew everything was about to change big time.

Chapter 14:
I'm Walkin'

"**B**et it doesn't get this cold in Boomer, West Virginia," I said after we'd left Glorious behind.

"It gets down into the 20s," Calypso responded, "but nothing like this. Why does anybody live here?"

"Who says this is livin'?"

She let that pass. This girl has seen what hopeless looks like, I decided, and apparently being cold doesn't qualify.

The thought crept into my head before I could swat it away—is it just possible that, as prickly as I am, she kind of likes me?

There was no question in my mind about my liking her.

"Mind if I smoke?"

"It's your car."

"Want one?"

"No, thanks. Camels, huh?" She observed.

"I'd walk a mile for one if I had enough wind. So you don't drink or smoke, huh?"

"Nope. Used up my quota of booze real early. Never did take up smoking."

"I suppose you're saving yourself for marriage, too."

She let that pass as well. If I ever made an unwanted move on her, she'd likely punch my nose up into my brain pan.

"You born and raised here?" she asked.

"Me? Hell, no!"

"You got family here?"

"Nope."

"So, why don't you pull up stakes if it's as bad as all that?"

I leaned forward and tried to wipe our breath off the inside of the windshield with my jacket sleeve. She grabbed the wheel to keep the car from sliding onto the shoulder.

"I'm on the ray-dee-o," I said, settling back in the seat. "I can't leave. I'm a star!"

When she didn't reply, I added, "One place is the same as another. Wherever you go, you bring yourself with you. If a drunk gets on the train in Chicago, a drunk gets off the train in Wisconsin."

"Is that where you're from?"

"Naw. I'm not a city boy."

"Where are you from then?"

"Little bump in the road called Slinger, Wisconsin."

"Where's that?"

"Near West Bend, if that helps."

"Not really."

"Well, like you said, about 25 miles from no place. Actually, it's about an hour and a half north and east of Madison. You've heard of Madison, right?"

"Sure. I was there before I came to Tyranny."

"I lived in Madison for 12 years."

"Yeah?"

"Oh, yeah. I was the number-one-rated morning drive-time DJ nine years running."

"Why'd you leave?"

"Got fired."

"Why?"

"They were looking for an excuse to fire me, and I gave them one—a joke I told that upset some folks. The two biggest accounts threatened to pull their advertising. I showed up at work the next day and somebody else was sitting in my chair."

"That's cold."

"That's radio. Not a whole lot of job security."

We let two miles of road crawl under the car in silence.

"Why is a woman like a frying pan?"

"Excuse me?"

I opened the window just enough to flick the remains of my cigarette out. The cold made her suck in air.

"It's a riddle."

"Okay. Why is a woman like a frying pan?"

"You have to heat them both up before you put the meat in."

She snorted. "They fired you for that?"

"Not in Madison. I got fired for a different joke there."

The "Tierney—population 2,417" sign floated by.

"Who's Jody Cartwright?" she asked.

"How's that?"

"Jody Cartwright? The sign said this is 'the boyhood home of Jody Cartwright.'"

"Cutright. You mean to tell me you never heard of Jody Cutright?"

"Can't say as I have."

"Famous television star."

"What was she in?"

"He. Jody was a he. *Gunsmoke,* for one."

"That's big time! There's a TV station out of Morgantown that still plays the reruns late at night. What part was Cutright? Was he the bartender?"

"Nope. He played Shuffles."

"Who?"

"He was only in one episode. Carroll O'Connor was in it, too. You've heard of Carroll O'Connor, haven't you?"

"Archie Bunker. The dumb bigot."

"That's the guy. Big star."

"So, Cutright was in one episode with Archie Bunker, and that makes him a star?"

"Before that he was a stunt man in the old B Westerns for years. When the cowboy jumped off the second-story balcony onto his horse? That was probably Jody Cutright."

"I still say big deal."

"Can you jump off a two-story building onto a horse?"

"Never tried. Probably could if I practiced."

"Then they'll put your name on the Boomer sign. Hometown proud, young lady. Every place has to be proud of something."

"What's Glorious proud of?"

"Me, of course."

"I didn't see your name on the sign."

"I think you have to die first. Here we are. Beautiful downtown Tyranny."

A few of the store fronts were vacant, their blank windows like gaps in a jack-o-lantern's grin. Many of the windows were covered with butcher paper and had "For Sale or Lease" signs with the name and phone number of a local realtor.

I braked, waited for a pickup truck coming the other way to clear, and turned into a parking space in front of a plain stucco storefront with a small sign announcing "Tierney Mission & Senior Center" over the door. Two large windows flanked the door. They were covered by beige curtains that probably looked second-hand the day they were made.

"Here you are, my dear. Come find me at Hoxie's Bar when the meeting's over."

"You don't have to wait for me. I can hitch a ride."

"It's too cold for that. Besides, I don't mind. My social calendar is clear this morning."

"Okay. Thanks! Where's Hoxie's?"

"We passed it two blocks back."

She opened the door, slid out, and shouldered her backpack. The air that seeped into the car hadn't gotten any warmer.

"Hey, why don't you come in with me? They'll have coffee and maybe donuts or rolls or something. Everybody's welcome."

"You sayin' I'm a drunk?"

"You sayin' I'm one?"

"Well, you were one, right? Or you wouldn't be going to an AA meeting."

"You never stop being a drunk. I'm recovering. Another two months and three days and I get my three-year coin."

"You must have started drinking when you were six."

"Ha ha. So, you comin'?"

"I'll pass."

"Okay. See you at Hoxie's."

"Until that time."

She slammed the door. I watched her stride without hesitation to the mission door, open it, and disappear inside. Brave little thing. She's had to learn to make her own way in this world at a young age. It had been that way for me, too.

I fired up a cigarette, buttoned my jacket tight at my throat, pulled my stocking cap down over my ears, and plunged into the frigid air. The dry snow crunched under my boots as I passed the Tierney Congregational Church, an insurance agent's office, an empty store front, a junk store. Across the street, the combination gas station and garage showed no signs of life but was apparently open for business. A small hardware store, another two empties, and a general store that promised food, clothes, ammunition, fishing tackle, and handmade dollhouses finished the block out.

At the corner—four-way stop, no signal—I crossed the street to read the historical marker in front of the general store. From it I learned that Tierney had been named for a John Tierney, who'd been in an artillery company in the Revolutionary War. Tierney, who had emigrated from Ireland to New England, suffered severe wounds in the Battle of Fort Ticonderoga and died after a field doctor amputated his leg. Members of his family moved to Wisconsin in the 1840s and settled at a spot called Frank's Corners. Family members later renamed it Tierney in honor of John, and the settlement grew into a thriving Irish town as farmers from New England and the East Coast moved into the area.

When had the town stopped growing and started the long slide down?

The next block consisted of a doctor's office, pet shelter, two empties, a tire store, the post office, a bank, and Frank's Diner—where a group of heavyweight men in ancient Oshkosh-B'Gosh overalls and flannel shirts sat humped around the center table, which was cluttered with plates still supporting the wreckage of fried eggs and hash browns studded with cigarette butts.

The newspaper office was between the diner and Hoxie's Bar. I'd already read that week's issue—I read the sheet every week, along with the other weeklies in the area, gleaning material for the show. Next door at Hoxie's, two men wearing cowboy hats sat at the bar, fingering their drinks and staring up at the television. I decided not to go in. I'm not sure why. I just kept walking, letting the cold air clear the cobwebs out of my head.

At the next corner, I'd exhausted the "business district," so I turned and shuffled up Church Street, passing a touristy variety store offering cheese, dried cranberries, cranberry muffin mixes, cake mixes, pancake mixes, fruit cakes featuring cranberries, postcards, trinkets, and who knew what else. The merchandise looked as if it had been sitting on the shelves for a long time. A bored-looking, middle-aged woman bent over the counter by the cash register, working on the crossword puzzle in the newspaper, a stubby pencil clutched in her hand like a club.

At the corner, a Catholic church on my side faced a Lutheran church across the street. In the next block the only functioning business was a machine and farm equipment repair shop that also did auto body work. The elementary school, its windows frosted over and smoke coming out of its chimney, gave way to a single block of shabby little houses, a rusted metal swing set knee deep in snow, a shutter hanging askew by one nail, a storm door with a hole in its window.

The road T-boned with a field of cornstalk stubble at the end of the block, so I started back the way I'd come, walking as quickly as I could to try to keep warm. By the time I reached Main Street, I wanted another cigarette but didn't want to take my gloves off to get it. I cupped a gloved hand over my face and tried to warm my nose with my breath, but it didn't help much. I glanced in at Hoxie's to see if Calypso might have come looking for me but saw only the same two cowboys at the bar.

How long did those damn AA meetings last? From what I'd heard, it was just a bunch of drunks talking about what skunks they'd been and how long they'd been sober this time and who had gone out and not been heard from since. First names only. I didn't know if they took up a collection or who was in charge.

One day at a time. Poor bastards. I'd known many a dry drunk, and they were some of the most miserable people in the world.

I was tempted to go inside the mission to warm up but didn't want to walk into the middle of true confessions, so I again kept walking, deciding I might as well see both ends of the dumpy little burg. I'd only been to Tierney a couple of times since I'd pitched my tent in Glorious and never found anything there that Glorious didn't have, which wasn't much.

The sun was out, and the air was still, which made the cold more tolerable. Who was the fool who invented "windchill"? I'd read somewhere that it had been invented, if that was the word for it, in the 1940s in the Antarctic. Wouldn't you think it was already cold enough there without putting the notion of "windchill" into peoples' heads?

I became aware of the persistent cawing of a huge crow perched on a sagging power line nearby and realized, the way you do, I'd been hearing it for some time without taking note of it.

I tried to imagine what the scene would be like when Calypso confronted Jubal. How would Jubal handle that—and right in the middle of the muddle with the Stoddard kid? Jubal, hell. How would Bee react? If there was no shillelagh close at hand, a frying pan would probably serve just as well.

Wasn't funny, really. Everybody in town knew Bee and Jubal had wanted to have a kid—she probably more so then he—and here comes Jubal's full-grown daughter sashaying into their lives. It occurred to me that maybe I shouldn't have told Calypso I knew who her daddy was.

I spotted the sign ahead on the left: "Tierney Raceway: races every Saturday night, Demolition Derby Wednesday night, July through September." Nothing there now but a deserted oval with a crumbling wooden grandstand and a couple of heaps, one with a large, barely legible red "21" in a white circle on what was left of the driver's side door, the other so demolished as to be unidentifiable even by next of kin.

Beyond that, construction or demolition or both seemed to be in progress on an old farm house. I decided to walk that far to have a look, then hustle back to the mission, stay long enough to get the blood circulating again, and tell Calypso the train was leaving.

I was thoroughly winded by the time I reached the farmhouse. A weathered, low, wooden fence lined the yard, with an equally weathered arbor offering admittance to a stone walkway covered with glare ice from snow having been trodden on by lots of big men in heavy boots, one of whom was on a tall ladder to the right of the path, hammering without much spirit at what was left of a chimney. While I watched, the man dislodged a brick and tossed it into a dumpster behind him in the yard. The tink-tink-tink of the hammer seemed to match the cadence of the crow, which had followed me and continued to give me hell from a nearby oak, whose dead leaves clung stubbornly to its branches.

From the back of the house, I could hear the hum of a generator and the grinding of a small engine, maybe a Bobcat, and of boards being ripped off, the nails screeching in protest.

A post to the left of the arbor tenuously held a black mailbox with "Barton" hand lettered in white on it and a tube for the weekly paper. A professionally made sign a few feet farther down the path announced "Future home of The Siren" in blazing red letters outlined in yellow.

What in hell was "The Siren"? I hadn't heard anything about it, and I was supposed to have my proverbial finger on the pulse of the area. Being careful not to slip on the ice, I approached the house and stood at the foot of the ladder.

"What's this thing going to be when you get done with it?" I called up.

The man stopped his dispirited tinking long enough to look down. He had a drinker's nose, red and veiny, and the deep squint lines around his eyes suggested a man who was outdoors a lot. A tool belt sagged under his substantial belly.

"Beats shit out of me," he said. "Restaurant? Bar? Maybe it'll be a strip joint. This town could use one."

"Good luck with that."

"Hey, you're that guy on the radio, aren't you?"

"I'm that guy."

"Yeah. I recognized your voice. You don't look like yourself."

"I know. I'm a lot better looking on the radio."

Ah, fame. I retraced my steps to the road, remembering an inspirational I'd stolen from someplace and used on the show in every town I'd been in. It seems these two men are digging a ditch. A passerby asks the first man what he's doing. "What's it look like I'm doing?" the first man snaps back. "I'm digging a damned ditch!" Undaunted, the passerby asks the second man the same question. He looks up, smiles, and says, "Why, I'm building a cathedral!" Moral of the story: it's all in the attitude. Wouldn't you think the man on the ladder would at least want to know what he was working on?

I halfway wanted to keep walking, but my fingers and toes had passed from stung to numb, a bad sign, and no amount of cupping and blowing could take the sting out of my nose, cheeks, and ears. Just my luck I'd probably get frostbite.

Walking as fast as I dared back toward town, I picked my way on the chipped snow and ice on the shoulder of the road. I'd ask around about The Siren when I got back to a telephone.

I was seriously cold and tired by the time I got back to the mission. Cursing myself for walking so far, I put a shoulder to the door and stumbled into the building, where the warm, smoke-filled air caused me to stagger.

I leaned against the door and surveyed the large room. Chairs lined the walls, three occupied by old men smoking cigarettes as if patiently waiting to die. The walls held religious pictures, landscapes clipped from calendars, a cross, and a bulletin board cluttered with announcements for "crafting workshop," "quilting bee," "Lunches served daily, M-F 11:30-12:15," and the like. A sign etched with a wood-burning tool in the hands of an amateur proclaimed, "When you give others the blame, you also give them the power." I spotted what appeared to be a portable altar with a kneeler along the side wall. Beyond that, a sign said "Meeting / Dining Room, Food Pantry, Mission Office" with an arrow pointing toward a hallway at the back of the room.

My fingers and toes were starting to ache as they warmed up. Soon I would barely be able to walk for the pain, but there was nothing to do about it except wait it out. What had I been thinking, walking that far on a day like this? I hobbled toward the hallway, which was dimly lit, and as I did, I heard a voice murmuring from behind a door to what must have been the meeting room, on the right about halfway down the hall.

I walked up to the door, hesitated, turned the knob and pushed the door open, first just a crack, and then enough to see into the room. Through the haze of cigarette smoke, I saw maybe two dozen people sitting on metal folding chairs toward the front of the room, where a battered-looking, old black man stood before them, hands jammed deep in the pockets of his long, ragged cloth coat.

"I finally learned," the old man was saying, his voice familiar, "that I didn't have to be the biggest noise in the room. I could just shut up and listen and be a lot better off."

A metal chair scrapped the tile floor, and Calypso got up and walked toward me.

"Sorry," she whispered when she got close. "Didn't know it would go so long."

But I was staring at that old man who was speaking. I'd heard him say that same thing before, about not needing to be the biggest noise in the room. It was my old pal Burleigh Grimes, big as life.

Chapter 15:
Douglass

The new day dawned clear and bright, with a stiff breeze from the south and white puffy clouds in the western sky. By the end of the day, melted snow flowed everywhere—including into basements—and folks emerged in short sleeves and shorts, baring pallid skin to the sun.

It's amazing how cold 42 feels in the fall and how warm it feels in the spring, after weeks of below freezing.

We'd been up late talking, Burleigh, Norah, Calypso, and I, in Burleigh's little cabin by the river. Actually, Burleigh and I had done most of the talking. Calypso and Norah mostly listened and seemed to be hanging on every word.

We'd finally gone to sleep, Burleigh giving the girls his bed and he and I bunking on pallets on the floor. Burleigh must have gotten up in the night to feed the fire, but I slept hard and woke up at dawn refreshed, even if my right hip and shoulder ached. I lay quietly, listening to the girls sleeping, their deep breath synchronized, Calypso snoring most prettily. Burleigh was already up and out for his constitutional, as he called it.

I'd almost drifted off again, despite my aches and pains when Burleigh came back, an old black Labrador hesitating and then slipping inside behind him. Although they came in as quietly as possible, and I tried not to make any noise getting up, Norah stirred and woke.

"Aw," she said sleepily when she saw the dog. "I didn't know you had a dog, Mr. Grimes."

"I don't. I think he has me. I found him in the woods. He was walking as if he had someplace to go. The moment he saw me, he came over to me as if I were the one he had been looking for."

The dog listened attentively, looking from face to face. His tail wagged tentatively. His muzzle was more white than black, and there was something off about his walk, the way his rear end dipped each time he took a step.

Norah got up and walked over to us.

"He's got a hitch in his get-along," Burleigh said, "But he's well-fed and clean, so he hasn't been wandering long. No collar, no tags."

Then I saw. The dog's left rear leg ended in a stump about a third of the way down. He looked up at Burleigh with eyes full of love, as if he knew that Burleigh was talking about him.

"Do you think somebody dumped him?"

"I do think so," Burleigh said.

"May I pet him?" Norah asked.

"Come in low," Burleigh said, "and hold your hand out for him to sniff."

She did, and the dog did, and then he rubbed his muzzle against her hand and she began to stroke him softly on his noble old head.

"What kind of a loathsome bastard would abandon a dog like that?" I said.

"Oh, maybe just somebody unwilling or unable to nurse him through his old age or have him put down. Neither one's easy."

"Come on! Only a real son-of-a-bitch would just dump him. He ought to be whipped."

"'Use every man after his desert, and who should 'scape whipping?'" Burleigh said.

"Isn't that Shakespeare?" Calypso asked. She was still wrapped up in a blanket on the bed but had been listening.

"Yes. *Hamlet*," Burleigh said.

"If you hadn't found him, he would have starved to death or been killed by a bear," I insisted. "The man who did this ought to be punished."

Calypso slipped out of the blanket, came over and squatted down next to Norah. She began massaged the dog's neck.

"Hate the sin," Burleigh said, "but love the sinner."

"Can't be done," I retorted, unwilling to let it go. "What about Hitler?"

"Don't start by trying to forgive Hitler. Start with something easier. Maybe the guy who didn't stop his car for you when you were trying to cross the street yesterday, something small like that."

Burleigh walked over to the big stone fireplace he had built by his own hand. The dog followed him. Burleigh got the fire restarted from the embers, went over, and sat down with a grunt in his rocking chair, which he'd also fashioned himself. The dog sat beside the chair, a contented grunt escaping him.

"Let me catch my breath and I'll hustle us up some breakfast. You-all must be hungry."

"I could eat," I admitted.

"Let's go to the Dinky for breakfast," Norah suggested.

"You ready to come back to civilization, are you?" Burleigh asked.

"Yes," she said. "If they want to expel me from school or arrest me or something, they'll just have to do it."

"They won't do anything of the kind," Burleigh said. "They'll be glad to see you, Jubal and Bee especially. And they'll stand up for you, too.

"And how about you, Calypso? Are you ready to meet your maker?"

"I guess so, but could I have first dibs on the bathroom *first*? I really have to go!"

We took turns hitting the head, ladies first. Burleigh had even installed the indoor plumbing, running a pipe from the well he'd dug. There wasn't much that old man couldn't do.

We bundled up and started walking to town, the dog at Burleigh's side, as if he'd been there all his life. The world we encountered was puddle-wonderful, as the poet said. Spring had come all at once. There was still ice at the edges of the river, and we'd no doubt have a couple more snowfalls, but winter's icy grip had been broken.

"What are you going to name him?" Norah asked, nodding toward the dog.

"I think Calypso would be a good name," Calypso said. "After all, we're both a couple of strays."

"We've already got our Calypso," Burleigh said. "I was thinking I'd call him Douglass."

The dog's ears flicked, and he looked up at Burleigh.

"I think he likes the name!" Calypso said.

"I've never heard of a dog named Douglass," Norah said.

"Neither have I," I said. "Why Douglass?"

"After Frederick Douglass," Burleigh replied. "He was an orphan, too, a stray."

126

"I think you're right about Norah not getting hassled," I said to Burleigh when the girls got a bit ahead of us. "But what about you? They might make trouble for you."

"I don't think too many people will think an old man like me was fooling around with her."

"You're wrong about that. There are a lot of small-minded, bigoted people in dear old Glorious, ready to think the worst about everybody."

"Aren't we're all small-minded and bigoted in our own ways?"

"Not like them. There's some flat-out fools in that town."

"You shouldn't call them that."

"I know. 'Love the sinner but hate the sin.'"

"That's it."

"No way could I do that."

"Why not? You've been doing it all your life."

"What are you talking about. What sinner have I been loving?"

"You'll see him the next time you look in the mirror."

"Me? I'm a sinner, maybe worse than most. But I sure as hell don't love myself!"

"No? You try to ease your pain, don't you? If you're too cold, you put on a coat. If you're hungry, you eat. And I'll bet you think you've got a good reason for everything you do. I know I'm that way. I let myself off the hook all the time."

Burleigh patted my arm and said, "If there's trouble, we'll take it as it comes. Don't worry."

I liked that, how he said "we." If he was in trouble, I wanted to be in it with him.

We caught up with the girls, who had stopped to examine some tufts of fur and some bones, all that was left of a small animal.

"Poor thing," Norah said.

"Owl probably got it," Burleigh said.

We walked in silence through the woods along the river, Douglass keeping right at Burleigh's side. I'd felt sharp pain in my fingers and toes the moment we'd stepped out of the cabin, but by the time we got to Glorious, they had warmed and it seemed I wasn't going to lose any of them, despite my foolishness the day before.

A crowd already filled the Dinky by the time we got there. As folks spotted us, the buzz of multiple conversations dissipated like lake fog at sunrise. We must have been quite a sight—me, Burleigh, runaway Norah, a pretty young woman almost no one in town had ever seen before, and a broken-down, old, three-legged dog.

Bee came out of the kitchen, stopped and stared for an instant, then hurried over to us, grabbing Norah and squeezing her so hard the girl squeaked.

When she let Norah go, Bee looked a question at Calypso, who stepped forward, introduced herself, and offered a hand for shaking.

"I'm Bee." She ignored the hand and gave Calypso a big hug, too.

"Looks like you're real busy," Calypso said when she got her wind back. "Can I help?"

Norah took Calypso by the arm and said, "Come on. I'll grab us a couple of aprons and order pads from the back. You want booths or tables?"

"Booths. They tip better."

I saw Burleigh slip out the back door with Douglass, no doubt headed to the newspaper to start getting caught up for the day he'd missed.

Waitressing had apparently been one of the trades Calypso had picked up in her young life. She zipped around the room like a swivel-hipped halfback dodging would-be tacklers, taking orders, refilling coffee mugs, hustling food, three or four plates running up her arm, bussing tables, and generally charming one and all with her smile and her down-home drawl.

Bee, who had been trying to service the room by herself, went back to tending the counter clientele and working the cash register, while Jubal sweated over the grill in back.

I pounced on the first table that opened up, ordered coffee and the meatloaf sandwich, open face, with a baked potato, gravy, green beans, and roll, with a slab of apple pie for dessert, no cheese, no ice cream, not heated, just pie. I hadn't been this hungry in decades.

When the room finally cleared out, Jubal emerged from the kitchen, dripping sweat, came over to my table, twirled a chair around and straddled it. Bee, Calypso, and Norah were in the kitchen attacking the dirty pots and pans.

"Where'd you find Norah?"

"I didn't. I ran into Burleigh up in Tierney yesterday. She'd been staying with him."

"I'll be switched. I never even thought of that possibility. Where'd the new girl come from?"

"She found me in Big Nose Rose's."

"Wait, now. You picked up Miss Daisy Mae in the bar and took her up to Tierney?"

"I took her to her AA meeting."

"You went from a bar to an AA meeting?"

"I just dropped Calypso off and picked her up later. When I went in to get her, Burleigh was up front, giving a talk."

"Her name's really Calypso?"

"It's a nickname her mother gave her. Real name's Corrina."

"And Norah was at the meeting, too?"

"No. She was staying in Burleigh's cabin. We went there after the meeting."

Jubal pounded on the side of his head, trying to get all this to settle in and make sense. "Did Norah tell you why she'd run away?"

"Her old lady hooked up with another low-life. He came on to Norah, but she gave him a kick in the family jewels and a quick chop to the throat and got the hell out of the house. I guess that's when she came to stay with you folks. She didn't tell me why she'd left you, though."

Jubal folded his arms on the back of his chair and sank his chin onto his bare arms. "She must have heard me and Bee arguing about her and thought we didn't want her there. We looked for her everywhere. How'd she end up with Burleigh?"

"Turns out he'd been coaching her on the fine art of throwing a screwball all this time. He said he let her stay with him because Norah figured the sheriff would be looking for her, and she was scared to go back."

"She needn't have worried about the sheriff. That old fool wouldn't have found her if she'd walked down Main Street beating a drum."

The dining room was empty except for two old farmers hunched over the counter. Everybody else was no doubt spreading the news, along with their own interpretations of events. In the kitchen, the old dishwasher was groaning and clanking through its wash cycle, the battered metal hood rattling from the force of the spray. I sopped up the last of my gravy with the bit of the roll I'd saved for that purpose.

Bee and the girls emerged from the kitchen, chattering like three old pals. "Ju-BAL," Bee called across the room. "I'm going to Eau Claire to pick up our order. Norah's going to come and help me load and unload. Get up off your lazy butt and help Calypso clean up out here."

"Aye, aye, Admiral," Jubal muttered. He put both big hands on the back of the chair and stood.

"You might want to have a word with Calypso first. She's got something to tell you."

"Tell me? Tell me what?"

"That's for her to say."

Bee and Norah went back through the kitchen and out the back door. I motioned Calypso over to our table.

"I'll leave you two to get acquainted," I said, standing as Calypso approached.

"Stay put!" Jubal hissed. To Calypso, he said, "Hello, there, pretty lady. You're more than welcome to join us."

Damned if he wasn't flirting with his own daughter.

Calypso slipped into the chair between Jubal and me.

"So, you're a friend of Norah's, are you?" Jubal began, remounting his chair. "I don't believe I've seen you around here before."

"I just met her yesterday," Calypso said.

"Well, listen to you," Jubal said, grinning. "Don't you have the sweetest Southern drawl?" He'd slipped into his own country cadence.

"Yep. West Virginia."

"No kidding? I spent half a season playing ball in West Virginia. I was a pro. Woulda made the bigs if I hadna burned out my arm."

Calypso said something.

"How's that?"

"'You pitched for the Emery Mountaineers."

"How'd you know that? Did Bee tell you?"

"You went 6-2, with a 2.5 ERA and more strikeouts than innings pitched. With a little more run support, you woulda been 8-0."

"Shoulda been 9-0. I left another game with a two-run lead, but the bullpen gave it up. But how did you … ?"

"My mother told me about you."

"Your mother…" Jubal's voice trailed off. He stared at Calypso so hard, I thought he might burn a hole through her. He glanced over at the door, as if checking to see if Bee had somehow snuck back in.

"Her name's Georjean."

"Georjean Durnion."

"You remember her?"

"Yes. Very well. How is she?"

"She's doin' fine. She said when I finally found you I should say 'howdy' for her, and 'no hard feelings'."

"You favor her," Jubal said, still not getting the gist.

"Leastways, I didn't get your nose."

"My…" The truth finally broke through. He reached up and touched his nose, maybe to see if it was still there. "Well, thank God for that," he managed.

Then he didn't know what to say.

"Hi, Pop," Calypso said, reaching over to offer Jubal a handshake.

Jubal stood. He was trembling a little. He opened his arms, and Calypso stood and stepped into his awkward hug.

"Now what do I do?" Jubal said, looking over Calypso's shoulder at me.

"Get her some food," I said. "She hasn't eaten all day."

Then I hightailed it out of there. When I looked back from the door, they were still standing, arms wrapped around each other, father and daughter, together for the first time.

Chapter 16:
Micah

When Bee and Norah got back to the Dinky, they found the door locked and the "CLOSED" sign in the window. Frowning, Bee set down the box she'd been lugging and fished the keys back out of her parka pouch.

Inside, they beheld an immaculate dining room. The floor had even been polished. The pass-through revealed a kitchen as clean as the dining room, at least the part they could see. The diner smelled of soap, disinfectant, and cigarettes.

"Oh, my," Bee murmured.

"What's the matter?" Norah whispered.

Jubal appeared in the kitchen doorway, sweat stains under the armpits of his old "Property of Glorious H.S. Athletic Department" sweatshirt, a large circle of sweat at his belly, and a streak of grease across his forehead. He was holding a dirty metal chunk about the size of a breadbox.

"Welcome back," he said.

"What have you…?" Bee started.

"Just tidying up a bit. I think I fixed the disposal we've been having trouble with for so long."

"I see that you've been 'tidying up a bit,'" Bee noted. "What did you do that was so terrible?"

They're going to fight about me again, Norah thought.

"Norah, maybe you should go up to your room and get some rest," Jubal said.

"You stay right here," Bee told Norah.

Jubal closed his eyes, nodded, then looked up. "Okay. Why don't you all get comfortable out here? I got something to tell you," he said." I'll fetch us some coffee. Anybody want some cheese curds or something?"

"Forget the cheese curds. Just get your butt over here."

132

"Yes, ma'am."

Bee yanked two chairs down from the nearest table and planted them on the floor, nodding toward one for Norah to sit on. Norah started to get down a third chair, but Bee said, "Let him get his own." Norah sat.

Jubal reappeared, the grease still on his forehead, a clean "Coffee's always on at the Dinky" tee having replaced the sweaty sweatshirt, a coffee pot in one hand and the fingers of his other hand hooked through three mug handles.

"Now then, ladies," he said as he affected a saunter over to the table, "let's relax and get our bearings."

"Where's Calypso? I thought she was going to stay and help you."

"She did. We had a good talk. Then she had some things she needed to do."

"You shouldn't have closed the diner early like this," Bee said. "Now the whole town will know something's wrong."

"Oh, I suspect most of them already do know, not that anything's *wrong*, exactly."

Jubal found a place for the coffee pot among the upturned chairs still on the table and plunked the mugs and coffee pot down. He pulled down a third chair for himself and straddled it but bounced up immediately to pour the coffee for them. Bee waved him away like shooing a mosquito, and he remounted his chair.

"What did you *do*, Jubal?"

"It's not something I did, exactly. Not recently. Not for a long..."

"I should really go over to the school library," Norah said. "I've got to study for a test I missed and have to make up."

"You stay, honey," Bee said, her voice softening. She put a hand gently on Norah's arm. "This is family business, and you're part of the family."

Relief flooded Norah. *A part of the family!* She hadn't ever known how sweet such words could sound, but she realized she'd been longing to hear them all her life. With the realization came awareness that, whatever the problem was, it wasn't anything bad about her.

"Okay. Here goes," Jubal says. "Better you hear it from me..."

"Hear *what*, Jubal?"

"Hear what I gotta tell you."

Bee seemed to sag. Maybe she'd seen what Norah had seen, that Jubal was actually afraid. He'd been stripped of his swagger and bluster.

"You can tell me anything, Jubal," Bee said.

"I never had anything like this to tell."

Norah realized she'd been holding her breath and released it as quietly as she could.

"You know I knocked around a lot before I met you. Lots of teams. Lots of towns. It's a ballplayer's life. This ballplayer's life, anyways. Koufax didn't spend one day in the minors."

"And lots of different women, I suppose," Bee said quietly.

"Not so many. I just hadn't met you yet."

"Go on."

"There was this one…"

"Jubal, I know this is hard for you. Please trust me on this. There's nothing you can tell me that would…that could drive me away."

Jubal stared down at the coffee mug he cradled in both hands. "Calypso's my daughter," he said. "I'm her daddy."

Nothing registered on Bee's face. It was as if Jubal had slapped her and she hadn't felt it yet. Then she set her jaw, as if to keep any of the words welling up in her from tumbling out. She shook her head slowly, never taking her eyes off Jubal. Norah sank down in her chair, wanting to disappear.

"I didn't know about her. I swear I didn't."

"Who's the mother?"

"You don't know her. Like I said, it was a long time ago, before I met you."

"I saw exactly how long ago it was, Jubal. She's a beautiful young lady. You must be very proud. Did you love this woman, her mother?"

"I really did think I loved her," Jubal admitted. "It was one of those 'at first sight' kind of deals. I… It just seemed …"

Bee's face didn't betray any emotion. That was frightening.

Jubal jumped up and went to Bee's side. He reached out to touch her shoulder, but Bee's expression—or lack of one—made him stop. He fell to one knee, looking up at her with beseeching eyes.

"I wish you'd just blow your top and yell at me, Irish," he said.

"I don't know what to say, Jubal. Maybe you should leave me alone for a while."

Jubal's face seemed to break into pieces without anything actually moving. He nodded his head slowly.

Without realizing she was going to, Norah reached out and took Bee's hand in hers. Bee put her other hand on top of Norah's, looked at her, and smiled weakly. "Looks like you got yourself a sister thrown into the bargain," she told Norah.

There were no tears on Bee's face, but they were in her voice. Bee turned back to Jubal. "Get over to the school and see what you can do to get things straightened out about Norah's missing classes. We'll talk later."

"You're right. I should get over there. You'll still be here, right? Won't you?"

"I'll still be here, Jubal."

Jubal went to the coat rack, dragged his jacket and cap off their pegs, and slipped out the door, closing it silently behind him. He went directly to the school, where he tried to explain that it was his fault Norah had missed school and that they shouldn't punish her for it. Lucy Euglem, the school secretary, said the principal wasn't in but that she'd deliver the message.

Jubal wasn't ready to go back to the diner, not right away. Instead he walked straight to the river and then north along the bank until he reached Burleigh's cabin. Seeing smoke dancing from the chimney, he knocked on the door, and the door opened.

"What brings you out here, young fella?" Burleigh greeted him. Douglass was standing by his right leg.

"Haven't you heard?"

"About you fathering an O-W?"

"Fathering a what?"

"'O-W.' 'Out of Wedlock.' 'Without benefit of clergy.' That's a polite way of saying 'illegitimate,' which is a polite way of saying 'bastard'. Come on in. Take a load off."

Burleigh stepped aside, and Jubal entered. Burleigh plopped down in his rocker by the fireplace. Jubal slumped down and sat on the floor, with his back against the wall, facing Burleigh. Douglass curled up beside the rocker. Jubal leaned his head back until it rested against the rough-hewn logs.

"I started smoking again," Jubal admitted.

"I smelled it on you."

"Do you mind if I smoke now?"

"I don't mind, but Douglass might, and you should. Going back to smoking after you went through all the grief of quitting ain't the dumbest thing you've ever done, but it's in the top 10. But go ahead. It might gentle you some."

Jubal felt Douglass's eyes on him as he fetched a half-empty pack of Camels from his jacket pocket.

"I hope you didn't come here seeking absolution from me," Burleigh said. "In case you never noticed, I ain't no priest."

"I haven't gone to confession since I converted. I guess you'd call me one of those 'fallen away' Catholics."

"I wouldn't call you nothin' of the kind."

Jubal tapped the bottom of the pack to get a cigarette to pop up. He brought the pack to his mouth, lipped the cigarette, and dropped the pack in his lap. He got a kitchen match from the same pocket, lit it with his thumbnail, and got the cigarette fired up.

The first cigarette, the fall-off-the-wagon cigarette he'd smoked a few hours before, had tasted and felt so good, he'd almost wept—even if it had made him dizzy and slightly sick. But by now, it was just hot smoke. His mouth was dry and his throat sore, and he felt nauseous.

"I hadn't met Bee yet," Jubal said quietly, "and the lady was more than willing. She might have even initiated the proceedings. If I'd known I'd gotten her... If I had... I woulda... Why don't you say something?"

"You've got the floor."

"You think I should get down on my knees and beg for forgiveness from Bee now for what happened years ago? Is that it?"

"Doesn't sound like a bad idea," Burleigh said.

"Maybe she'll forgive and forget, huh? Is that your thinking?"

"She'll forgive, all right. But she won't forget. And it wouldn't be good if she did." Burleigh put his hands on his knees and leaned forward. "Do you want justice, or do you want mercy?"

When Jubal again didn't answer, Burleigh said, "Go back and do the right thing. You know what it is. You were born knowing. You just don't want to do it."

Jubal started to say something, took a long drag on his cigarette instead, and blew the smoke away from Burleigh and Douglass.

"You're right." he finally said.

"I know I am, but that don't make me happy," Burleigh replied. "I hurt for you and Bee. But she's going to get through this all right. She's a strong woman, and a strong woman is stronger than any man."

"But what if she kicks me out? What if she can't stand the sight of me anymore?"

"Then I guess you'll get the justice instead of the mercy. But I don't think that'll happen. I'm thinking you two can come through this even stronger than before. And you just might get a daughter out of the deal. Another one, to keep Norah company."

"You think Calypso might stay?"

"She come a long ways to find you. And this ain't such a bad place to be."

"No," Jubal allowed. "I guess it isn't at that."

"Maybe Calypso might turn out to be as good a ballplayer as Norah."

"You think Norah's that good?"

"I know she's that good. I coached her, didn't I?"

"No way they'd let her pitch on the team, if that's what you're thinking," Jubal said, relieved that the subject had shifted to baseball.

"Who's this 'they'? Aren't you the coach? I thought you told everybody she'd be on the mound for Glorious on opening day."

"'They' is the school board, and if I do try to put Norah on the team, they'll can me."

"So you didn't mean what you said at the diner?"

"I meant it then. I've just been thinking about it since then."

"There's your trouble right there—thinking. You'll never know how it might play out unless you do it. We both know she's good enough to play, and we know she deserves a chance to try."

"Can't you talk her out of it?"

"Wouldn't try even if I thought I could. That's her decision."

Jubal sighed. "And then it's my decision. The damage is already done with Calypso, but now I gotta… I'll have to …"

"Calypso isn't damage, Jubal! She's a lovely young woman. She's a beautiful soul longing to know her daddy."

Jubal stood up too fast, got dizzy, and had to sit down again.

"Whoa, now," Burleigh said. "You're gonna have to walk through this thing slowly."

Jubal nodded. "Damn cigarettes," he said.

"Give 'em here." Burleigh reached out.

Jubal fumbled the pack out of his pocket and handed it over. Without looking, Burleigh pitched it over his shoulder into the fire behind him.

"That one, too."

Jubal made it to his feet successfully this time, walked over to the fireplace, and pitched the butt in.

"The journey of a thousand miles, Jubal," Burleigh said. "You just took that first step."

"How'd you get so damn smart, old man?"

Burleigh laughed. "I am old," he said, "but I ain't smart. I'm just finally figuring out that I don't know nothin'."

Burleigh and Douglass followed Jubal to the door.

"Go in peace, son," Burleigh said, putting a hand on Jubal's shoulder. "Love what's good. Do what's right. Walk humbly with your God."

"Yeah. You, too," Jubal mumbled.

Jubal walked out into the fading afternoon sun. The burbling of the river over the stones seemed to laugh at him and his troubles. When he reached the edge of the little clearing, he turned and looked back. Burleigh and Douglass were still standing in the doorway. Burleigh raised a hand, and Jubal waved back. Then he plunged into the trees, not even sure if he was headed in the right direction.

Chapter 17:
Ms. Carolyn and Mr. Grimes

Had Jubal meant it when he said Norah Stoddard would be his opening-day pitcher for the Glorious High School varsity baseball no-names? He had, but he was going to need some help to follow through on that intention, which I have come to see as rather noble.

And Halle LuLu, he got that help.

A group of women, led by Eulalia McKenzie Bledsoe and Bee Cooney, found themselves a high-priced Madison lawyer who would take their case pro bono (that took some doing) and filed suit against the school board under Title IX of the Education Amendments, which prohibits sex discrimination in all aspects of education programs that receive federal support.

By putting their "no women allowed" policy into writing, the board had made themselves an easy target. The high-priced Madison attorney won, at least temporarily. The court issued an injunction against any enforcement of the school board's policy.

But what of Norah's status? She would have to be a student in good standing, with at least a 2.0 grade point average, to qualify to play for a WIAA team.

Hurtle jumped. After urging from both Jubal and Bee and strong editorial support from the *INQUISITOR-NUGGET*, the principal allowed Norah to take a make-up exam for the one she missed, and her teachers all certified that she was in fact making A's in their classes.

So let's get to that historic baseball game, right?

Not so fast. We've got some new business to attend to first, the matter of Ms. Carolyn Henniger having been caught *in flagrante delicto* with Myron Mickelson who, although having reached the age of 18, was still just a senior in high school. Just how flagrant was Ms. Carolyn's delicato?

I'd say being caught naked in the sack with an equally naked Myron, and by Myron Mickelson's mother at that, was plenty flagrant enough.

Mama had left work at the grocery store early because she was having one of her headaches. The headache got a lot worse, I suspect.

By sunset that very day, Ms. Carolyn had been relieved of her job as editor, effective immediately. The absentee owners had never particularly liked her anyway, she being too young to be editing a newspaper, and a woman to boot. I don't know who tipped them off so quickly, but I certainly have my suspicions.

So talk of baseball will have to wait.

Ms. Carolyn snuck into the newspaper office the next morning before sunrise, hoping to pack up and go before anyone saw her. She heard the clacking and banging of the old fire-breathing Linotype; as always, Burleigh had beaten her there. She stood in the doorway. The clacking and banging stopped, and Burleigh appeared in the doorway of the back room. Douglass peeked out from behind his right leg.

"Hello, Ms. Carolyn," he said.

"Hello, Mr. Grimes." Because of her harelip, his name always came out 'Gwimes.' "What must you think of me?"

"I've always thought very highly of you, Ms. Carolyn. I think no less of you now."

"After what I've done?"

"You've done nothing to harm me, and I suspect you did the young man a world of good."

"I'm public sinner number one, Mr. Grimes, a corruptor of youth."

"'Let the one without sin,' Ms. Carolyn. You won't catch me flinging no stones."

She smiled. She wouldn't have thought she could, not then, but she did.

"Nobody else seems to share your opinion," she noted.

"That doesn't make me wrong. It just makes me lonely."

Now he was smiling with her. Then she noticed the dog.

"Who's this?" She bent down, and Douglass came over, tail swishing, and sniffed her proffered hand.

"That's Douglass. He thinks you're all right, too. And there are others on your side."

"Name one."

"Kenny."

"How do you know that?"

"He told me. If you tune in to his show this morning, you'll hear him tell everybody else. He says it's a witch hunt."

"And I'm the witch."

"You're no witch. You're young, you're principled, and you're smart—maybe not so smart in this one thing, but smart otherwise. You should shake the dust from your sandals and march on out of this town with your head held high."

"That's nice of you to say, but…"

"I'm not saying nothin' to be nice. I'm signifying to the truth."

Carolyn walked to her desk and sank into her chair—or at least what had been her chair until very recently.

"You're the only person in this town I respect, and the only friend I've got," she said, mostly to herself. "Well, except Myron, who says he'll marry me now that he's 'despoiled' me."

Douglass limped over and sat down beside her, offering himself for patting.

"See? There's another friend you've got," Mr. Grimes said, "and ain't he a mighty fine friend to have?"

"Yes. And so are you. I just wish you'd get the respect you deserve."

"Well now, Ms. Carolyn, if we all got what we deserved, who would escape a whipping?"

"You are the only person in this town who could make a reference to the Bible and Shakespeare in the same conversation."

"If I am, you're the only one who would have known I'd done it."

She looked down at her hands, folded in her lap. They had started to ache, and she saw that they were locked so tightly, the knuckles had turned white. She forced herself to relax them and used one to start stroking Douglass's back and gently massaging his neck.

"Do you think I deserve to be fired?"

"That ain't mine to decide."

Burleigh had been leaning against the composing table, but now he walked over and stood on the side of the chair opposite Douglass. He got down on one knee and put his arm around Ms. Carolyn, gave her a quick squeeze, and handed her a clean handkerchief from his vest pocket. She dabbed at her eyes.

"Go ahead and blow," Burleigh advised. "I got another one."

She blew her nose, blew a second time. When she could get her voice under control, she said, "What else have you been hiding, Mr. Grimes? Besides your erudition?"

"I'm not hiding nothin', Ms. Carolyn. Nobody else ever looked."

Burleigh got up with a grunt, fetched two cardboard cartons that gallon cans of ink had come in, and helped Ms. Carolyn pack the tools of her trade—her *Strunk and White*, her *Words Into Print*, a graduation present from her grandfather, her *AP Style Manual*, her *Merriam-Webster Dictionary*, and her assorted notebooks, pens, pencils, and papers—all of which fit into the cartons with room left over for her camera.

Then there was nothing left to do.

They carried the boxes out to the car and put them in the trunk. The sun was just up. The day was dawning clear and crisp, a promise-of-spring morning.

"What's your real name, Mr. Grimes?"

"David Henry Thoreau Grimes," he replied without hesitation.

"Don't you mean Henry David?"

"No, ma'am. David Henry. That was his birth name. He switched it around later."

"You know a lot, David Henry Thoreau Grimes."

"I know a little about a lot of things, Ms. Carolyn."

"Are you really kin of that baseball player?"

"I doubt it, Ms. Carolyn. That other Burleigh was about as white as an albino snowman."

She laughed. "Oh, Burleigh. I'm going to miss you so," she said.

"You don't need to miss me. I'll be right here. I'm done rovin'. But if you ever need a good back shop man, you just give me a call, okay? Me and Douglass will come runnin'."

"I will."

"Where you headed?"

"Wherever someone will hire me. Mrs. Johannson said she'll let me stay on until I find something."

Mrs. Johannson was a widow who rented out a room in her farm-house—the only part of the farm she'd been able to keep after her husband died.

"Go where somebody will appreciate you and let you use your smarts and learn and grow," Burleigh said. "And write and tell me where that turns out to be."

"I will. I promise." She was crying freely now.

"Wherever that is, you'll land on your feet. I know that."

She got up on her tiptoes, a hand on his shoulder for balance and, seeing her intent, he leaned in to receive her kiss.

"Anybody see you do that, they'll put you in the stocks, Ms. Carolyn," he said, grinning.

He stood and waved as she drove off.

David Henry Thoreau Grimes, with help from Ms. Sylvie True from the neighboring *Tierney Lighthouse*, got out the next issue of the *INQUISITOR-NUGGET* on time, maintaining the paper's record of never having missed an issue. Nowhere did the paper mention the firing or the scandal that triggered it.

The owners hustled in a replacement editor, another raw rookie fresh out of journalism school, this one a kid named Philip Pierpoint. They soon converted the operation to MacIntosh computers, scrapped the Linotype and hot-lead press, started having the papers printed at a central plant in Wausau, and told Mr. Grimes his services were no longer required.

Burleigh and Douglass went back to their cabin by the river. They were both done rovin'.

Chapter 18:
Morning Dove

I hate morning.

I know, I know. I'm the morning man, all bubbly and manic and making funny noises to help other folks face the day. That's what I do. Who I am would rather stay up until sunrise and sleep until sunset. Maybe I'm part vampire.

But a man gotta do what a man gotta do, like they say, and if you want to be anything in this business, you gotta be drive-time, preferably the morning man—even if you've sunk so low as to work for a little five-watter in Bumluck, Wisconsin, where drive-time means a couple of pickup trucks and a stream of 18-wheelers barreling too fast through Main Street.

I've got an alarm clock that could wake the dead—and probably anybody who lives within two country miles of me—and when that sucker goes off, my heart beats like a conga drum. I by-god get up and do my little show, and I'm the morning man.

The morning after Carolyn Henniger got fired for doing what comes a little too naturally, a bad dream woke me up in the pitch dark even before the alarm went off. I've had the dream many times before; it's always different and it's always the same. I knew I wouldn't be able to get back to sleep, so I hauled my carcass out of the rack, took a couple of aspirin dry, pulled on my shoes and a jacket, and went out for a walk in the dark.

A few of the spring birds were back from their vacations in Florida or Mexico or wherever they'd been, so I had something besides the crows for company. The sky was just starting to get light in the East, and those birds were singing to it. Maybe they thought their songs make the sun rise, and for all I know, maybe they did. The crows were already gathering in the big catalpa tree that's always last thing to bloom each year and seems to go from dead sticks to a riot of white overnight. The crows set up a ruckus as I walked by. They were like the old men who gather for coffee even before the Dinky opens, sitting on their roosts solving the world's problems and exchanging stories about how stupid we all are, themselves included.

It was too early even for the Dinky, although I saw a light on upstairs and knew Bee was already up. All the other stores were dark and shuttered, except Mr. Marisnik's, where the lights were also on. I looked in the window and saw Mr. Marisnik hauling a box out from the back of the store. I tapped on the glass and mouthed the words "Need any help?" He waved and shook his head 'no, thanks' and gave me his big, toothy grin.

There was no sign on Mr. Marisnik's store, no hours, not even a name. He was open when he was there and not when he wasn't. He sold all manner of weird stuff, herbal teas and creams to rub on where it hurts and remedies for bee sting and poison ivy and frostbite, soaps that smell like anything and everything but soap, beads, Tarot cards, the I-Ching, and the *Kama Sutra*—in Glorious, Wisconsin! He kept Halloween costumes hanging on the back wall year round, and he was just as likely to have Christmas lights in July and firecrackers in December. He'd had the store for less than a year, and I couldn't imagine he was making a go of it. I was pulling for him, though, even mentioning the store on the show sometimes, even though he didn't buy air time.

He seemed content to spend his time sitting on a stool behind the counter when he wasn't tidying up. What the hell. To each his own, I say.

* * *

I decided to head down to the lake while I waited for Bee to get the coffee perking, and as I neared the shore, I spied Calypso perched on a rock, her back to me.

"Good morning, young lady," I called out while still a few paces away.

She turned and smiled at me and patted the rock beside her, so I sat. The horizon now held some light, although the sun hadn't made an appearance yet. There was still ice in the center of the lake, but it probably wouldn't last the day. The trees across the lake were bare silhouettes.

"You must love mornings like I do," she said. That drawl of hers was like syrup on grits.

"Not me."

"I think morning's the nicest part of the day, everything so quiet and peaceful. It's my bell."

"I don't hear any bells."

"I mean it's my song. It makes my heart sing."

I was still half in the dream that had pushed me out of bed and wasn't ready to make conversation at that level, so we sat in silence looking at the lake and the sunrise, the clouds at the horizon going through their progression from purple to yellow to just clouds, while I fought off the fidgets and tried to think of something smart to say.

"If you don't like morning, how come you're up so early?"

I couldn't think of a good reason, so I told the truth. "Nightmare."

"Really? Tell me about it."

"There's nothing as boring as somebody telling you his dreams. I'm in the business of being interesting."

"You don't bore me, and this isn't business," she pressed. "This is just two new friends getting to know each other."

So I told her the dream. Once I got started, the words gushed out of me.

"I'm usually up in the mountains, but sometimes it's a city I know I've been in before."

"Which was it this time?"

"Mountains. But not like the ones where I worked in Colorado, all lush with pine and fir and spruce and cedar. The mountains in my dream are rock piles, with brush and a few straggly sumac. There's usually a lake, but not a pretty one. There aren't even any trees around it."

I glanced over at her. She gave me a little smile of encouragement, so I kept on.

"I'm always with a group. Sometimes I know some of the people, but sometimes they're all strangers. Whichever, I always feel like an outsider."

"Why?"

"I've babbled enough. I believe I'll take Will Rogers' advice and take advantage of this opportunity to shut up."

"Please keep going. Why did you feel like an outsider?"

"I don't know."

146

"What happened next?"

"Oh, I get separated from the group, and I'm trying to find my way back to where I'm supposed to be. I'm hungry, and they're going to be serving a meal for all of us. I have to be on time or they won't feed me. Everything looks familiar enough, but things keep getting moved around, and I wind up going around in circles, lost and frustrated."

"Who's 'they'? Are you at some kind of camp or retreat?"

"I guess."

"Go on. I'm interested."

"Can't imagine why. Anyway, I come upon a place that sells food, a little store, but there isn't anybody around and nothing there for me to eat. So I am still lost and hungry. That's when I woke up and decided to try to walk off the feeling from the dream."

"Maybe you're always in a group in the dream because you're always alone in real life."

"What do you mean, 'alone'? I'm around people all the time."

She was silent, which made me nervous. I was about to crack a joke or something to break the mood when she said, "Tonight, before you go to sleep, tell yourself that this time you're going to find your way back, and they'll be plenty to eat when you get there."

"What good would that do? You can't make your dreams turn out the way you want."

"Have you ever tried?"

"No. I've never jumped off a cliff and tried to fly, either."

I got up and started to walk back up the gentle slope, feeling like I'd just made a babbling idiot out of myself.

"Where away?"

"To grab some coffee at the Dinky and head over to the station."

"Mind if I tag along?"

"Free country. Or at least that's what an old piece of paper says it's supposed to be."

She slipped her hand into my big, clumsy paw and gave it a squeeze.

"So, you're a night owl and I'm a morning lark," she said.

"I guess."

"They say that night owls always pair up with morning larks."

"They do, huh? Maybe that's so somebody's always awake to stand guard."

She turned her head, shaded her eyes, and looked up.

"What?"

"I heard a Cooper's hawk. Across the lake. I'm trying to see if I can spot it, but I probably need binoculars."

I hadn't heard anything. "You a birdwatcher, are you?" I asked.

"Not really. I just love them, and I try to learn the names of the things I love, so I can address them properly. I don't believe I know your full name, Kenny the morning man."

"Kenneth Remington Kellogg. 'Kenneth' after my father and 'Remington' for the western painter and sculptor. A relative of mine died at Gettysburg, I'm told."

This time I did hear a bird call. "Now that one I know," I said. "That's an owl."

"Nope. Mourning dove."

"It goes 'hoot HOOT, hoot, hoot, hoot'. That's an owl!"

"I'm pretty sure it's a mourning dove."

"Have it your way. I don't give a hoot."

She giggled. I loved the sound of it.

The Dinky wasn't open yet, but Bee waved us in. The good smell of coffee met us, and I heard Reb in the back, rattling pots and pans. Suddenly I felt hungrier than I had in a long time.

We took the table for two by the window, and Bee brought over two mugs with steam coming off them. She gave me that raised-eyebrow, half-grin, cocked head look that meant, "What are you up to, you devil?"

"Do you take anything in your coffee?" she asked Calypso.

"No, ma'am. Just hot and black."

"You ready for breakfast?"

Calypso squinted up at the menu on the chalkboard over the counter.

"What's the 'Big Mess'?" she asked.

"Scrambled eggs with chunks of bratwurst, layered with hash browns and onions, some peppers, chopped tomatoes, salt, pepper, paprika, a little tabasco sauce. Comes with a biscuit."

"I want that."

"Good choice."

"You should have it, too," Calypso told me.

"I'm a two-aspirin and four-cups-of-coffee man in the morning."

"Breakfast is the most important meal of the day," Calypso insisted. "We want two Big Messes."

"Thatta girl."

"If I throw up, don't take offense," I said. "I don't think my gut can stand the shock."

"Two messes," Bee called out as she walked back to the counter, where the three old wise guys were already perched on their stools.

When Bee brought out two hot messes, Calypso sailed into hers like she hadn't eaten in a week. When she slowed down enough to talk, I did what I usually do when I'm nervous; I started interviewing her. But she kept turning the conversation back on me, asking me questions. She seemed to want to hear the answers, which is the great trick to getting people to open up to you.

"Did you always want to be on the radio?"

"You know, I think I did. I listened to the radio all the time when I was a kid. Soap operas, *The Breakfast Club*, ballgames, Jack Armstrong, the All-American boy, everything. I even listened to the man read the Sunday comics.

"I used to get one of those rolls the toilet paper comes on and pretend it was a microphone and put on my own show. I always wished I'd have a nice, deep radio voice, but I wound up with this squeaky frog's croak. I do have a face made for radio, though."

"I think you have a perfect radio voice, and just look how successful you've become. You've fulfilled your boyhood dream."

I laughed at that. "I don't know as I had any boyhood dreams. I just liked to play radio."

"More coffee, you two?"

Bee was hovering over us with the coffee pot.

"Yeah. Thanks," I said.

"No more for me," Calypso said. "I'd float."

Bee topped off my coffee, gave me another look, and walked back to the counter.

"What was your first radio job?" she asked.

"Covington, Kentucky. A little five-watter like here. I don't even think the signal made it across the river into Ohio, and the big stations in Cincinnati would have drowned it out if it did."

"Was that show like the one you do now?"

"Some. I really wanted to do interviews, but I couldn't get anybody to come on the show. So I started interviewing myself, doing different characters, making up bits."

"How long did you stay there?"

"A year and a half. Then I got a big break. They needed a fill-in on one of the stations in Cincinnati, which as you know is a pretty good-sized market, and I guess the station manager had heard my show and liked it enough to take me on. I was close by, and I was cheap."

"And you were good! You were so good, they hired you permanent."

"Two weeks. I lasted two weeks."

"Why just two weeks?"

"They hired somebody else. They said they'd gotten complaints about a joke I told."

"Same joke about the frying pan?"

"No. A different one."

"Tell me."

"You really want to hear it?"

"Of course I do."

Bee was back, without the coffee pot.

"Shouldn't you be on your way? It's about seven minutes to show time."

"Geez…" I jumped up, grabbing for my wallet.

"Pay me tomorrow. You're going to have to hurry."

"I'm coming, too," Calypso said. "If it's okay?"

"Sure. Come on along."

When we got to the station, I had to bend down, hands on my knees, to catch my breath.

"Can I come in and watch you do your show?" she asked, not breathing hard at all.

"No watching. If you come in, you have to be part of the show."

"Not me! I'm no radio star!"

"Have you tried it?"

The door seemed to be stuck. I pushed harder and realized it was locked. I fished my keys out of my pocket, but when I tried the station key, it wouldn't open the door. I only had three other keys, for my car, motel room, and the studio door, and I tried each one, and then tried the station key again. No go. I pounded on the door, waited, pounded some more, but nobody came.

"Don't worry. I'll get us in," Calypso said. "That's a cheap old lock."

She dug a knife out of her pants pocket, and in about two shakes, she'd picked the lock. She grinned as she waved me in first.

The lights were off, and there was nobody there, not even old Droopy Drawers. Either the 'bot was running the station, or we had dead air.

"Hello?" I shouted.

Nothing.

"Come on," I said, taking Calypso by the arm and hustling her down the hall. My studio key still worked.

"What's happening? Where is everybody?" she asked.

I flipped on the studio light and turned on the broadcast feed to the studio speaker. The 'bot was putting people back to sleep with the big band sounds of the '40s.

"I'll tell you what's happening. We're going to launch the first edition of a brand-new show, 'The Kenny and Kalypso Koffee Klatsch'."

The words surprised both of us.

"Oh, no," she protested. "I don't know how to talk on the radio."

"It's a lot like talking without the radio. You're a natural. Trust me."

"I'd be too nervous."

"No, you won't. You'll be just the right amount of nervous. A good shot of adrenaline will keep you sharp."

I flicked on the lights, got the mic positioned and my new co-host and me into headphones. There was only one chair, of course, so I gave mine to Calypso and stood next to her. I had to lean down to push the button moving the feed from "automation" to "studio," waited for the song to end, potted down the automation, potted up the mic, and proclaimed to the waiting world…

"Good morning, Glorious! Time to rise and shine, Sunshine! You're listening to WCOW, the cow! The mighty 690, six-nine-oh on your ray-de-oh, the voice of the Trempealeau Corridor and the only station in America that gives a damn about Glorious, Wisconsin!

"I'm Kenny, and this is the very first and possibly only edition of The Kenny and Kalypso Koffee Klatsch. With me this morning is my new co-host. "Introduce yourself to the nice folks, Calypso."

She stared at me with those hazel eyes and shook her head.

"This is radio, sweetheart. You have to use your words."

When she still didn't speak, I said, "Tell the nice folks 'howdy.'"

"Howdy," she stammered.

"Good start. Now tell 'em where you're from and five fascinating facts about you that even your own mother doesn't know."

"My name is…"

"Naw. Your mother knows your name. Tell them where you're from, honey. We'll start with the easy stuff."

"Boomer. That's a little town in West Virginia."

"What's Boomer, West Virginia famous for? Besides you, I mean."

"Ain't famous for anything. Just some nice, friendly people and a few stinkers, all of them trying to make a livin' and raise their families."

We went on in this fashion for a few more rounds, but she still had micphobia.

"Tell the folks what we had for breakfast this morning," I tried, hoping to trip her switch.

"The Big Mess."

"That's right, folks. This nice little lady demolished one of The Reb's famous Big Messes, a wonderment of good eating. Reb and Bee are serving up messes and all their other delights right now at the Dinky. Come on down and join your neighbors for lots of big grub for just a little dough. They'll have the radio on, so you won't have to miss the show. That's the Dinky Diner, official sponsors of the Kenny and Kalypso Koffee Klatsch—although they don't know it.

"And speaking of The Reb, our very own genuine ex-professional baseball player, they got a baseball team just down the road from your hometown of Boomer. Isn't that right, Calypso?"

The light came on in those hazel eyes of hers, with the little flecks of gold in them. She started talking about how fun it was to go to the games with her mama, starting when she was just a little girl. She listed some of the players who had gone on to Triple A ball and one who even made it to 'The Show.'

"What was that player's name, honey? Anybody we'd know?"

"Willie Thompson?"

"You're sure about that?"

"Absolutely."

"Because I remember a Willie Thornton who played a little ball for Pittsburgh, but I don't recall a Willie Thompson."

"No. I'm sure it was Willie Thompson."

"Well, as Will Rogers said, 'It ain't what we don't know that gets us in trouble. It's what we know for sure that t'ain't right.'"

"I think Mark Twain said that."

"No, ma'am. It was Will Rogers."

"Twain. And the player was Willie Thompson. I even got his autograph."

"Nope. Rogers and Thornton."

"Wanna bet?"

"Absolutely. But tell us some more about Boomer. Is it anything like Glorious?"

We were rolling now. She'd forgotten about the microphone and started describing the hills and valleys and trees and birds around Boomer, while I grabbed the record I wanted from my shelf of vinyl. I positioned the record, got the turntable spinning, and levered the arm until it was poised over the cut I wanted.

I let her ramble, sticking in a wisecrack or two, until she came up for air, realized she'd been talking—on the radio!—and turned a perfect shade of pink.

"Let's give the folks a sweet song to help ease them awake this morning, what say?" I had to stoop to talk into the mic, my face almost touching Calypso's.

I lowered the boom, and Harry Belafonte's voice filled our earphones with, *"Down the way where the nights are gay..."*

Calypso's jaw dropped, and she gave me the strangest look. But then she closed her eyes and started to sway with the music, and pretty soon she was singing along.

"But I'm sad to say I'm on my way..."

She had a beautiful singing voice to go with the beautiful rest of her. She was smiling, her eyes closed as she sang. I potted up her microphone and Harry's feed down so the folks could hear her on-air singing debut better.

When the song was over, I said, "And that of course was the great Harry Belafonte singing *Jamaica Farewell*, with sweet harmonies by our very own Calypso the chanteuse, right here on the Kenny and Kalypso Coffee Klatsch on W-C-O-W, the mighty 690, six-nine-zero, with me, your hero."

Both buttons on the phone pad were blinking green. I punched up phone line one.

"Hi. You're on the air with Kenny and Calypso. Whatcha got for us this morning?"

The station phone started ringing out at the receptionist's desk.

"Who's that delightful young lady you've got with you this morning?" line one asked.

"Good morning, Gladys. So nice to hear from you this morning. That's my new cohost, Calypso Durnion. Gladys, Calypso. Calypso, Gladys."

"Hi, Calypso, honey. You've got a beautiful singing voice. You should be on the radio all the time."

"That's very nice of you to say," Callie managed, turning pink again.

"And you're right. It was Mark Twain."

"Will Rogers, Gladys. Trust me. I've got another caller waiting. Good to talk with you."

I punched her drop button. The light on that line immediately turned flashing green again. The station phone stopped ringing but started again immediately.

"This one's probably for you, too," I said, grinning at Callie as I punched up line two.

We fielded phone calls non-stop for a while, all the callers wanting to talk to and praise Calypso. Two more deluded people claimed I was wrong about the Will Rogers quote. I played more cuts from Harry's record, including *Banana Boat*, and Calypso sang along. We ad-libbed a pretend news broadcast and kept working the phones. We had a full head of steam up now.

Then someone was crying on line two. I mean really crying!

"What's going on, caller?"

"It's not fair!" a male voice said. "It's not fair."

He started sobbing, and the line went dead.

"Somebody moved to tears by Calypso's beautiful singing," I said, trying to keep the flow going. I put on another Belafonte song so we could regroup.

The studio door swung open, and the boss, Bob "Bottom Line" Bonner, appeared in all his fat, blustering glory.

"What in hell are you doing in here!" he snapped.

"We're making radio history, *mi jefe*," I informed him.

The station phone started ringing again.

"Could you get that for us, please?" I asked, ever so sweetly. "The receptionist seems to have stepped out."

El Jefe frowned, hesitated, and went to answer the phone. The phone kept ringing every time he finished a call, and that was the last we saw of him until it was time to have Calypso and Harry sing us off the air with a reprise of their greatest hit, *Jamaica Farewell*.

I faded on Calypso and Harry as the song ended, told the folks so long until tomorrow and advised them to be good to themselves. I put the station back on the 'bot, gave out a whoop, pulled Calypso out of her chair, and gave her a hug that like to squeeze the air out of her.

"That was fun," she gasped.

"That was damned fine radio, that's what that was. I told you, you are a natural."

Bonner was still on the phone as we left. "Yes, ma'am," he was telling whoever was on the line. "We just thought it was time for something a little different, so we went out and found this young lady to brighten things up. Yes. Yes. I'm so glad you liked it…"

We walked together to the Dinky. My legs were sore from standing so much, but I hadn't even noticed while the show was going on. The room erupted in cheers the minute we walked in.

Then I went to walk the paper route with Billy, went back to my cave, and slept the sleep of the unencumbered, best sleep I'd had in years.

I didn't see Calypso again until the next morning, when she met me at the station door, ready to do another show.

The door was unlocked. Loni Marlowe was back at her post at the receptionist desk, already on the phone. We had a few minutes before air time.

"Did you find your way last night?" Calypso asked. "In your dream, I mean."

The station had provided a second chair, and we both settled in.

"I don't think I had the dream, at least not that I remember. I didn't dream at all."

"Oh, you always dream," she said. "Everybody does. You just don't remember."

"You sure about that?"

"As sure as I was about Mark Twain."

"I looked it up at the library, and darned if they didn't have it wrong there, too."

She smirked. I went to the record shelves to pick out a few albums for the show.

"How did you find that record so fast yesterday? The Harry Belafonte?"

"Just luck, I guess."

"That wasn't luck. That was a Godwink."

"A whatssit...?"

"That was God winking at you, saying 'I got you covered'."

"'Godwink,' huh. Where'd you get that one?"

"I made it up."

"Do you really believe in that stuff?"

"I sure do. How else do you explain some of the things that happen?"

"Well, I imagine I plucked the record out first try because I've been doing this so long, I know where every record is."

"They're right in here," I heard Loni say in the hall.

The studio door opened and Ms. Carolyn Henniger stood before us.

"Are you in need of a newswoman?" she asked.

"You applying?"

"I am. I suddenly find myself between jobs."

"I don't know as you'd be paid. I don't know if I will, either, to tell you the naked truth."

"That's all right. I need the experience, and it will look good on my resume."

Glorious

And that friends, is how the Triple K Koffee Klatsch got its start, with a kid singer, a newswoman with a harelip, and a clown for a host.

After the broadcast, Carolyn told us that she'd been fired from the newspaper—and why—and then I remembered the mysterious caller who had wept and hung up the day before and realized it must have been poor Myron.

Chapter 19:
Singin' in the Rain

I t had rained hard all night, and the flashes of lightning and deep rumbles of thunder had come close together. Each time Burleigh awoke, he patted Douglass, lying on the rug next to him, and imagined them in the hands of God. He prayed, "Thy will be done" and went back to sleep.

It was the prayer Ada Walker had taught him, the prayer of the simple, the prayer of the child he had been and was still.

The rain slowed some at dawn. Burleigh arose and went down on his knees to pray. He saw no flashes of light and heard only distant rumbles of thunder and decided his prayer would be better done outside, in the rain.

Douglass followed him outside. The rain was cold at first, stinging his skin, and Douglass kept trying to shake off the water. But after they had gotten as wet as they were going to get, it no longer seemed to bother either of them.

They walked slowly to the place where Burleigh best loved to sit and gaze at the river and listen to the stirrings of the trees, which were said to scream in a voice no human could hear when they were suffering from flood or drought or fire or the axe.

Flooding was always a danger for all who lived by a river when the rain came hard and fast.

"Rain down," he chanted softly, his deep, rumbling voice even deeper and thicker with lingering sleep. "Rain down on Your people. May Your Word find rich soil here, and may it yield 30 or 60 or 100-fold. Your will, not mine, be done. Rain down, God of love."

He recited the commandments, slowly, thoughtfully, pausing after each one and murmuring "Amen." There is one God; there is no other. You shall love God with all your heart and mind and spirit and energy. You shall not make graven images and worship them. You shall not take the name of the Lord thy God in vain. You shall honor the Sabbath, a gift from God, and keep it holy. You shall honor your father and your mother." He didn't remember his birthmother and had never known his father, but he prayed for them and for Ada Walker, who was his real mother.

There was no light in this dawn, but Burleigh believed that the sun shone no less brightly above the clouds, although he couldn't see it.

Then the shalt-not's. *Don't kill. Don't even hate. Don't commit adultery.* He smiled at that. He didn't have to worry so much about that one anymore, although he knew it was still possible to commit adultery in your heart by lusting. *Don't steal. Don't covet,* not your neighbor's wife nor his ox nor his ass nor his wife's ass. *Don't envy those who have more than you.* You have been given everything. How many coats can you wear at one time? And who has more than 10 fingers on which to put a ring?

And finally, *don't bear false witness against thy neighbor.* No lying, especially the lies that make you seem more or better than you are, the lies you tell yourself.

"I love you, Lord, and I know You love me, and I know I need reminding 30 and 60 and 100 times a day."

Douglass peed on a nearby tree and asked his master with a look if they might perhaps come in out of the rain now. Burleigh looked up into the rain, letting it strike his face. It made a sussing sound in the trees, and the river ran hard and fast as it rose slowly in its banks. He believed in hell. He thought maybe each person made his own hell while still on earth, and that hell was being aware of God's love and aware that your sins—the people you had hurt and the good you hadn't done—separated you from that love by your own choice, because you wanted to be God instead of God's creature.

Still inclining his face to the rain, he thought of the old spiritual. "*Up above my head, there's music in the air.*" He sang the cantor's part and then the people's, and his voice grew louder until he noticed it and sang more softly again. You don't have to be the biggest noise in the forest, he reminded himself.

"*There's music in the air,*" he sang. "*There must be a God somewhere.*"

He sat for a while longer, his baggy nightshirt clinging to his skin, letting the rain wash him clean and listening, lest he miss the still, soft voice of the Lord.

"I do hope I've done the right thing," he said aloud. "I do hope I understood. Your will right and that it wasn't just me tryin' to be a hero. If I didn't get it right, don't punish her for it, Lord. Let it be on me."

Then he recited the only words Jesus said he really needed, said them slowly, pausing often to keep his mind still before going on.

"Our father

"Who art in heaven

"Hallowed be thy name.

"Thy kingdom come

"Thy will be done

"On earth as it is in heaven."

"Do we really mean that?" he'd once heard a preacher say from the pulpit. "Or do we just want God to do our will and pretend it's God's?"

God's will can be a fearsome thing.

Burleigh cupped his hands, letting the rain fill them.

"Give us this day our daily bread."

He thought about breakfast and pulled himself back to the prayer. We are to ask for the bread and the grace we need for this day only, he reminded himself. Let tomorrow take care of tomorrow and ask again then.

"Forgive us our trespasses

"As we forgive those who trespass against us."

And make me aware of my sins, Lord, please, but not so's to overwhelm me and make me lose hope.

"And lead us not into temptation, but instead deliver us from evil."

He had heard a Catholic priest recite what he had called an embolism here, and he said the words to himself, because it was the priest's part.

Deliver us from every evil and grant us peace in our day. In Your mercy keep us free from sin and protect us from anxiety, as we wait in joyful hope for the coming of our Savior, Jesus Christ.

You get no peace until you're free from sin.

He opened his eyes and again lifted his face heavenward. The rain had slackened, and as he got to his feet, it stopped. Water continued to drip from the trees. "Tree rain." Burleigh's arms seemed to rise of their own accord as he prayed, "For Thine is the kingdom, and the power, and the glory, for ever and ever, Amen."

He was stiff from sitting in the rain, and his body was glad to be moving again as he walked slowly back to the cabin. His home. *Did the Lord build this cabin, or did I?* he asked himself. Which blade of the scissors does the cutting? The Lord had built it, using his hands. He paused at the door to whistle for Douglass, who emerged from the trees, his hind quarters swaying, sleek black fur plastered to his old, thick body.

"Shake," Burleigh said softly, and Douglass sent up a spray of water.

"Good boy," Burleigh said, and they went inside for breakfast.

Chapter 20:
Some Enchanted Evening

Like a bumblebee flying, it was impossible, and yet it happened. I fell in love with Calypso—Callie—and she fell in love with me. Me! The class clown, the blowhard, the jokester, always keeping people at arm's length with my barrage of babble—I was in love.

Infatuation, followed by inflammation, followed by I-want-to-be-with-you-for-the-rest-of-my-life love.

I'd thought such love didn't exist, or if it did, I'd never experience it. I'd even convinced myself I didn't want it. Such nonsense was only for fools, I told myself.

Now I was one of those fools.

I didn't take her to bed. She didn't take me to bed. We just wound up in bed together, as if we'd had an appointment to meet there all our lives.

I'd had sex with many women. What I had with Callie was lovemaking. I was as much concerned with pleasuring her as I was with being pleasured. We pleasured each other.

How could this beautiful young woman love me? I'll never know the answer.

She didn't try to change me, didn't nag me about my drinking or my sloppiness. She never asked me to go to an AA meeting with her. But I saw that she kept going, and when I asked her why, asked her if she wasn't cured already, she said you're never be cured and that the meetings sustained her. She was able to help others there, she said, and that helped her.

Only when I asked did she tell me her story. When she was six or seven years old, she took a nip out of her mother's glass, just to see what it tasted like, when her mother had left the room to go to the bathroom. She had liked the way it made her feel. She started drinking to get drunk by the time she was 12, and by the time she was 14, one drink always screamed for another.

She hated herself for getting drunk and kept getting drunk anyway. Her mother tried to help her. Detox, counseling, therapy, rewards, threats—they all made perfect sense, and none of them worked. Then she went to an AA meeting with a school friend named Lucille, just to see what all those drunks did there. None of what she heard and saw there made any sense, but she went back, and over time, and after a couple of relapses, she stopped drinking, one day at a time.

One night I asked to go to a meeting with her. I went back and kept going back with her. I realized that I was one of them, a drunk who would eventually hit bottom if I kept drinking. Only the lucky ones, they said, hit bottom before drinking killed them.

Not drinking was bloody hell at first. Sometimes it still is. I learned that it wasn't just about not drinking. It was about a new way to live.

I wasn't cured. I understand that. I'd never be cured. But I could be in a continual process of recovering. I started to see things clearly. I started to tell myself the truth. I was still a jackass, but now I was a sober jackass, and I had a chance and a future again.

Getting sober doesn't make your problems go away. In fact, they come into much clearer focus, along with all your failings and sins. You finally have to start doing something about them. It's very painful, this business of coming out of your cave, into the light.

But after a lifetime of self-sabotage, I was at least starting to get out of my own way and let the goodness of life come to me.

The Kenny, Kallie, and Karolyn Koffee Klatsch became the best work and the most fun I'd ever had. I didn't have to force my manic patter all the time. I didn't have to be the one getting all the laughs. I found myself getting more satisfaction out of setting Callie or Carolyn up for a good laugh line as I did in pulling off some great piece of material myself.

I felt like the Grinch whose heart grew three sizes. I was Ebenezer Scrooge buying the Christmas turkey and hugging Tiny Tim.

One night, I lay quietly, still entwined with Callie, just floating, hearing a song in my head. It was that one from *South Pacific*, about falling in love across a crowded room. You know the one I mean. I fell asleep listening to it, and when I woke up, Callie was propped up on one elbow, looking at me with a warm, sleepy smile on her face. She'd let the sheet fall off her beautiful sweet breasts but made no move to cover up. I smiled back.

I didn't make a joke. I didn't say anything. We just smiled at each other, and for once in my life, I didn't need to make a sound.

This was my song. I wasn't playing it. It was playing me.

Chapter 21:
Take Me Out to the Ballgame

We interviewed Norah and Jubal on the Klatsch the morning before the game. Norah was quiet and deferential, trying to deflect attention away from herself and onto her teammates. Jubal was full of every sports cliché ever coined and then run into the ground.

"I'm not trying to make any statements or anything like that," Norah said quietly, in answer to Callie's question. "I just want to play baseball."

"Is this the most important game of your coaching career?" I asked Jubal.

"No, Kenny. We're treating it like any other ballgame."

"Just another game, huh?"

"That's right, Kenny."

"Sure, Coach. If you say so. If Norah does well, does she earn another start?"

"We take 'em one game at a time. We're just focused on playing good baseball tomorrow."

"How do you like your chances?"

"Regis is a tough opponent. We have a lot of respect for them. We know we're in for a real battle out there. They'll have their ace, Reggie McCammon, on the bump. He's a senior, a big, strong kid. We've seen him before, and he's mighty tough."

"Do you think we can beat 'em, Coach?"

"They put their pants on one leg at a time, same as us. If we play our game, stay alert on the field and patient at the plate, we've got a good shot."

One leg at a time. I loved that. Picture somebody jumping into his pants two legs at a time.

"How about you, Norah? Do you think you can *beat 'em*?" Callie asked.

"I don't know if I will, but I sure believe I can."

* * *

Opening day for our Glorious High School No Names, taking on the Regis Ramblers on their home turf in Eau Claire, dawned clear and bright. The Wisconsin Tourism Bureau couldn't have fashioned a more perfect day—temps in the mid 60s, blue skies, puffy white clouds sliding slowly to the north and east—the sort of day we'd waited for all winter.

About half the townsfolk of Glorious and a pretty sizable number from Tierney climbed into their cars, trucks, manure spreaders, whatever had wheels and could move, and made the trek north, just as they had for the tryouts.

Callie and I drove up together early, along with the equipment necessary to do a remote broadcast. I had no idea how to run the stuff, but Callie said she'd figured it out just fooling around with it one afternoon. She could do that sort of thing. Me? If I sorted my socks right, it was a minor miracle.

Carolyn would be working the board back at the station, keeping us on the air and doing the station breaks and ads. We'd sold lots and lots of ads for the game, just as we had been for the show, which was of course what was keeping us in management's good graces. And the advertisers, God bless 'em, didn't mind having Carolyn read those ads, even though she sounded, well, different.

I'd call the play by play for the mighty six-ninety, and Callie would provide the commentary. She knew more about baseball than I did.

I knew the radios would be on at the Dinky and every other place of business in town, for anybody who hadn't made the trip to the park, and some folks had even brought transistor radios to the game, hoping they could pick up the signal and listen to us describe what was going on right in front of them.

We were in a beautiful, little, wooden bandbox called Carson Park. There was no room for Callie and me in the "press box" at the top of the bleachers behind home plate, but we'd gotten there early enough to stake our claim to seats in the first row. Callie got the equipment set up and tested while I went down on the field to get the line-ups and ask some of the Ramblers how to pronounce their names.

History would be made that day, and the stands filled fast, the throng overflowing the bleachers until folks were standing five deep down the left and right field foul lines. There seemed to be as many fans for us as for the home team.

A huge cheer rose up when Norah came out of the dugout to warm up in her traveling gray uniform with "Glorious" curling in ornate block letters across her chest, the sort of chest no Glorious varsity baseball uniform had ever covered. She wore number 32, for Sandy Koufax, her pitching hero. As she warmed up with her catcher, Mike Cavanagh, I figured she must have had a tornado in her belly and bees in her bonnet, but she seemed calm and focused.

Burleigh Grimes, volunteer pitching coach, stood behind her, watching her warm up and speaking to her softly from time to time. Burleigh was the first black man to coach in any capacity for Glorious, so we were making history in that way, too. A baggy uniform hung on his tall, skinny frame. He bore number 42, in honor of Jackie Robinson, the first black man to break the Major League color barrier back in 1947.

We all stood, took our caps off, and covered our hearts for the national anthem. The Regis High School band, dressed in uniforms that could have been hand-me-downs from the Three Musketeers, screeched and clattered its way through the stars and spangles. Callie, standing next to me, sang beautifully while I squeaked along, breaking on the high notes.

Everybody sat. In the moment of silence before the beautiful ballet of baseball was to begin, Callie nodded to me, flipped a switch, and I began.

"Glorious baseball is on the air," I intoned, hoping to sound like Vin Scully or Curt Gowdy. "A good afternoon to you, wherever you may be, and thanks for sharing this beautiful afternoon with us.

"Today, your Glorious varsity nine go up against the tough Regis Ramblers of Eau Claire. We're perched on the shores of Half Moon Lake, in the thick forests of Carson Park, where Hammerin' Hank Aaron made his professional debut with the Eau Claire Bears many years ago, and you couldn't ask for a more beautiful day for baseball.

"So pull up a chair and enjoy the game, as the Regis Ramblers take the field!"

I held the mic out to pick up the crowd cheering as each player sprinted out to his position when the PA announcer introduced him, to roars of approval from the home crowd.

"I'm your announcer, Kenny Kellogg, and with me this afternoon is Ms. Callie Durnion, and Callie, what should we watch for in today's game?"

While she opined on the history-making match-up, I studied the chart I'd drawn with up the Rambler players' names and numbers by their positions on the diamond and tried to memorize them. I'd also be keeping play-by-play scorer's notations on each player at bat for each team.

Big Reggie McCammon emerged from the dugout last and took his time sauntering out to the mound to throw his eight warm-up tosses to his catcher, a skinny kid named Borschard. Burleigh stood on the top dugout step and barked out, "Drew up, Starrett on deck, and Akey in the hole!" and our shortstop emerged carrying his war club to the on-deck circle to take his practice swings. Starrett, the second sacker, stood behind Drew, watching McCammon throwing.

Then the ballgame was underway, and time stopped for the duration. As you may know, there is no clock in baseball. A game could go on forever.

Starrett worked a one-out walk and got all the way to third on an Akey sacrifice bunt and a wild pitch uncorked by McCammon. In between pitches, Callie told us what McCammon was throwing—all fastballs so far, which she described as having "plenty of gettie-up but not a lot of wiggle"—and informed us that he was trying to crowd the hitters in on the hands. She also described the positioning of the fielders for each Glorious batter. The kid really knew her stuff.

Our clean-up hitter, first baseman Joey Posthuma, stood in, hoping to drive in Starrett from third base, but McCammon served up three sizzling fastballs, which Joey waved at and missed. Side retired, no runs, no hits, no Rambler errors.

We threw it back to the studio in Glorious, where Carolyn was supposed to read the ads and give the station breaks.

Callie and I—and I figure everybody else in the park—watched Norah as she walked out to the mound amidst cheers mostly, but some catcalls as well.

"Here we go," Callie said, putting her hand on top of mine and giving it a quick squeeze.

"Here we go," I answered, my throat suddenly dry. I was that anxious that Norah do well, for her sake, for Jubal's, and for a lot of other folks, too. She may not have wanted to be a symbol or a hero, but whether she liked it or not, a lot of people were rooting for Norah to be spectacular or to fall on her face, depending on their disposition on the matter of equal rights for women.

She'd face Borchard, McCammon, and first basemen Olsen in the home half of the first. I hoped she'd strike out the side on nice pitches—an "immaculate inning," they call it—or at least not get shelled before she even got properly settled in.

She walked Borchard on four pitches, none of them close to bring strikes.

"She's overthrowing," Callie analyzed. "Trying too hard. She's got to just pitch her game."

McCammon drove a base hit to left field, putting runners at first and third.

"Curve ball that didn't break," Callie said. "Caught too much of the plate. She's lucky he didn't hit it out of the park."

The catcalls increased. "Get a real pitcher out there," someone from nearby yelled, probably loudly enough for the mic to pick it up.

Norah went to two balls, no strikes on Olsen, gave him something too good to hit, and he drilled opposite field triple to right, scoring two runs.

Down two zip with a runner on third and no outs.

And still, she was such a sight to behold out there, this beautiful young woman with a long, reddish ponytail flowing out from the back of her cap. She turned her back on home plate, gazed out into centerfield, where Barr was playing deep in deference to clean-up hitter Hughes' power. Puffy white clouds looked down on the pines and firs behind the centerfield fence. She took a deep breath and glanced over at the dugout, where The Reb stood on the top dugout step, shoulder to shoulder with Burleigh, both men watching her, giving her time. Maybe praying.

Burleigh said something to Lefty, who nodded, and Burleigh walked slowly out onto the field, whistling at the umpire to call time.

Norah seemed impassive as she watched him coming. Burleigh climbed the hill for a brief summit conference, a few words, a pat on the back, and the old man walked slowly back to that top dugout step with Lefty.

Norah looked in for the sign from her catcher, nodded "yes," smiled.

She went into her smooth wind-up, hands high overhead, right leg bending up until her knee was above her waist, her body turning, gathering for the thrust off the left leg, left arm coming up and over, right leg licking forward. A little grunt as she released the ball, her left hand, now empty of its missile, nearly scraping the ground on the follow-through, her left leg flying out behind her.

Poetry, or as close to it as I ever saw in this world.

"Hike!" the home plate umpire bellowed, punching the air with his right fist.

"Good backdoor curve, caught the outside corner after the batter had given up on it," Callie said.

Norah was ready to go again as soon as she got the ball back.

"Hike!" the home plate umpire barked again.

"Slider, down and in," Callie said. "Right at the knees. Perfect pitch."

Again the nod, the smile, the kick.

"Hike!" came the call. "Batter's out!"

The Glorious faithful erupted.

"There it is!" Callie gushed. "The scroogie, starting way inside but then kicking back to catch the inside corner!"

Still just one out, runner at third, as Callie described for the uninitiated just what a screwball was and how you throw it.

The count went full on Rambler third baseman Holder. Callie uncorked another screwball that didn't break quite enough, walking Holder to put runners at the corners, first and third.

A strike out for shortstop Wilson, two outs.

A walk to left-fielder Sturdevant. Bases loaded.

No action in the Glorious bullpen. Norah was on her own, with Morgan, the centerfielder and number eight batter at the plate.

"Good morning, good afternoon, good night!" Callie crowed after Norah sent Morgan back to the bench with three straight strikes, the last one a frustrated swing at a ball up around his eyes.

Two runs, two hits, three walks, three strikeouts. What kind of a crazy first inning was that?

You'd have thought she'd just won the World Series, the way her teammates met her at the dugout. Not an immaculate inning, that's for sure, but then, life is messy, isn't it? A living, breathing contradiction wrapped in an enigma.

As I look at my hen-scratchings in the scorebook now, I can still see that afternoon in Carson Park vividly, but I still can't quite believe any of it really happened.

Norah stuck out the first two batters she faced in the second inning and got out number three, McCammon, on a lazy fly out to center field, one-two-three.

In the third, Hughes got on with one out on what should have been an out in right field except the ball squirted out of Bradburn's glove for an error. Holder promptly tripled him home, and we were down another run. But Norah stranded the runner at third, getting Wilson and Sturdevant on ground outs. In the fourth, she hit a batter, the number nine hitter, McKeever, got a seeing-eye single up the middle, and both runners scored on ground outs before Norah fanned the cleanup hitter to end the inning.

Five runs in four innings. Not good. But our boys had gotten off the snide in the top of the fourth, plating Bradburn, Cook, and Drew, so Norah was only down two runs.

I figured The Reb would pinch hit for her then and give her the rest of the day off, or maybe move her out to center and let someone else pitch, but in the top of the fifth, she led off with a triple, Cook walked, and Foster White clubbed a three-run shot way over the right field fence to put Glorious ahead. Drew doubled, stole third, and scored on a ground out, and when the dust settled, Glorious and Norah had a two-run lead.

Given new life, Norah struck out two in the fifth and the side in the sixth, and when The Reb finally brought in a relief pitcher to start the seventh, the crowd, or most of them, anyway, stood and cheered and cheered until Norah, now playing centerfield with McGuire taking over on the mound, finally had to take off her cap and wave it to get them to stop.

The score stood. A 7-5 win for Glorious.

And that's how Norah Stoddard entered her name in the eternal celestial scorebook—first female to pitch in, start, and win a game in the history of Glorious High School or anyplace else we'd ever heard of.

I was there. I saw it. It happened just that way.

Chapter 22:
Rebel at Appomattox

The post-game celebration overflowed the Dinky and went on well past normal closing time. Even with Callie and Norah helping, clean-up lasted right into the new day.

Now the girls were upstairs in the room they were sharing, talking, occasionally giggling, too excited and happy and exhausted to sleep yet.

Bee and Jubal sat facing each other at the little table for two in the back corner by the restroom in the otherwise empty dining room. To use a term she'd heard her little point guard, Kerrie Merry, use more than once, Bee was scared shitless.

Reb had initiated a conversation! A man who ordinarily jumped out the nearest window at the hint of serious talk had suggested that they needed to talk!

He led her to the table in the deserted Dinky, held her chair for her, and fetched coffee for both of them. Who was this man? What could possibly have pushed her man-child to such desperate action?

"I'm really proud of you, Rebel," she said, to break the ice. "What you did took a lot of guts."

"Norah did the hard part," he said. "And they could still fire me, you know."

"They won't dare. They'd get run out of town."

She reached across the table and took his hands in hers. His were ice cold. She warmed them in hers and stroked the callous that had formed on the tip of the index finger on his pitching hand years ago and never gone away.

"You didn't do it just because of me, did you?"

"I did it because it was the right thing to do," he said. "Right and smart. I was wrong. I'm sorry I was such a jerk. Sorry about everything."

He swallowed hard, as if he had a piece of humble pie stuck in his throat.

She swallowed harder. He'd never said anything like that before.

He seemed to relax now, at least a little. "I'm sorry about what I said about Norah trying out for the team and women's rights and all that. I'm sorry for what I said about you being... oh, you know what I said, and it was mean and stupid and wrong and I'm sorry. I'm really, really sorry."

Those were tears on his cheeks!

She'd seen him cry twice before. The first time was when he'd gotten word that his daddy had passed, and she had wept with him. The second was when she'd miscarried, and the doctor said she might die if she ever tried to have a child again. He had wept with her that time.

This was the third time.

"Even if she'd stunk the place up—which she kind of did before she settled down— she deserved a chance to try."

"Will you give her another start?"

"Yeah, if I'm still the coach. She was nervous. She'd be better next time. And she did strike out an awful lot of them, didn't she? I imagine they heard about it when they got back to the bench, too." Jubal swiped at his tears with the back of his hand. "Struck out by a mere girl!"

"Downright mortifying," Bee said, with the tip of her finger gently catching a tear he had missed. "I was afraid you weren't going to stick with her when she gave up those runs early."

Jubal took the finger that had wiped his cheek and kissed it. "I've been afraid you weren't going to stick with me," he said.

"Oh, Jubal, if I were going to leave you, I'd have done it long ago."

"I suppose that's true enough."

"I love you, Jubal. You know that."

"I guess I do. But I sure as heck don't know why."

"There's no 'why' to loving someone. I could tell you all the things I love about you, but that wouldn't explain it. I think God must have made us for each other."

"Then he sure must have a weird sense of humor."

"She certainly must."

Jubal was fighting to find his next words. She waited, but she wasn't scared any more.

"What made you change your mind about letting her try out?" she finally prompted.

"You were a big part of it. I won't deny that. I've seen how you've had to fight for your girls, how dedicated you are to them. But it was something else, too. It was her."

"She is an amazing athlete."

"Not just that. She's good enough to make the team, to be a starting pitcher, even our ace, and I know how hard it is to learn how to pitch like she can. But it's more than that. It's her determination, her courage. She's a really quality kid. She deserves every chance."

Bee waited. This wasn't all Jubal needed to say.

"There's something else," he finally said in his smallest voice. "We haven't talked about Calypso and my…" He frowned, not sure what word he needed.

"Indiscretion?" Bee prompted.

"Yeah, my indiscretion. That's a nice word for it. You've been so good, so amazing, about taking her under your wing and treating her like your daughter."

"She isn't like my daughter. She is my daughter. You're her father, and I'm your wife. That makes her my daughter. And a pretty amazing one at that."

"Yeah. She's something, all right. And she and Norah are just like…"

"Sisters?"

"Yeah." He took a sip of his coffee and made a face. It was no longer steaming hot, the way he liked it. "You wanted so bad to have a baby. We both did. And now here we are with two teenagers. It's kind of the final irony, isn't it?"

She'd heard him use that expression, "the final irony," before. He had attributed it to a teammate in double-A ball, someone called the Iowa Kid, a lanky pitcher from Iowa City named Herbert Spitzer, who was, Jubal said, the best pool hustler he'd ever seen or even heard of.

They sat quietly for perhaps a full minute.

"Are we okay?" Jubal asked.

"We're okay. There's one thing I'd like to ask you, though."

"What's that, Hon?"

"Did you really not know you had a daughter?"

"Heck no, I didn't know! You don't think I would have told you?"

"I think there's a chance you wouldn't have. I think there are a lot of things you've never told me about yourself. There's a part of you that's shut up inside, a part I've never been able to reach."

She thought he might get up then and escape into the night for one of his walks, but he stayed.

"I'd like to think that I would have," he said at last. "But honestly, I'm pretty sure you're right. I'm pretty sure I wouldn't have."

"But why, Jubal? We shouldn't have any secrets between us!"

"You would have been mad as hell! And hurt. You know you would have!"

"I have a *bit of* a temper."

"A bit of a temper?!"

"Am I as bad as all that?"

"Not bad. I usually have it coming."

"Jubal, don't you think it's important that we share our honest feelings with each other, good and bad? You wouldn't want me to hold it all in, would you?"

"Hmmm, maybe a little bit of holding in wouldn't be bad, at least until after you'd had your second cup of coffee in the morning."

She laughed with surprise. Her laugh triggered his. They kept the laugh going a little longer than merited, but it was a great release, and now words came tumbling out of Jubal.

"I've told you that my mama was drinkin' most of the time I was comin' up."

"Yes."

"Well, sometimes when she was drunk, she'd get really, really mad at me over something I'd done. Like the time my dog and me came home with skunk stink all over us because I'd throwed a rock at a mama skunk who was with her babies?"

"I can't believe you'd do a thing like that!" Bee frowned.

"I didn't mean to hit her! I was just trying to make her run away. And I hadn't seen the babies before I flang the rock. But Mama, she flew into a rage and made me take off all my clothes, right there in the yard, and hosed me down for 10 minutes, screamin' at me all the while.

"Then she made me gather up my clothes and take them to the incinerator out back of the shed, me still dripping wet and cryin' and buck nakid, and throw them in with the trash and light the whole deal on fire. Then she locked me and the dog out of the house for hours, just sittin' in there, drinkin' her beer and hatin' on me."

"Oh, Reb," Bee said quietly. "How awful."

"It wasn't the hosin' or the swearin' or even the makin' me sit outside wearing nothin' but skunk stink. It was the hate I seen in her eyes and heard in her voice. It was like…"

Jubal was crying again, for that little boy, dripping wet and naked, facing his mother's fury.

"She didn't hate you, Jubal. The drink had hold of her. She couldn't help it."

"I've told myself that. But I still can't get past what I saw in her eyes."

"Jubal," she said quietly. "I ain't your mama! I'm not going to lock you out, especially not if you're buck naked. I just lose my temper sometimes."

She got up, went to him, hugged him. She cried with him until he stopped.

"I'm glad you told me that story," she said.

"I guess I'm glad I did, too."

She hugged him tighter. "You learned a lesson, then, huh?"

"What's that?"

"Don't throw rocks at skunks."

He laughed. The moment passed. Now it was alright for them to go upstairs to bed together. And that's just what they did, hand in hand, as they climbed the stairs.

Chapter 23:
Justice and Peace Shall Kiss

Burleigh awoke before dawn, as was his lifelong practice. He wouldn't have called it discipline, although it would have appeared so to others. He loved the morning best, loved the sunrise, the bird songs, the singing of the river in warm weather, the profound stillness of a new snowfall and the groaning of the ice in the cold.

As he had gotten older, he needed more sleep, so he took a nap after lunch but kept getting up just as early. Perhaps he knew the number of sunrises left to him was dwindling and couldn't bear the thought of missing even one.

Each one was different. This he had learned.

He did his morning inventory of his body, to see which parts were working well and which would need special attention and found that only his right knee seemed to complain at the notion of movement and weight-bearing. This was a good report.

He thanked God for waking him into the new day, then read his Scripture, opening the book to wherever it fell but steering it to the New Testament this day. God gave him two of his favorites, Psalm 85 and the Gospel story where Jesus bids Peter to walk on the water, and both spoke directly to his heart.

> *Kindness and truth shall meet.*
> *Justice and peace shall kiss.*
> *Justice shall spring forth from the ground*
> *and peace shall look down from heaven.*

Burleigh didn't need the book for this passage. He had it by heart, and he treasured its promise.

He also knew the Gospel story well and thought perhaps he had trained his Bible to fall open to it more often than chance would account for. In it, the Christ appears to the disciples walking on the stormy waters. They fear Him as a ghost, but he bids Peter to walk out to Him. And Peter does—does, that is, until, he takes his eyes off the prize and focuses on the wind and waves. That instant, he begins to sink and calls out for Jesus to save him.

Burleigh pictured Jesus reaching out to grasp Peter by the wrist, Peter's hand clutching his Savior's wrist as Jesus pulled him swiftly, but gently to safety.

"Oh, you of little faith," He had said, but not as a reprimand, Burleigh thought, but as a gentle, perhaps sad observation. Or maybe he was laughing as he said it. "Why did you doubt?" he had asked.

That was Burleigh, too, a "little faith." Many times, he had reached out in desperation for Jesus's hand to keep from sinking.

"I believe, Lord," he said aloud in the empty cabin he had made with his own hands. "Help me in my unbelief."

Peter would go on to deny his Lord three times, Burleigh reminded himself, but then the risen Christ had given him three chances to atone, asking him three times, "Do you love me?" and three times instructing him to "feed my sheep."

The tender light that comes before the sun filled his little cabin. It had come earlier each morning for many days now. It was time for his walk.

He thanked God for the sunrise, for the crisp, clean air, and for his relative absence of pain, thanked God, too, for rain and snow and pain when it came.

After he gave thanks, he brought his concerns and needs and shortcomings to his God as honestly as he could. For years, he had foolishly tried to impress God with his supposed piety, as if God were some visiting potentate, but God knew Burleigh better than Burleigh knew himself.

How could faith and anxiety still coexist in him? Why did he still doubt? Why was he still such a "little faith"?

He heard the call of the Cooper's hawk, and he returned it with a sharp, crisp series of high-pitched whistles. There was a nesting pair nearby; they tried to drive him away from the eggs or baby hawks every time he passed. The hawks were keeping the other smaller birds away from the area, but Burleigh walked far up river until he began to hear the little ones greeting the dawn and bringing the sun up, singing because God had given them a song, and they were returning it to God.

Burleigh answered each one, and they replied, so good was his imitation.

Burleigh remembered an old, dear friend. They had known each other since they were little children, "friends of longest duration," they called each other. His death, over a year ago now, had so saddened Burleigh that he felt the weight of it on his heart for weeks after and prayed for his friend every day for a long time. It had been a while now, and thinking of his friend brought a gentle ache for his loss, but also the warmth of good memory and hope for the resurrection.

He prayed for his enemies, those who had fired Miss Carolyn and Kenny. God had turned evil into good and made them a team with Calypso, she with the beautiful gift of song.

He prayed for the children. Many of them had begged him to teach them to whistle as he did. He smiled at the thought. They called him "Willie the Whistler." He demonstrated for them and told them as best he could how he formed his mouth, but none of them could ever make the sounds like the birds. He had never met anyone else who could until Calypso. She had been able to replicate the sounds perfectly. She listened and heard and took the songs inside herself.

He had no job to go to now. He had dearly loved that job. But instead of advising him to move on, as he had always done before, God told him to stay where he was. He probably had enough money to last him all his life—his needs were simple and few and he had always saved most of what he earned once he had stopped drinking. He had found a place where he would wait for God to call him home.

So what was his job to be now? He was an unpaid pitching coach, wearing a baseball uniform again after all these years, but that was only in spring and then again with the Home Talent town team Jubal managed in the summer. What would be his winter job?

God would show him. He had only to pay attention so he'd hear the call when it came.

Leave for tomorrow the problems of tomorrow. You are living right now, and now is all you have and all you've ever needed.

He tried to be patient with himself and his little faith. God had been patient with him, not forcing awareness on him until he was ready for it, teaching him only a little at a time, light for his path, but only a few feet ahead, not into the far future. That's where the faith had to come in.

"Grant me Your mercy for this day," Burleigh said aloud.

A rabbit ran right at him and then bolted off the trail into the brush, trying to get him to follow. A mother with a nest of babies nearby, he figured.

"I won't hurt your babies," he murmured softly. "I never would."

"Why do you doubt?" he heard Jesus say again.

"I am your little faith," he replied. "I believe. Help me in my unbelief."

Chapter 24:
Jamaica Farewell

Wisconsin continued to lose its small farms, and our town continued to cling to survival. Did, that is, until the TV cameras rolled into town and turned the spotlight on little Glorious for all the world to see. I'll come to that presently.

Norah won 13 games and lost only one and set a Division IV record for strikeouts in a season that year, carrying our scrappy baseball team all the way to the state championships, where they lost 1-0 in the semi-final game on a walk-off suicide squeeze bunt in the 13th inning. Norah pitched the entire game.

Our town was mighty proud of her and The Reb and the rest of them and let them know it. There's a trophy case in the entrance hall of the high school extolling the achievements of our Glorious Chiefs/Rebels/Eagles. Along with the trophies, there's a plaque, very like the plaques that hang in the Baseball Hall of Fame in Cooperstown, bearing the likeness of Norah Stoddard and delineating her achievements.

Norah's mom died just after baseball season ended. The last in the long line of bad men in her life beat her to death. I can't even imagine the mix of feelings Norah must have had, but Bee and Jubal were there for her, and they wound up adopting her, legal recognition of what the heart already knew.

Despite Norah's pitching heroics, the school board managed to get the lower court's decision reversed, *after Norah had graduated*, codifying its ban against women participating in traditionally men's sports. Perhaps as a sop to those outraged by such stubbornness, and having failed to agree in meeting after meeting on a suitable mascot, they opened up the matter to a vote of the students, who elected in a landslide to call themselves the Glorious Rebels, a salute to the man who had stood up for women's rights, as his supporters maintained, caved to pressure from his better half, as many others suspected, or simply wanted the best possible team on the field, which meant Norah on the mound.

Years later, there would be a revolt against the notion of any school seeming to glorify the institution of slavery, and the Rebels became the Eagles, in honor of the majestic birds that nested where the river stayed open all winter because of a hot spring that fed into it a mile south of town.

Although the name "Rebels" no longer remains, a more important legacy of what Norah and Bee, Jubal and Burleigh, did lives on in the Glorious High School Lady Eagles. Yes, the school finally funded women's athletics, and the Lady Eagles basketball team even won a Division IV State Championship.

In other important sports news, Tierney's own Mary Kay Haskens (no relation to the Haskins whose farm turned into a cranberry bog) won the annual State Cow Chip Toss in Prairie du Sac over Labor Day weekend, having bested Glorious' own Sid Bundren in the local qualifying contest with an epic fling of 137 feet 6 inches, a state record. She went on to represent the state in the national competition in Beaver, Oklahoma, finishing just out of the money, a respectable fourth. A young bronc rider from Tennessee took the gold.

Carolyn proved to be an able news director at the mighty six-ninety, and her dry humor played off beautifully against the more spontaneous Callie. The Triple-K Koffee Klatsch flourished for a time—the time of my radio life—and I wouldn't have traded sharing the mic with those two ladies and being the morning man of Glorious, Wisconsin, with anybody, not even Howard Stern.

Carolyn and Myron were over as an item, but the young outlier was voted "Person Most Likely to Succeed" at the end of the school year.

For a short time, Sylvie True took over our little jewel, the Glorious *INQUISITOR-NUGGET*, doing double duty by getting out both the Tierney and Glorious sheets every week, with a huge assist from her back-shop man and *de facto* managing editor, Burleigh Grimes, who got his own column, upper left page one, right under the banner.

But after six months, a local chain owned by one Benjamin Franklin Devers, who had already bought up the little weeklies in Wild Rose, Iola, Blair, and Whitehead, bought the *Lighthouse* and the *I-N* and replaced the old-fashioned Linotype with little boxes, all in a row and all named "Mac." Devers printed all their papers out of a central plant in Eau Claire, and Burleigh was out of a job.

The new editor continued to run Burleigh's column, however, paying him pocket money and solidifying his status as the sage of Glorious. He would also continue as volunteer pitching coach for the Glorious Rebels for ten more years. He'd socked away enough money over the years to live out his life among us, his nomad days over. A man living alone in a cabin by the river with no phone, let alone a television set, and who caught fish and grew his own vegetables, didn't have much need for money.

He was a hero one more time, he and his old dog, Douglass. They walked to town early one morning, as was their custom, arriving just as the sun crested the horizon, and this particular morning, they happened on Billy Coates, making his morning delivery from the bakery to the Dinky. As Burleigh and Douglass approached, a gang of juveniles, out of school, out of work, and no doubt out of their minds after drinking all night, descended on Billy. Not content to simply taunt him and make him cry, one picked up a rock and threw it at him, and another charged at him, brandishing a stick.

The rock missed its target, and the charger with the stick never got close. Douglass broke from Burleigh's side and raced to meet the foe, teeth bared, an ominous low growl rolling out of him, raced as only a dedicated and pure-of-heart three-legged dog could race. The thugs scattered, and one of them, the one who had thrown the rock, stumbled and fell. Douglass was on him and might have done some real damage, but Burleigh's shrill whistle stopped him. The old dog turned and limped back to his master, who was standing with his arm around Billy.

Burleigh got down on one knee, stroked Douglass tenderly, and talked to him, the two of them eye to eye. Douglass seemed to take in every word, and when Burleigh was done, Douglass licked him right on the lips. Burleigh didn't even rub it off.

Callie and I were on our way to the Dinky for our pre-show coffee and saw the whole thing. I think that's how I'll always remember Burleigh, down on one knee, gentling that old dog and receiving his kiss.

Having pitched the Glorious softball team to three straight State championships, Norah got a scholarship to a small college in northern Indiana and pitched for the previously all-men's baseball team. She fell in love with her catcher, and they got married after graduation and gave The Reb and Bee two grandbabies to adore. After making a few appearances with the Independent Northwoods League St. Paul Saints, thus becoming the first woman to pitch and win a game in a professional men's league, Norah retired to run a daycare center in Upland, California, her husband's hometown.

She came back to visit her adoptive parents often, bringing her family. Her husband, Gary, seemed like a good egg, although nobody could have been worthy of our Norah. She and Sarah remained good friends. For a woman who had written her name into history, or herstory, Norah remained the modest, quiet soul she'd always been.

Kristi and Annette carried out their plans to turn what had for generations been the Haskins' farm into a cranberry bog. I went with Carolyn to do a remote from the auction when the sale on the farm closed; I've experienced very few things in life sadder than a farm auction.

The sale didn't include the house and that little chapel Gram Lydia built, and she stayed in that house for the rest of her life. One of her grandsons and his wife moved in and are raising a family there now.

Callie and I were together for a time more, a time that seems like a dream to me now. But it wasn't the sort of thing that could have lasted. Garrison Keillor, while on his way back up to St. Paul, Minnesota, stopped in at the Dinky, maybe for a piece of rhubarb pie, and heard Callie singing on the Koffee Klatsch. He sought her out—we even got to interview the great man on our show—he was a queer duck who never looked at you when you talked to him—and invited her to be a guest on *A Prairie Home Companion*. On the basis of that appearance, she signed a recording contract and went on to be a star on the Grand Ole Opry. She recorded some duets with Dolly Parton—and more than held her own. You've no doubt heard her sing. Her big crossover hit, number one on the pop charts, was a song Dolly wrote for her. Maybe you've heard it. It's called *Odyssey*, and it has that nice Jamaican beat.

On my last morning with Callie before she left for St. Paul to meet her destiny, a chilly, coming-of-winter fall morning, I woke up before dawn and watched her steady breathing, studying her face and her curves under the blanket, feeling her warmth, committing her to memory—as if I could ever forget her.

When those beautiful hazel eyes fluttered open, she smiled at me, reached out, and traced my lips with her finger.

"What time is it?" she murmured, still stoned with sleep.

"Early. No hurries, no worries."

"Time enough for your Robert Frost and my Emily Dickinson to get together?"

That was a little euphemism she had invented after I'd played a Simon and Garfunkel song called *Dangling Conversation* on the show.

Yes, there was time enough for Bobby and Emily to get together.

"I knew you'd have to leave," I told her after. "You belong to the world. Besides, I'm too old."

"You're not too old," she insisted. "I'm too young. I'm not ready to settle down yet."

"And I'm pretty damned settled down."

"I'll come back."

"Don't go teasing me with false hopes."

"I'm not. And when I come back, you'll write a sequel to the book you're writing about us."

"I might not even show that thing to anybody else."

"Yes, you will. You'll be proud of it, and you'll want others to read it. And lots of people will read it and want more.

"I should live so long."

"You'll live a long time. Just stay off the booze."

"Without the booze, it'll just seem like a long time."

She laughed and brushed my lips with hers.

"You're a good man, Kenny Kellogg," she said. "You've got the best heart of anybody I've ever known, except maybe my mama."

Heart? Me? I'd never thought of myself much in terms of heart.

"Sing me the goodbye song," I said, realizing that I was going to cry.

She smiled. "Sing it with me, sweet love," she said.

So we crooned a little duet, her sweet, crystal-clear high voice carrying my gravely, growly low one.

> *But I'm sad to say I'm on my way.*
> *Won't be back for many a day.*
> *My heart is down, my head is turning around,*
> *I had to leave a little girl in Kingston town.*

I offered to drive her to St. Paul, but she thought it best if she took the bus.

"When I'm hugely famous," she told me as we waited for the bus to arrive at the depot in Eau Claire, "I'll give you exclusive interviews on your radio show."

She didn't know how right she was about the hugely famous part.

But even she couldn't have foreseen the change she would bring to our beautiful Glorious, slumbering by the crystal-clear Trempealeau River. After her breakout hit with *Odyssey, Hartmann from the Heartland* and his traveling road show came to town and introduced our little slice of heaven to the world as the "Town Where Calypso (she was famous enough to only need one name) Got Her Start." He taped a segment with me on the radio with Carolyn doing our silly thing, captured the morning crowd at the Dinky, and did an interview with Burleigh—with Douglass, of course—the old coach talking about his protege, Norah Stoddard. Then he followed Billy on his rounds for a day. The whole deal aired on *CBS Sunday Morning* in an 18-minute segment.

The rest of the media ran with the story, and Glorious became a tourist destination. Just to cement our fame, Mr. Hartmann, "Charley" to us, came back in late summer to tape a segment on the Cow Chip Fling.

We even got our weekly newspaper back, the *INQUISITOR-NUG-GET* again rolling off the presses every Wednesday night, its circulation swelled by out-of-town subscribers and the tourists who came in driblets all year and droves in the summer.

Looking back on that fateful day, as her bus rolled out, taking Callie toward her destiny as a star, I remember how she opened her window, leaned out, and gave me that piercing whistle Burleigh had taught her.

If ever she whistles for me again, I'll come running.

For the first time in my life, the term "broken-hearted" seemed quite literal. I cried like a little kid all the way back to Glorious, carrying a weight in my chest that made it hard to breathe.

Like Roger Miller used to sing, *the last word in lonesome was me.*

I wanted a drink worse than I'd wanted one since I'd quit, and that's plenty a lot. I parked in my usual spot behind the by-the-week motel but then couldn't bear the thought of going inside. Callie had told me I deserved something nicer than the little rathole I lived in, but I'd always figured it suited me. Now I didn't think I could even stand the sight of it.

I headed for Big Nose Rose's Saloon, but Calypso's singing our good-bye song ran through my mind and turned my feet. I cut through the alley between the Dinky and the newspaper and walked up-river to Burleigh's cabin. The air was so sweet and clear, you'd swear you could live on it without food or water. As I walked, I cried and howled and sang *Jamaica Farewell*.

Burleigh and Douglass seemed to be waiting for me, sitting on the stoop outside their cabin, Burleigh working udder balm into his old catcher's glove. I sat down next to Burleigh; he looked up and nodded to me, squinting against the late afternoon sun.

"The young lady got away all right?" he asked after a while.

"Yep. She's on her way."

Usually I get very nervous if somebody doesn't talk, and I rush to fill the silence with my nonsense. But with Burleigh, I felt comfortable to just sit, sharing the sounds silence makes in the woods.

"I could rustle us up some supper if you'd like," Burleigh said.

"Thanks, but I'm not hungry."

"I suspect not. You got too much else going on inside you that needs digestin'."

"How about one of your Bible quotes? You got one handy for the occasion? Scripture for broken-hearted lovers?"

"I got one that fits all occasions," he said. "Micah 6. *Love what's good. Do what's right. Walk humbly with your God.*"

I chewed on that for a while. "Yep," I said. "Can't argue with that."

"Go on inside and get the other glove, why don't you? We'll have a catch," that wise old man directed. "Maybe I'll teach you how to throw a screwball."

So I had a catch with Burleigh, the first time I'd touched a baseball or had a glove on my hand since I'd hit puberty.

I was fighting off having to go back to my hovel, and as if he were reading my mind, Burleigh offered to let me live with him. I was mightily tempted, but the thought of making that walk into town in the winter in the dark to do my radio song and dance seemed daunting.

"Something else will turn up then," he said.

I believed him, and that something did its turning up right away.

When I got back to town, I saw a light on in the Dinky, which had closed hours before. When I looked in at the window, I saw Jubal hunched over the center table. He'd covered the table with old newspapers and was working on that damn garbage disposal of his. Seemed like he had to fix it every week or so. He looked up, spotted me, and waved me in.

"How about a Rebel Burger?" he greeted me.

"Naw. You'd just have to clean the grill again."

"You're supposed to clean those suckers? Well, I'll be hogswaggled."

He got up and headed for the kitchen. "It's on the house," Jubal said over his shoulder.

He fixed me my burger—two beef patties, spicy brown mustard, and fried red onions—and I sat at the table with him and wolfed it down while he went back to tinkering with the garbage disposal.

"Norah and Callie's old room's empty now," he said, casual like, just as he pulled out a great gob of gunk that had been clogging the disposal. "Would you have any interest in parkin' it over here instead of livin' in that pleasure palace of yours?"

"You gonna adopt me, too?"

"Can the kid be older than the father?"

"'The child is the father of the man'," I said.

"Yeah. And 'I'm my own grandpa'."

"Never mind. You sure that would be all right with the Boss?"

"She suggested it."

"I'll go get my junk. It won't take long."

It took about 15 minutes to pack up my entire estate and walk back.

Then I went to a meeting and just sat and listened, an activity I had very little experience with and definitely needed to work on.

The next morning, I dragged myself to the radio station, wondering if I could even do a show without Callie—though I'd been doing them for decades without her before she walked into my life. For four hours, Carolyn and I did our thing, and Callie's empty chair didn't hit me in what was left of my heart more than four or five times a minute.

After the show, I walked the paper route with Billy, our weekly ritual.

"Nothing lasts, for good nor ill," I told Billy, putting a hand on his shoulder. He had hardly spoken as we folded and tossed our papers; any change in his world upset him profoundly. The new editor had already told us he planned to switch to delivery by an adult with a car, so that one person could do the whole corridor, and Billy would soon be out of a job.

"I don't know what I'll do without I deliver the papers," Billy said.

Not having a better one, I gave him the same answer Burleigh had given me, Micah 6. He seemed to chew on that, same as I had.

"You know what I wish?" Billy asked me.

"What do you wish?"

"I wish I could be a milkman and bring folks their milk and butter and eggs and cottage cheese."

By now, we'd finished delivering to the by-the-week where I'd lived for so long and the old folks' home where I hope I'll never have to live.

"You'd be real good at that," I told him.

He would, too. We hadn't had dairy delivery in years. but maybe…

"Why couldn't you start your own once-a-week milk route? You could bring folks their dairy and maybe some other groceries, too, and even keep delivering the papers. I could drive you. A lot of old folks have trouble getting out, especially in the winter. This would be a godsend for them. I could talk it up on the radio, get the word out that way."

He nodded eagerly, a big smile on his pumpkin face.

I prayed I wasn't raising false hopes, but I really did think it had a chance of working. Besides, everybody needs something to hope for, not just people like Billy but all of us, don't you think? I figured I was going to live on the hope that Callie would come back, as she said she would. Did I really believe she'd do it? Well, as Butch said to Sundance, or maybe it was the other way around, "I will if you will."

As for Glorious, which seemed to have been close to dying before all this happened, it has thrived in a way its founder, Ansen Knutson, never could have imagined. The tourists mostly come because of Calypso's fame as a singer, but if they want to know who really turned this town around, they should go see that plaque in the trophy case at the high school and learn just what Norah and Bee and The Reb and Burleigh did. They're the heart and soul of it. They, especially Norah, put this little burg on her feet, gave her back her pride. Calypso came from the outside and graced the town with her presence for a while. But Norah, she was homegrown, and she showed what a nobody from Glorious, and from a shattered home at that, could do.

I think old Ansen's pretty proud of the town he founded and thanks his maker for the day he came upon our little bend in the Trempealeau River, the just-risen sun glittering on the water like fallen stars, and proclaimed it "glorious."

That's how Glorious got its name, and Glorious it should always be.

About the Author

Marshall J. Cook is a Professor Emeritus who taught writing at the University of Wisconsin-Madison. He edits *Extra-Innings*, an online newspaper for writers and others who love words, teaches in the UW Odyssey Project, and creates and hosts *The Writers and Their Words* radio program and podcast, originating at WLSP-FM Sun Prairie, WI.

He has been married to Ellen since 1968, and they live in Madison, Wisconsin with one mini-Schnauzer and two Persian princesses. Ellen and Marshall have one son, Jeremiah, who is married to Kimberly, who presented them with a granddaughter, Liliana Lenore, thus guaranteeing that they shall inherit the entire family fortune.

When not writing or teaching, Marshall likes to read, lift weights, walk the dog, and talk back to the television (not all at the same time). He's a retired jogger and a passionate baseball fan, loves 50s-60s rock 'n roll, Bruce Springsteen, roads, and eats in small-town diners.

wwww.sunprairiemediacenter.com
www.odyssey.wisc.edu
www.continuingstudies.wisc.edu/writiing/extra-innings